SHARDS OF STASIS

SOUL COURT ASCENSION BOOK TWO

MEL HARDING-SHAW

CORUSCATE PRESS

CHAPTER 1
HEL

Eyes burning with flame glowed in the darkness as the shadowy bodies of the starhounds slunk closer. The ambient light was just bright enough to reflect off the venom dripping from their hinged fangs.

Fuck. This was a terrible idea. Why had she let Morrigan talk her into it?

Hel stood at the top of the stairs beneath the imposing façade of the old National Library building with its levels of concrete like so many computer chips layered on top of each other forming an architectural bunker. If only she was planning to take shelter there instead of following through on this madness. The hounds had been appearing more and more often across the city since the huge portal she'd sensed her father opening on the edge of her range, but she still had no idea where exactly they were coming from. The residual power signature she could've used to track the portal had disappeared from her senses almost as soon as it arrived, screened by something.

Back when they'd found Tir, she'd thrown the hounds off

her track when her portal had drawn them away from the City of Souls to the Fire Lord's territory in Europe. But something must have tipped off her father to her current location, probably the damn gossip sites running stories on her 'love life' with Bast. She'd been stuck in the Tower for weeks, hiding. She needed to draw his attention away from the city before the hounds killed any more people, which is what today's insanity was all about.

Hel and Bast had kept her power and the news of their inadvertent mating bond tightly under wraps. The ever-deepening link to his soulweaving power was likely to kill her and the mating bond meant she'd take Bast with her. If anyone found out how dire things were, the city would panic and the vultures would start circling.

They had shared some of Hel's eccentricities with the ruling partnership of the city, though. Like the fact she'd once stopped the hounds with nothing more than a command. When the trail of dead bodies continued to grow despite the scouts' patrols, their captain Morrigan had suggested she try simply ordering the hounds away. Hel had realised, or hoped, she could do one better and use them as misdirection to get her father off her tail. If Bast hadn't been avoiding her like he was the plague to try and slow her succumbing to the deadly taint of his magic, he probably would've forbidden what she was about to do. She almost wished she'd let it slip as the hounds' chilling snarls carried on the wind.

Morrigan was flying somewhere above her, ready to swoop to the rescue if needed, but her azure blue and deep grey wings blended into the night sky, rendering her invisible. Even the knowledge that Hel wasn't alone couldn't calm her racing heart. A lifetime of fear running from her father's hounds didn't disappear because of a single experience.

This really was a *terrible* idea.

She was downwind of them, but as soon as they caught her scent, they'd call for reinforcements. The closer the hounds stalked, the more the sweeping lines of Bast's mating mark, like tattooed angel wings on her back, tingled with power. Its reaction to the threat sent chills through her body. If only the man himself would deign to come anywhere near her, she might've been a little more confident about facing down her hunters.

Actually, fuck that. She straightened her back a little as her hand hovered near the blades concealed in her baton. She'd protected herself just fine her whole life and now was no different.

As if to prove her thoughts wrong, she felt the delicate icy touch of the souls, who followed her to screen her portal signature from her hunters, swell into a crushing mass as they sensed the threat to her. Joining with the souls from this sector of the city, they converged on her location. The irony was that it was their compulsion to swarm as they tried to protect her from danger that put her at greatest risk of the soul taint the mating bond had left her exposed to. The cacophony of their voices threatened to lay her out cold, especially when they flocked together like this. Wincing, she stumbled back, despite the fact she hadn't been moving.

She wouldn't last long like this. The only question was whether the souls or the hounds disabled her first. Wrapping her power around herself in the hopes it would create a buffer, she reached inside for the voice of command she'd wielded once before on that day by the fountain when she'd ridden a griffin to Matiu Island.

"Stop," she growled.

The hounds froze in place. Three of them. Three creatures from her nightmares that were now so close she could make out the scar on one's ear and the faded whiplike burn from a phoenix tail on another's flank. She'd practised what she'd say before she came here, wary that her fear would paralyse her. It was more a concept that she forced into each beast's mind than words. One by one, she took over their awareness and whispered into their essence—*I was never here. You never scented me. You will find me elsewhere.* She accompanied the words with a driving urge to chase a phantom trail to a series of far distant locations.

"Go," she whispered.

They scattered just as the little breathing space she'd desperately held for herself collapsed under the pressure of the tide of souls converging. It wasn't just voices now but images, memories. Despite the souls' good intentions, the memories that pierced her defences were those of their deaths. She lived each one as if it were her own—crushed by a crumbling building, disembowelled by a feral griffin, peppered with a dozen bullets until she tumbled from the sky, flesh torn by teeth that paralysed her muscles and sent agony searing through every vein.

Hel whimpered. Distantly, pain flared as her body crashed to the cold rough ground.

"Stop," she whimpered to the dead. "Please, just leave."

The hounds had listened.

The souls did not.

"Hel! Stay with me!" She could feel the brush of feathers against her arm, but Morrigan's voice was thin and reedy to her ears, sounding like it was travelling from an impossible distance away.

4

She didn't know how long she lay there in the cold of night before a wave of fear and guilt washed over her, not her own, and something pushed back against the souls hovering close.

"What the fuck did you do?" Bast sounded just as distant as Morrigan.

The memories holding her trapped receded to a gentle lapping on the edge of her awareness, and the voices of the dead quieted.

You can't swarm around her like that. You'll kill her, Bast's voice boomed through her mind as he addressed the dead, equal parts fuming and terrified.

We had to save her. And we can't resist her, one of the souls replied. His voice was rich and old, his death a quiet slipping away into sleep that left Hel less raw than the others.

Strong arms wrapped around her shoulders and legs as Bast scooped her up. Hel nuzzled her face into his chest, letting her eyes slide closed in exhaustion as she drew in a deep breath of his familiar scent. She was slowly coming back to the world of the conscious, but she clung to this in-between state, knowing the arguments would start soon.

He'd been avoiding her for almost two months, hoping to prevent their bond from deepening and causing just this kind of problem. The feeling of sinking into his embrace was like reconnecting with a missing piece of her soul. An ache that had become so constant she no longer noticed it eased, and her body relaxed into the man holding her. Bast tightened his fingers around her in wordless response and his lips brushed the silver streak of hair that now stretched from her temple.

"Get her out of here before anything else attacks," Morrigan's clipped voice said.

The souls surrounding them surged closer at the mention of a threat and Hel groaned as their memories followed once again. Bast's fear for her searing down their connection only made it worse. The sensations threatened to throw her somewhere dark and endless that she wasn't sure she could return from. Hel reached for her power and wrapped it around them both, letting its searing blue sunshine entwine with Bast's cold starlight as it was always so desperate to. She'd meant it to calm him so she could focus on fending off the souls, but as their magic stroked against each other in a way their bodies hadn't since that single mistake of a night when they'd mated, all it did was create a new kind of distraction. She barely noticed as they surged into the air, floating in sensation until they reached the safety of home.

Home?

Her eyes flew open as that thought hit. When had she started thinking of the tower as home?

As Bast carried her into the penthouse from their balcony, Hel let out a long breath in relief. The souls that followed her to protect her from discovery when she was out in the world were a constant irritation. It was only here, inside the powerful shields anchored in the twisting black metal covering the tower, that it was safe enough for the souls to leave her be. Their overwhelming presence against every window of the building might feel like a tsunami waiting to hit, but it was still better than the voices and images that sank into her skin when they were even closer.

"What the fuck were you thinking?" Bast hissed at her,

but his hands had gentled as he lowered her into her bed and stroked a strand of hair from her face with a trembling finger.

Hel scowled up at him, her words coming slowly as she struggled to pull herself together. "I was thinking there's no point losing lives when I could just order the hounds away."

"Did Morrigan put you up to this?"

"Believe it or not, I occasionally do things just because it's the right thing to do. Something you might have realised if you were ever in the fucking vicinity," Hel said.

She struggled to sit up, every muscle in her body screaming in protest. The after effects got worse each time the souls swarmed her. She hated feeling weak. Hated what Bast's magic had done to her when they'd become mates.

Bast placed a hand firmly on her shoulder, pinning her in place. "Stop it. You need to rest," he said, his voice softening and threaded with guilt.

"Did you sedate me with our connection?" Hel asked, still dazed.

Bast's hands jerked away at the accusation in her voice, but he didn't leave. "No. That was all you spacing out," he corrected. "And if you could start taking some responsibility for *anything at all* when you're a willing participant, that'd be great."

The guilt that surged inside her was her own this time. Hel's scowl deepened as she realised Bast would be able to feel it, just like she could feel his. She didn't want him to know that she felt bad every time she lashed out at him like this. Didn't want him to know that she understood that her power reached for his every bit as much as his reached for hers. She'd blamed him for their mating bond, but she knew she was equally at fault.

"I'm working on it. I'll find a way to fix it," Bast muttered as if she'd spoken out loud. He was looking down at the bed instead of meeting her eyes.

"Fix the mating bond or fix the souls trying to kill me?" Hel asked, and immediately regretted the question, because she wasn't sure how she actually felt about the former and she didn't want Bast to find out through their connection.

Everything had happened so fast, and with him avoiding her there'd been no time to process the shift from viscerally hating him to ... whatever they were now. Wasn't it fucking typical that, just as she'd discovered she wasn't really indentured at all and she could've left the city at any time, the universe would throw this bond at her and she was back to being forced to remain? Was it too much to ask for a little choice?

"Both. They're the same thing," Bast said.

They weren't. And they both knew it. Their mating bond had opened her to a deadly vulnerability when it exposed her to his power, but there was a big difference between 'fixing' their bond by severing it and fixing the danger to her some other way. Everything in her rebelled at the thought of losing their connection, despite her confusion. Was she that desperate for connection that she would risk death by soulweaver? Severing their bond hurt too much to think about. She didn't want to know why.

Dragging her thoughts back to the present, she stared down at Bast's hand where it rested on the covers, her eyes tracing the tendons that revealed their strength. If he moved it a little to the right, it'd be touching her thigh. She could still remember the feel of his fingers against her skin the night it had all changed. The way he'd held her pinned to the wall. The desperate way he'd grasped her hips as their powers became impossibly tangled...

Ugh. That train of thought was even worse. She licked her lips and looked away as Bast groaned softly, sensing her arousal through their connection.

"You're killing me here," he rasped.

"Pretty sure that's the other way round. You'd know if I was killing you because you'd be bleeding out on the floor," Hel snapped back, cursing the feedback loop of their connection that made it impossible to hide their desire.

This was part of why they'd been avoiding each other. But his absence from her days had only heightened the tension between them every time they finally came back into each other's orbit. Fabric rustled as Bast's hand drifted closer to her body.

"Don't," Hel said. She hated the weakness in her voice, the plea.

Bast sighed and moved away. The heat of the arousal she'd sparked in him tingled across the wings tattooed with power across her back, and she watched as he rubbed his chest where her mark was now seared into his skin above his heart.

"Can I see it?" The words fell out of her mouth before she could stop them.

She'd never gotten a chance to look at it when it formed during their mating. Bast had run away too quickly, leaving her lying in bed with his words spinning through her dreams —*This may be the worst thing I've ever done.* The few times she'd seen him since, his shirts were buttoned high enough that there was no hint of its presence. He was hiding it. From her and everyone else. Hiding the proof of the depth of their mistake.

"Only if you want to deal with the possessive lust it's going to spark in you," Bast smirked, but his arrogant expression was belied by the bitter yearning she could feel from him.

Hel swallowed hard, annoyed that even the thought alone sparked some of that lust. "Leave it, then."

"Your sensitivity to the souls is getting worse," Bast observed.

Hel nodded.

"There's no point keeping our distance from each other anymore. I'm going to have to bring you with me when I travel. I need to be nearby if you have another episode. We can't let the souls keep screening your power, either. They're too dangerous that close to you."

Hel frowned. The escort of souls Bast had put in place before they bonded was the only thing that allowed her to portal to safety without her father's hunters finding her. Without them, she couldn't risk using her power, and if she was stuck travelling with Bast that was going to mean some long flight times in his arms. He'd been flitting from continent to continent containing all the known outbreaks of the contagion, and they still kept finding more.

"I thought being near *you* made it worse," she said.

Bast's guilt surged again. "No. I'd hoped it would slow the progression, but the bond is too strong already. The bigger risk is me not being there to pull you back in time."

Hel sighed and nodded. He was only speaking the truth. She didn't know how much longer she could've survived the onslaught of deaths. "How are you not affected by them?" she asked.

Bast stared at her for a long moment, and seemed to decide she deserved an explanation after her brush with death.

"My power is like a lodestone for the souls, drawing

them closer. I can shift the power they channel to me but I can't shift *them*, and it's their proximity that causes the soul taint. They can't resist the pull toward my power in you, especially when they think you're in danger, and they can't avoid the transference of their deaths when they come into contact with you. The longer my magic weaves through you, the less the souls will be able to respond when I beg them to leave you be. It will become a compulsion they can't resist."

Hel knew the feeling. The annoyingly reassuring presence of the man beside her with his black eyes ringed in silver and guilt was a compulsive temptation. Bast looked away as he continued explaining and she kicked herself for mourning the loss of his gaze.

"Most soulweavers die before adolescence when the deaths overwhelm them, but every few generations, one manages to form an instinctive shield in childhood a bit like a magical immune response, which is what I did. My shielding filters the soul's voices from their essence, so I only receive their words and power instead of the trauma of their death. I'm studying my shield so I can try and replicate it for you, but it's not something I ever consciously made. The shielding is anchored in the structure of my wings. That's part of why they glow with power the way they do. I don't know how to recreate it for you without that anchor. But I won't stop trying." Bast raised his hand as if to hold hers and then dropped it again, standing up. "I'll text you next time I get called out to deal with the contagion. You'll have to come with me," he said.

Then he strode from the room as if her father's hounds were chasing him. Leaving her alone. Again. Because why would he spend any longer in her presence than he absolutely had to? And why did she want him to? Ugh. She needed a drink.

Hel's entire body protested as she tried to sit up. The residual ache felt like her soul was trying to tear itself away from her bones, one painful tendon at a time. She wasn't going anywhere fast. Fine. If she couldn't go to the whiskey, it would have to come to her. She flicked a quick message to Morrigan and Ra, dragging her pillow higher so she could at least sit upright in comfort. Screw Bast. If he was going to abandon her again, then he could deal with her stealing his friends.

I think your man would literally kill me if I got you drunk right now, the Scout Captain replied a moment later, to Hel's disgust.

A soft knock at the door distracted her from her scathing response and she looked up in time to see Ra pushing it open with a sly grin on his face. There was a man who didn't care he was pissing off the lord of the city. Or, rather, there was a man who took perverse pleasure in trying to force Bast to face their bond even though he still had reservations about her.

"You called, m'lady?" he said, sweeping an ironic bow, one hand clutching a bottle of whiskey and two crystal tumblers in the other.

"Not a lady," she shot back. "Is that Bast's reserve stash?"

"If you didn't want to be a lady, you shouldn't have mate bonded to a lord. It's too late now. And if I'm putting my friendship at risk to bring you alcohol, then it's going to be *good* alcohol."

Hel rolled her eyes and let him pour them both a generous helping. "Please. I know where mine and Bast's non-relationship stands compared to your friendship, and it's so far down it's not funny. You're not risking anything."

Ra gave her a sideways look as he settled on the bed next to her, stretching his legs out across the covers and making himself right at home. "That's not true, and you know it. I can feel how much he cares for you through our connection. You must feel it ten times stronger."

Hel took another sip of the smooth whiskey that warmed her all the way down and decided it was time to change the subject. "Speaking of feelings, how're you and that Earth Lord of yours doing?"

Ra's phone vibrated with a message at that moment and his expression turned carefully neutral as he read it. He had a great poker face, but the fact he'd had to don it was obvious.

Hel broke into hysterics. "Ra Cooper! Are you sexting the Earth Lord?"

"No! You really are a brat. No more whiskey for you."

Hel leaned over and snatched his phone away from him before he realised what she was doing. Her eyes widened as she read the message. "Awww. That's kinda sweet. I think I just vomited in my mouth a little."

Mica had sent a picture of the sun setting over the forest near the cave system that made up his stronghold on the Asian continent with a message saying it reminded him of the hills surrounding the City of Souls. It was short, formal and totally neutral in tone, but the fact he'd seen a beautiful sunset and sent a photo to the human second-in-command of a ruler the courts barely tolerated said it all. Not sexting then. But probably as close as Mica got to it, Hel thought with a smirk. He was such an odd match for the playfully irreverent man sitting beside her, but she could tell from Ra's uncharacteristic embarrassment that he was just as interested as the Earth Lord.

Ra grabbed his phone back and shoved it into his pocket. "Stop interfering."

"I will if you will. When are you going to see him next?"

"How are you feeling, anyway?"

"Subtle topic change there, bro," Hel said, her smirk widening. Then she sighed as Ra just kept looking at her expectantly until she caved. "My physical injuries are all healed up."

"And the mating bond?"

"Is not ideal."

"Give me a bit more to go on here. I need to be prepared," he said, some of his deep concern for Bast showing through.

"For me to succumb and die, you mean? I'm not there yet."

"Hel!"

"Fine. When I'm inside the tower, I can ignore the slow degeneration because that bastard being here and *never wanting to see me* is enough of a distraction. When I'm outside the tower, it's like I'm cloaked in deaths and as soon as I'm in danger they pierce me from every direction. It's worse each time. Bast says I need to stay near him now so he can pull me out if I'm dying."

"Well, shit. That sucks," Ra said.

Hel barked out a bitter laugh. "Yup. Pretty much. Would not recommend."

"Is there anything I can do?"

Hel shrugged. "Bring me whiskey when I need it?"

She wouldn't admit it, but after years of isolating herself from everyone, she'd quickly grown addicted to the company she'd found here at the tower—Ra's teasing, Ana's mothering, Kaia's curious enthusiasm. She wasn't alone anymore, and she wasn't sure she'd survive going back to that loneliness if she had to run. Luckily, it looked like Bast's soulweaving magic would take her out long before her father would hunt her down, anyway.

She didn't have a connection to Ra, but he must have sensed the turn her thoughts had taken because he slung an arm around her shoulders and pulled her close.

"It'll be ok. Bast will figure it out. Now, try and look like you're having fun, so I can take a selfie and rub his nose in what he's missing."

At some point, Hel must've given in to exhaustion and Ra must've left because she woke to a flurry of feathers smacking her in the face as a cheeky twelve year old bounced on her otherwise empty bed.

"Wake up, Auntie Hellkitten! You promised you'd let me try out your blades today!"

Hel groaned and tried to shove her head further under her pillow, but Kaia wasn't having any of it.

"I brought you kawakawa tea!"

Hel prised an eye open to see the tea balanced precariously on her side table, dangerously close to the girl's overexcited wings. Hooking a foot around Kaia's knee, she used a grappling move to shift Kaia to the other side of the bed and then propped herself up enough that she could rescue the magically infused steaming energy boost.

"Hey! No fair!" Kaia complained, now lying on her tummy and propping herself up on her elbows to glare at

Hel. The electric blue of her outer feathers spread across the bed like a second blanket.

"Life isn't fair," Hel said, feeling every day of her twenty-five jaded years as she took a sip of tea to hide how her expression had turned dark. She didn't want to be the one to take away this girl's carefree happiness. Although, with the way Kaia's power was blossoming, it wouldn't be long before the danger forced her to move to one of the courts for training. Then it would only be a matter of time before she lost that beautiful innocence.

Kaia poked out her tongue and blew a raspberry at her, startling a chuckle from Hel that almost sent tea spraying down her front. She smiled and ruffled the girl's white-blonde hair that was so close to the cream colour of her inner wings. Her Māori heritage was there to see in the facial features and beautiful skin tone that echoed her human mother's, but even ignoring the wings, there was so much of her father's elemental heritage in her appearance. Hel felt a moment of pain for the girl that she'd never known her father. Not that Hel had ever known hers either, but Kaia's sounded like he'd been a genuinely nice guy. Whereas Hel's was still trying to hunt her down and kill her, and she didn't even know why.

"Are you done yet?" Kaia asked, flapping her wings in excitement.

The draft she generated sent strands of Hel's dark hair into her mug, and she quickly fished them out and drank back the rest of the spicy brew before the girl could send the cup itself flying.

"Let me have a shower and some breakfast. Then, if you can throw me three times I'll let you handle a *practice* blade."

Kaia pouted. "But you *promised*."

"I promised I'd teach you blades. I said nothing about letting you use mine."

Kaia sniffed and rolled off the bed. "Just for that, I'm going to throw you *four* times. And I'll get Uncle Ra to film it and show Uncle Basti."

Hel hid her smile and made her way to the en-suite.

When she returned to her bedroom wearing a pair of old black jeans and a faded tank with her hair braided out of the way ready to train, a very sad-faced girl was sitting on the bed holding Hel's satellite phone.

"Uncle Basti texted. He said you need to go meet him on the roof."

Hel gently took the phone from her and glanced at the message. It had no other information. Rolling her eyes, she went back to her wardrobe to grab some warmer clothes suitable for flying long distances. Luckily, she didn't feel the cold like a human would. She assumed he was needed somewhere to deal with the contagion. Strapping her baton to her thigh holster, she shrugged on her leather jacket as she walked out the bedroom door. By the time she reached the kitchen, Ana was ready with homemade protein bars to stash in her pockets and a small flask of water she could hook on her belt.

"Sorry, kid," Hel murmured to Kaia as she finished securing everything she needed. "We'll practise next time I'm home."

Kaia threw herself into Hel's arms, squeezing her tight. Hel swallowed the emotions that rose in response. Kaia was all-in, always. A bundle of curiosity and affection wrapped up in endless enthusiasm. She sent a silent wish to the universe, not for the first time, that the girl never lost that.

"Be careful, Auntie."

"I will, sweetheart. Be good."

Ana snorted at that and gave Hel's shoulders a half-hug in response before gently disentangling Kaia and pushing Hel toward the door. "He's waiting."

Hel rolled her eyes. "He could've come and fetched me in person if he was in a hurry."

She took the stairs two at a time up to the roof terrace and, despite her fear of leaving the safety of the tower, she couldn't help her tremor of excitement at getting to fly once more. She loved the rush of the ground falling away beneath her feet and the cold, clean air of the upper reaches of the sky. Even if it meant she'd have to be wrapped in the arms of the infuriating man who'd been avoiding her, held against his taut muscles with that deliciously surging motion of his wingbeats.

CHAPTER 2
BAST

Bast did his best to pretend every nerve in his body didn't stand to attention when Hel stepped out onto the terrace. The morning light glinted off that ever-thickening streak of silver in her hair, making her seem beyond mere human beauty, which she probably was. She'd never responded to his accusation that she wasn't human, but it was the most likely explanation for the deadly mate bond they'd formed. He had no idea what else she could be. Other than the Archivist Tir, there were only humans and elementals on the Melded Earths.

Their connection thrummed between them now they were within sight of each other, like a rubber band pulled tight for too long and desperate to return to its natural state. His eyes flicked down to her luscious lips and the leather jacket that hid too much of her beautiful body from him as she stalked in his direction.

"You're late," he said, turning away from temptation to face the twenty-nine storey drop that would be dizzying to someone without wings but made his blood sing.

"I was in the shower when you texted."

Her clipped words short-circuited his brain, filling his mind with the image of her naked and wet and sending a surge of arousal straight to his cock. He bit back a groan. The past two months of avoiding her had been an exercise in self-torture, but he refused to let his magic drive her to an early grave. He'd hoped the distance he'd forced between them would be enough to slow down her susceptibility to the souls that surrounded the city. It hadn't.

"Was it something I said?" Hel asked with false innocence.

Bast glanced over at her and saw her sinful mouth twist up in a smirk, but she wasn't immune either. Her breath was faster than it needed to be, especially for his hellcat whose breathing was usually unnaturally slow. Her tongue flicked out to wet her lips as he watched and the movement held him captivated. Need surged through the strands of their power that had woven together. Mating bonds were rare among his kind and he'd never paid much attention to the details about them, but even he knew the weeks after a bond formed were usually spent together, in bed and everywhere else. He physically ached for her. And that was nothing compared to the ache in his soul.

"We need to get going. Mica's had another contagion outbreak." He held out his hand to Hel and waited, wings flared out slightly for balance as the wind gusted across the roof.

The first touch of her fingers to his both soothed and exacerbated the ache filling him. As he tucked her in close to his chest, he felt her breathe a silent sigh of relief. His hands skimmed up her sides beneath her jacket as he prepared to lift her into his arms. For a moment, he lost himself in the feel of her body against his. Her jasmine and steel scent washed over him as his thumbs stroked her ribs and one hand drifted to her lower back, pulling her closer still. He let his head drop until his nose was brushing against the softness of her cheek, not sure if he wanted her to turn her face up so their lips could meet or to pull away. He wished things could be different. Wished his power wasn't consuming her. That her secrets didn't fill him with distrust. As the ever-present wind picked up, he wrapped his wings around them both, keeping the cold air from her face.

"Bast," her soft voice cracked on the word and he couldn't tell if it was a warning or a plea.

It was his turn to sigh. Scooping her up into his arms, he launched them out into the open air before he could make any more mistakes. He smiled despite himself as he felt Hel's uncontained joy at flying fizzle down their connection like champagne bubbles against his soul. Her eyes shone as she watched the harbour waters pass far below, and he pressed a kiss to her neck. She'd wrapped her legs around his waist so he wasn't carrying all her weight in his arms and there was no hiding exactly how much his body appreciated hers pressed against him.

It was going to be a really fucking long day.

"I'm going to use my magic to shield us from the wind and speed us up. It shouldn't draw the souls any closer and we'll be clear of most of them soon anyway, but let me know if it becomes a problem."

Hel stiffened in his arms as he reached for his power and channelled it to propel them faster above the ocean that now stretched endless to the horizon.

"You okay, Hellkitten?"

"It's manageable," Hel said.

Bast frowned in concern. He'd released the souls he'd had following Hel to screen her power, but he had his own invisible entourage as well. He couldn't risk making them back off because that would leave him reliant on only the power reserves he could store in his wings. They would be flying too far from any populations of the dead for him to draw magic from.

"I could ask a scout to come accompany us and carry you," he offered, even though every cell in his body protested that she was his to carry, his to protect.

Hel shook her head and nuzzled in closer to his chest. "The pain of being so close and not touching you would be worse," she whispered after a long silence.

Bast searched for a topic that might distract them. "I feel like I spend half my time in other territories dealing with the contagion right now. We keep searching for some pattern to predict where it'll come next, but we can't figure it out. They're usually somewhere close to a stronghold or major city, but out of the way enough that they don't behave like that outbreak we dealt with in the childcare centre. Luckily. If we had one growing that fast and I couldn't get there in time, I don't want to think what might happen."

Bast shuddered as he remembered holding back that contagion while Hel and the scouts cleared the building. It had been mindlessly ravenous, a life-sucking sinister ivy that left pure absence in its wake. A black hole that devoured reality. The unpopulated locations he'd been dealing with recently had been bad enough, but when it had formed so close to so many lives, everything about its behaviour had changed—the speed it spread, the way it tried to cut off any escape. It was truly terrifying to imagine what it would do in a city if it wasn't caught quickly. He'd barely been able to rein it in on that one building.

"Will your containment shields hold?" Hel asked.

"I don't know. For now, they will. They have to. They're anchored well and the way my power repels the contagion means it's not actually touching it to contain it. In theory, it shouldn't erode or weaken over time. But I can't imagine a force like that remaining quiescent. And I don't know what will happen if I die."

Hel's arms tightened around his body at the reminder and, despite the depressing topic, he felt a surge of satisfaction at the possessive hold.

"Tell me something I don't know about you."

"Still trying to get me to spill my secrets?" Hel sniped.

"We can work up to that. Tell me anything. Tell me about teenage Hel growing up on the streets of the City of Souls. I'm sure you must've given Ryker some grey hairs."

They flew in silence for another few minutes before Hel's soft voice murmured in his ear. She didn't spill her secrets, not on purpose, but she did gift him stories from her time in the city they shared. He knew she thought she was giving him nothing, merely recounting the routine dangers faced by a courier. But her tone and the feedback down their connection all told him far more than she meant to.

Her pointed remarks about debt were designed to injure him. It was a running argument despite the fact she now knew the truth that he had no part in her indenture and even Ryker had only bought her debt to keep her safe. But mostly what she revealed when she spoke about her debt and employment was a deeply rooted sense of fairness and equity that extended far beyond herself. Perhaps not as far toward the elementals as he would hope, but even there she was softening. He could feel it in her emotions as she spoke, and he'd seen it in her fledgling friendship with Morrigan. She was not the selfish, uncaring person she'd first seemed.

Her stories of learning parkour in the alleyways running between elemental and human buildings fit with that shock of joy he felt from her every time they took off. She loved heights and the adrenaline rush of speeding through the air as much as any elemental. She even laughed when he recounted his own childhood attempts at parkour when he'd been grounded, literally, by his foster-parents. Coordination was a challenge for oversized wings on a body that was growing too fast to find its centre of balance.

"Oh shit, talking of grounding. Ana had to resort to threats to stop Kaia from launching off the roof yesterday," Hel said.

Bast smiled. "She's growing up so fast. It won't be long before she'll need that practice."

"Before you send her away, you mean?" Hel asked sharply, but Bast could feel there was no real heat in her words.

She understood the dangers of leaving Kaia's power untrained. Another part of his essence thawed toward this woman who was already so fiercely protective of the family he'd chosen.

"Yes. Before then."

"Has Mica agreed to take her yet?"

"He seems amenable. The bigger challenge will be getting him to accept someone from home to accompany her. Teens rarely bring anyone with them, but power of that level runs in families who give their loyalty to a single court. Students usually have plenty of familiar faces around them, either at the stronghold teaching or as part of the city's mage force. Kaia won't have that. Her father's family disowned him when he abandoned the courts to move to the Free City, and I don't even know what court they belong to."

"What's Mica's problem with having someone go with her?"

"We get along for now, but that doesn't mean he trusts having one of my people in his stronghold. He'll assume they're a spy, if not a saboteur. It's just the nature of court politics."

"And would they be?"

"Of course. Spy, not saboteur. But I wouldn't let it put Kaia's education at risk. She would be the priority."

"I bet he'd be okay with Ra," Hel said, smirking, and Bast's laughter filled the air around them.

"The thought has occurred to me. He's my back-up plan if all else fails. I need him at home, but Kaia will need someone more."

"Can't Ana just go with her? They won't see a human as a threat."

Bast sighed. "Even if it wouldn't be deeply uncomfortable for Ana as a human in an elemental stronghold, I don't think that would be the best idea. She didn't have long enough with Kaia's father to learn about our children and there are so few young elemental families in our city for her to see what is normal for a child of Kaia's age. I love her, but she is overprotective. Learning to control power like Kaia will have is dangerous. We can't protect her from that process, because if she fails, she'll die. If any of her mother's fear or doubt affected her, it could have catastrophic consequences."

"So, we'll talk Mica round then. He's in your debt."

Bast couldn't help but kiss her again in response to that

assertion and the way she'd made it their shared goal. If only they really could be a partnership. He couldn't do that to her, though. She'd die if she stayed with him. He had to find a way to sever their bond.

If everything went well, Hel would've run far away from him by the time Kaia was ready for training. If everything didn't, they'd both be dead.

THEY ARRIVED in the elemental city that bounded the Earth stronghold in the early afternoon, a little over twelve hours after they set out. The strength of Bast's power supplementing his flight meant the travel time to the Asian continent was less than most others of his kind would've taken, but he'd held back a little to conserve his strength. He wasn't going to put his mate at risk by exhausting himself and leaving them vulnerable to attack.

The Earth Court's organic elemental structures slowly emerged from the tropical forest below them. Soaring turrets of limestone twined through trees like they'd pierced up through the earth from the extensive caves that riddled the earth beneath. Rows of white stalagmites supported arching covered bridges that protected Mica's people from aerial attack as they traversed between buildings nestled in the canopy, just as the causeways between high-rises in the City of Souls did. There was little sign of human architecture. Mica's lands might have fallen prey to the most ravenous incursions of the contagion in the last few years, but he had avoided most of the fall-out from the Melding by virtue of his city occupying land that had been a nature reserve in the human earth.

The warm, humid air was cloying and Bast's muscles ached as he shifted a sleeping Hel in his arms. She might be prickly when awake, but contentment filled him that she was comfortable enough to rest in his arms while he kept an eye on the increasing numbers of elementals soaring below him. Years of fleeing his homicidal brother had left him wary of his own people, despite the positive turn his relationship with the other courts had taken recently. Well, half the courts anyway. His brother Tyson wasn't actively trying to kill him anymore, as far as he knew, but he wasn't talking to him either. And if the reports of his spies were anything to go by, the ruler of Air Court, Lady Aliya, was gathering fighters around her. He wasn't sure whether that was to defend against his presumed wrath or to launch an attack and finish what she'd started with Tyson when they'd killed Bast and mounted his body on her wall. At least the power he'd demonstrated with his resurrection had made her cautious enough to stay clear for now.

A flash of sun reflecting off shining copper wings nearby pulled him back from his reflections and Hel groaned into his chest as his hands tightened around her, waking her from her sleep.

"I think every muscle in my body is cramping," Hel complained.

"We'll land soon. Mica's heading our way."

Bast gently rearranged the woman in his arms until her legs wrapped around his waist again. He couldn't help but let out a silent sigh of relief as he redistributed the drag of her weight. His mate was relatively slim, but she was dense with muscle. He thought he'd masked the sound, but his discomfort must have travelled along the bond regardless, because his usually grumpy hellkitten started kneading his shoulder muscles, massaging out the pain. His wingbeats stuttered in surprise, and they dropped a foot before he recovered. Hel's laugh tickled against the skin of his neck and his own mouth twitched in response.

"Watch the road, mister," Hel said, her voice still slurring a little as she woke up.

A sensation of giddy sleep deprivation sneaked down their connection. He knew it wouldn't last. Any moment now she would shake off whatever dream had softened her sharp edges and they'd be back where they always were. Wherever that was. They'd lost their way somewhere between guilt and anger. Never quite made it to bargaining and depression.

He pulled himself together as Mica's strong wingbeats brought him within earshot ahead of them.

"Bastion. Helaine. It is good to see you," the Earth Lord called. His voice was laced with tiredness and he looked unusually dishevelled, his white collared shirt half untucked beneath a silk waistcoat.

"Lord Mica," Bastion said, holding a hover mid-air as he nodded in greeting.

"Can I offer you somewhere to rest before we head out?" Nothing in Mica's voice or expression gave away anything but calm, but Bast could see the tension across his shoulders and arms that were too stiff by his sides. He was worried.

"You always were too polite for your own good. We can rest once we've sorted the outbreak," Bast said.

Relief flashed across Mica's face before he simply said a quiet "Thank you" that held a raft of emotion. "This way."

Mica banked to the west, leading them to the far outskirts of the city. Hel shifted in Bast's arms and he glanced down at her face to see she was frowning and biting her lip in thought.

"You okay?" he asked her, resisting the urge to take over biting her lip for her.

"Yeah. Mica's stronghold is saying hi. And I can feel the contagion ahead and ... something else. Something new."

"New good or new bad?" Bast asked as he gently explored the sensation of Hel's awareness of the stronghold through their bond.

He'd been the tiniest bit jealous that she had the ability to communicate with the courts' strongholds like every elemental except him could. For the first time in his life, he could feel the wary but welcoming presence of the stronghold through Hel. It didn't surprise him it had a deep calm that mirrored its unflappable elemental lord and sank deep into the maze-like limestone cave system below the earth's surface that made up its body.

He treasured the experience Hel had given him. Without her, he would've spent an immortal lifetime blind to this presence he'd never been able to conceive was so fundamental to elemental lives and society. Her face softened as she sensed the wonder and gratitude he was hiding and her hand pressed to his heart briefly, reaching for her mark on his skin.

"New bad. Whatever it is reeks of the same power as my ... hunter," she said, replying to his earlier question he'd almost forgotten he'd asked.

The long pause in her sentence before she'd found the word hunter had Bast wondering what she'd almost said instead. Secrets filled the silence between her words until he could almost taste them on his tongue and her body thrummed with tension at whatever this unknown new threat was.

"Is it safe for you here? I could take you to Mica's stronghold and return alone," he offered.

Hel shook her head. "I need to see what's going on."

Ahead of them, Mica descended in a tight spiral to green pasture nestled in between the steep forested hills. The cleared space among the otherwise tropical jungle provided farmland to supply food to the stronghold. He could see why Mica was so worried. There might not be many people here at risk, but if they lost this land they'd have to clear more or replace the local supply by trading with those further afield. Just like Bast had made Soul Tower a self-sufficient ecosystem to protect his family, Mica wouldn't want to rely on anyone else for the basics they needed to live.

The point of contagion on the pasture's edge was as clear as an inkblot on an otherwise blank page. Seething darkness absorbed the bright daylight until even the surrounding air became washed out. Colours lost their vibrancy and each breath of air was a little harder to take than the last.

"You should stand well clear," Bast murmured into Hel's hair as he brought them down next to Mica on the grass.

Ignoring her scowl, he braced her body while she took a moment to regain her balance after so long being carried in his arms.

"Why did you bring her?" Mica asked him.

"She can hear you, asshole. She's standing right here," Hel snapped at the Earth Lord.

Mica blinked and swept into a bow. "Forgive me, Helaine. Why are you here?"

Bast hid a smirk as Hel figured out what to say in response. She must've felt his amusement because she glared at him again. He loved feeling her anger. The way her eyes glittered with emotion. The sense of building recklessness that he knew if he could just nudge in the right direction might snap their control and ... fuck. He needed to calm down. This mating bond was making everything between them too acute. Hel was picking up on where his thoughts had gone and he could see her breaths coming faster, the movement of her chest's rise and fall holding him captivated. They couldn't be this for each other. They needed to break this bond, not feed it. He locked everything down.

"She just can't bear to be away from me," Bast said, knowing it would throw her back toward burning rage.

Rage was good. Rage was safe. It was that other heat they needed to steer well clear of. The usually reserved Mica broke into laughter and Bast cocked an eyebrow in question.

"You are a braver man than me, Bastion. Shall we?"

Bast waited for Mica to head toward the black absence of the contagion nearby and then turned to Hel. "Can you still feel the new threat? Is it here?"

Hel looked like she was struggling not to spit expletives at him. Bast watched as she swallowed hard and squared her shoulders as if being polite was an act of impossible strength.

"It's nearby. Somewhere that way," she said, jerking her chin toward the rock-strewn scrub in the distance.

Bast nodded. "We can check it out on the way home."

"Go do your saviour-complex thing so we can leave already," Hel snapped, turning her back on him and starting a series of stretches that left him biting back another groan as she showed just how flexible she was.

Bast shook his head in disgust at himself and spun toward Mica, striding away from the temptation behind him. He was all for fucking who and when you wanted, but this burning need was more like an addiction he had no control over. The bloody mating urges would be the death of him. He flinched at the thought that was too close to the truth. If only this damn contagion would take a rest for a week, he'd be able to focus on sorting out how to shield Hel from the souls that fuelled his power.

"Ready?" Mica asked him as he drew alongside the copper-winged lord.

"Always," Bast said, already calling to the dead of this place and drawing their power to him.

This was his fifth trip to help Mica deal with the contagion. Something about the Earth Lord's territory seemed to attract the darkness that destroyed reality more than anywhere else. The two of them were well-practised in weaving their magics toward this common aim now. Mica seamlessly stepped in to anchor the containment sphere to the ley lines flowing beneath them as soon as Bast's soul-weaving compressed the danger as tightly as possible within its bounds.

Bast staggered as he released the magic and his vision blurred. A firm hand gripped his arm, holding him steady.

"Come, Bastion. You need to rest. Let's get you and Helaine back to my stronghold," Mica said.

Bast regained his focus at the sound of Hel's name. Turning toward the spot where he'd left her, he blinked slowly. The only movement was the slight breeze through the grass. There was no sign of his hellcat. He was about to call out to her when a shock of terror stabbed through their bond.

He was launching himself northward before he'd even had time to process the sensation, following the pull of her essence on his soul. Every beat of his wings felt like he was hauling lead weights from the earth that was speeding too slowly beneath him. Still breathless from the effort of the power he'd expended, the air in his lungs now sliced like broken glass as he fought to fly faster.

"What's wrong?" Mica asked as he swooped alongside him, not nearly as exhausted by their efforts as Bast was.

"Hel's in danger," Bast said, his eyes scanning the rocky outcrops for any sign of her black-clad form. How had she travelled so far, so quickly?

"You're certain?"

Bast's head snapped around and he fought back the anger that would distract him from his purpose. "Positive," he snapped back.

"Interesting," Mica murmured from beside him, but he didn't have time for the Earth Lord. He needed to find his mate.

As they crested the ridgeline, the reason for Hel's fear became clear. A dozen of the starhounds that hunted her were slinking back toward a point on the far side of the small gully, no doubt sent packing by her strange ability to command them. Her commands had made no difference to the shadowy humanoid shapes still attacking her. Their wraithlike forms drifted on the breeze until they lunged in sudden bursts. The ringing clang of their swords against her metal baton said they were far more tangibly dangerous than the ethereal ghosts they appeared to be.

As they surged again, he felt Hel's pain radiate through him as the pommel of a sword caught her cheekbone. Bast watched in horror as she sunk to her knees and the hand holding her baton dropped to the ground. Hel's knuckles were white as she clenched tight to the metal of her favourite weapon, but her arms seemed to have lost the strength to wield it. Bast felt a fist clutching his soul as the wraiths closed in, and then he panicked even more when he realised what the sensation actually was. Not a metaphorical fist, but a desperate grasp for his power from his mate. A strangled cry left his lips as he let her take his power as his own, unable to deny her and desperate to keep her safe.

An explosion of death magic shuddered out from Hel, shattering the incorporeal forms of her attackers. He would have rolled his eyes at the crudeness of the strike if he wasn't so terrified he'd just let her kill herself with his power. It was so very her. He hadn't even realised they could use each other's power, and she just grabbed it and made a fucking bomb. Every soul in the surrounding region turned their attention her way, powerless to resist the call of his power in her body and the threat to her person. They were distant but closing in fast. The temporary quiet on the plane of the dead like the waters that receded before a tsunami hit the shore.

Bast landed next to his mate's crumpled form so hard he was driven to his knees, barely noticing the sharp scree that pierced his clothes.

"Hel. Talk to me, sweetheart. Say something."

Silence.

Scooping her body up into his arms, he was relieved to feel the tiniest puff of breath against his neck when he nestled her head into his shoulder.

"You're exhausted, Bastion. Whatever was attacking her is gone. Let me take her," Mica said, his voice gentle as if he was cajoling a recalcitrant wild animal.

"No. She's mine," Bast snapped, holding her tighter.

He knew he needed a plan. Knew he shouldn't be revealing anything to Mica. He couldn't make his brain form thoughts past his need for the woman in his arms to wake up.

He needed to get her as far from here as possible before her hunters called for reinforcements.

"I can see that. I'm not stupid enough to get between a man and his mate. Let me help," Mica kept cajoling.

Panic whipped through Bast as he realised the secret of his connection to Hel that wasn't even known by his own people was now exposed. He pushed the feeling back. There wasn't time to think about it. As he looked in the direction the hounds had disappeared, he noticed a cave-mouth in the distance. But every time he tried to look at it, his eyes slid sideways and the air blurred until the lines of the rocky hill face became softened and indeterminate. Remembering Hel's earlier words, he drew a little on that strange power of hers that had writhed through every part of his soul.

Looking with his mate's power instead of his own, he could see a huge shard of metallic stone piercing the earth at the cave's entrance. The clouded forms of the wraiths regathering around it were punctuated by the shining blood-red eyes of the starhounds who'd retreated. They wouldn't stay away for long now that Hel was unconscious, and Mica and his people wouldn't be any help if they couldn't even see them.

The Earth Lord's concerned face entered his field of vision, blocking off the view as he remained oblivious to the threat behind them. "Bastion, please."

Bast jerked back, every instinct screaming at him to hold Hel close, to take her home where she'd be safe from her hunters. With his mate's magic still flowing through him and her body cradled limp and vulnerable in his arms, the intensity of his need was enough to overwhelm his common sense. If she could use his power, he should be able to use hers. Hel's magic responded to his desperation, channelling through him to shape a portal before he'd even consciously thought about making it happen.

"Fuck," he whispered.

He'd just have to hope Mica's sense of honour and obligation kept him quiet until he'd figured out how to explain this to him. Portalling was something no one but Tir could do.

As he stumbled through the gateway, the shiver of Hel's power mixed with his own and their interwoven magic teased across his skin like a caress. He landed hard on his tailbone, sharp pain radiating from the lower edge of the wing he'd crushed beneath him as he twisted to keep hold of Hel. He'd already been running on fumes before Hel had dragged his magic from him to use for that explosion; draining him beyond what his body could take. He didn't so much close the portal as sever it from all power the second they crossed its threshold.

The souls embedded in the Tower's defences surged around them, desperate to protect Hel from whatever had rendered her unconscious and putting her at far greater risk as they did so. The only thing that kept them from her was Bast's desperate scream and the vast balancing pull of the magical metal vines coating the Tower they resided in. For now, it was enough to keep them hovering just outside. But as the soul taint progressed in her, even that wouldn't be enough to keep them away.

CHAPTER 3
HEL

The ceiling slowly came into focus as Hel woke. It was dark blue, and the sheets twisted around her limbs were black. She'd woken in Bast's bed. Alone. Again. Only this time, she couldn't even remember the night before. The last thing she remembered was the chill of the wraiths pushing down into her and drowning in the screams of the dead. Shivering, she sat up and groaned as her skull throbbed. A quick glance to the other side of the bed left her no wiser as to whether her infuriating saviour had shared it with her. Why take her to his bed to recuperate if he wasn't even going to stick around?

A flash of relief down their bond told her Bast had realised she was conscious. The connection that had turned her body into a compass with him as true north was an ever-present gentle tug downward. He was probably hiding in his office on the floor below. The background noise of the Tower's souls seemed to have increased in volume while she'd been gone. They were now an ever-present pressure around her like she was inside a soap bubble waiting for it to pop and expose her to their violent power. It was their drive to protect her that caused that hyper-focus, and it would probably kill her. All she could do was project calm and safety and hope they stayed clear.

Someone had left painkillers and a glass of water on the side table, which she gratefully downed before leaning back against the headboard and waiting for everything to stop feeling so much. That's what she told herself, anyway. She definitely wasn't waiting to see if someone was going to come check on her. Just like she wasn't breathing deep as Bast's lingering scent enveloped her.

She was about to attempt standing when the door cracked open. A smile spread across her face despite her headache as Tir drifted into the room, the tentacles cascading from their scalp undulating softly toward her in concern.

"It is good to see you awake, Helaine," they said, standing awkwardly near the bed.

"Where have you been all these weeks? Come sit down. I'm going to get a crick in my neck looking up at you, and I'm sore enough as it is," Hel replied, patting the bed beside her.

Rows of razor-sharp teeth appeared between too many lips as Tir smiled in reply, but it didn't bother her. She felt a strange affinity to the Archivist despite how different they appeared. Tir had called her a distant cousin not so long ago, and she wondered how true that might be. They were both the only ones of their kind on this world. Not that she had a clue what she actually was because her guardian had shapeshifted her to a human form as a baby and now she was stuck that way. She and Tir were also the only beings in the Melded Earths who could portal. She frowned a little, fighting confusion as the thought prompted a vague memory of Bast channelling her power at the Earth Court.

As if they'd read her thoughts, Tir volunteered the answer to her unspoken question. "Bastion borrowed your power to portal you home. It was quite clever. I thought I'd better come and check on you."

"How long was I out?"

"A little over a day."

Hel smiled as Tir produced a plate from behind their back with a flourish. The delicious aroma of buttery scones filled the air as they both tore open the fluffy dough to scoop jam and cream on top despite the fact it was the middle of the night, judging by the darkness outside. They sat in comfortable silence as they ate. Apparently Tir could sink their razor fangs into a still-twitching giant winged spider monster for dinner and still fancy a Devonshire tea.

"This world's not all bad," Tir said as they swallowed their last bite and licked the crumbs from their deceptively delicate fingers.

"Where are you from?" Hel asked.

Tir's terrifying smile returned to their face as they deflected. "How are you feeling?"

Hel shrugged and picked at the woollen throw beside her. One of the tentacles wreathing from Tir's scalp snuck across her lap and twined around her hand, tugging it away before she could damage the threads.

"I don't know how much longer I can take it. I'm safe from the hunters here, but this is the epicentre of his power. The sensation of the souls that shield the tower crawling on the edges of my awareness is driving me mad. Each time they swarm while I'm out is worse than the time before," Hel said finally.

"If anyone can take it, it's you. You have the strength of both your parents."

Hel froze in place and she could swear even the dust motes hanging in the air stopped dancing. "You know who my parents are?" she whispered, half terrified and half hopeful. She knew it was her father whose hunters she fled, but she'd never known who her mother was.

"Don't worry. I won't tell anyone. Your secrets are yours to share. Or not. Your mother sacrificed her life to keep you hidden. I'm not going to betray that. Amira would come back across the veil and haunt me forever if I did," Tir said.

Hel blinked in shock. She'd always wondered if her guardian was more than she seemed, but Amira had refused to answer any questions about her parentage. Hel had outright asked her if she was her daughter and her answer had been—*you are my atonement*. An atonement her mother had left instructions with Tir on how to betray.

Tir seemed oblivious to the bombshell they'd just dropped on her.

"For what it's worth, I think you could tell your mate it's your father hunting you. Amira clearly thought you were the key to stopping him. Bast might be able to help you figure it out through your mating connection."

Well, that explained a lot. Tir had misunderstood the message Amira had left—*I thought we were leaving him to burn, but the contagion's darkness slipped in behind us through the gate. Watch for his vanguard and the shards of stasis. He is the self-proclaimed Emperor of Suns. The Melding was his firebreak. Do not let him repeat it. When there is no choice left, call for my atonement.*

Hel had been born shortly after the Melding of the human and elemental earths into one reality. The Melding had killed millions, created mass destruction of the world's cities, and resulted in years of power struggles between the two species forced to co-exist until the elemental courts took full control of the world. It would've been hard enough trying to raise a child through that apocalypse at the best of times, let alone while fleeing someone as powerful as her father.

Perhaps Tir had known her guardian in happier times, before the rage and running. Before the endless shame and thinly veiled hatred that now made a sick kind of sense. How had Amira come to be pregnant to Hel's monster of a father? It didn't bear thinking about. No wonder she'd always pushed Hel away. Their whole short time together, only thirteen years, had been about denying her father, not protecting Hel. It was a life of flying below the radar, being nothing more than a shadow wherever they went, and never, ever, calling attention to themselves. When she'd written to *Call for my atonement,* she'd meant to shout Hel's existence to the world and draw Hel from hiding. She'd meant they should serve her child up to the man who wanted her dead. But Tir had no idea Amira had called Hel that.

Hel delayed responding to Tir's suggestion by shifting her plate off the bed and rolling to her feet. She'd spent enough time lying down. It was making her feel weak. Vulnerable. There was no way she was going to share who she was with Bast. He already knew she wasn't human, but if she told him everything, it would only be a matter of time before he put two and two together. He'd figure out she was the atonement her mother's note had said to call for. From there, it wouldn't take long to figure out why.

Would he sacrifice her to her father to save them from the ravaging contagion or another Melding like the one that

41

had killed so many and destroyed so much? If he wouldn't, then one of the other courts sure as fuck would. The rulers had all been there when Tir recited Amira's note from memory. They'd sacrifice her in a heartbeat. Some of them would even enjoy it. She wasn't selfish. She wouldn't let the realities collapse again just to save herself. But when the time came, it would be her choice and no one else's.

"Like you said. That's my choice to make, not yours," she said softly, as she hunted for some clean clothes.

Her eyes hitched on her reflection in the mirror as she scooped up a pair of jeans. The silver streak in her hair that had formed the night she mated with Bast was growing wider, and she touched it with a trembling hand before she caught herself.

"The black of your hair colour is all your father. Amira's was a bright blood red that told you everything you needed to know about her in one look. It's amazing your human shape has lasted so long past her death," Tir said.

"I don't even know what I really look like. I don't know what she really looked like. Or my father. I don't know anything." Hel had never been one for crying, but she could feel tears threatening.

She was adrift, and she didn't know how to get back to shore. If Bast wasn't avoiding her maybe she could've used him as an anchor, but he remained painfully, noticeably absent. Movement flickered in the reflection and then Tir was standing behind her, pushing the silver strands that had grown with her mate bond behind her ear.

"I met your mother in her true form a few times long ago. She was one of the few who knew I had come to this planet. She was a lot shorter than you, but all muscle. No one would ever call her small. She was a war-leader, and she had the most beautiful twisting curled horns that framed her hair. Three sharp points on each side. They were black, but they glinted with reflection in the sunlight like shards of obsidian. She used to smear dirt on them in battle so she wouldn't become a target. I never saw your father, but I have heard stories from those who have. It's hard to know what is truth and what is exaggeration. They all say he towers over those around him. His sword is called Starkiller and his power is so great the name could well be fact. He has wings, but not like the elementals. His are made of power and stardust. And his hair is like flowing locks of molten ebony."

Hel snorted. "Did that last bit come from someone with a crush on him, by any chance?"

Tir chuckled. "Why, yes. I believe the man to whom I was speaking had spent the previous month trying to seduce him with no luck. Sol was too busy taking over another star system at the time to notice."

"Sounds about right. So, I may or may not have wings and horns and fuck knows what else, and they may or may not start showing if Amira's magic ever wears off?"

"Yes. It could be difficult to hide who you are if that happens."

"No shit," Hel said, rolling her eyes.

Sometimes the fact the Archivist was from another planet and had spent most of their years on the Melded Earths hidden away in a pocket dimension became painfully obvious. Talk of wings and horns reminded her of that last glimpse she'd had of Amira before the hounds dragged her dead body into her father's portal all those years ago. Amira had temporarily paralysed Hel with drugs before shifting her only human friend's shape into something to fool the hounds. She'd given the decoy both horns and wings. Had

Amira based the form on what Hel really looked like, or had she just guessed? There was no way to find out.

"If you ever decide to stop hiding, I might be able to help disperse Amira's magic. It's almost as entangled in your body as your mate's," Tir said.

"Not gonna happen," Hel said, shifting uncomfortably. "Anyway, I've been meaning to ask you something. We've been trying to identify a human I saw talking to Lady Aliya in the hydroponics garden before we found you. It sounded like he was the one who tipped you off we were coming that day in the bus tunnel. It's driving everyone nuts that there's a traitor in the Tower we haven't identified. Do you know who he is?"

Tir became still as a statue, every writhing tentacle motionless. "He was serving the Lady of Air?"

They sounded deeply concerned, which wasn't surprising. They might be scary looking and eat monsters for breakfast, but she'd known Tir was good from the first time their eyes had met. Aliya—the Lady of Air—on the other hand, was renowned for exploitation, torture, and oppression. She'd *killed* Bast, for fuck's sake. And then mounted him on the wall of her crystal stronghold like a trophy. Hel would never forgive her for that.

"Yes."

"And he is putting you in danger?" Tir asked.

"If he's reporting back to Aliya, yes. Ra says it looks like she's preparing an attack force."

Tir was silent for a long moment, deep in thought. "There are humans I help sometimes because I know what it is to be powerless."

"Separatists?" Hel asked.

"Yes. I don't care what their politics are. I only care that they are oppressed, and that they do not seek to harm anyone."

"This man is working with Aliya. That fact alone means he's definitely harming someone," Hel said.

"I understand. All the elemental rulers are ruthless, but the Lady of Air is uniquely cruel. I will help you find this man. But none other of the ones I have helped."

"He's the only one we want, and I'm pretty sure Ra and Niko meet with a bunch of separatists on behalf of the ruling partnership, anyway."

Tir burst into motion, stepping into a clear space in the room. "Then I shall take you to him."

"You know where he is?" Hel asked, grabbing her baton and strapping it to her thigh.

"No. But I know him. I can use him as a focus and portal to him," Tir said.

Hel briefly considered fetching Bast or Ra, but the traitor was likely within the Tower and, between her and Tir, they could easily deal with one human. The familiar liquid shadow of Tir's magic slipped across her awareness, and a shimmering black portal formed in her bedroom. Hurrying after Tir's undulating form, Hel stepped through their gateway into a wall of thumping bass and a seething mass of people dancing. They'd emerged in The Crypt—the nightclub in the lower floors of Soul Tower.

She barely had time to process the assault on her senses before Tir grabbed the arm of a man a little shorter than her dancing nearby.

"Tir! Hi!" he said, clearly a little too drunk to realise how unusual it was for the Archivist to be in such a space.

As the surrounding people noticed the writhing tentacles and razor-sharp teeth in their midst, they edged away, creating an empty space on the dancefloor.

"Marcus. You betrayed my trust," Tir said, the sibilance in their voice becoming stronger as their anger showed.

"What are you talking about? I've got your back. And your tentacles. Can I touch one?" Marcus said, words slurring.

Hel rolled her eyes. This was the guy who'd sold them out to Lady Aliya? He was pathetic.

"You need to come with us," she said.

Marcus blinked in her direction, finally seeming to realise she was there and that everyone around them suddenly wasn't. "I don't do portals," he said, shaking his head and pulling away from Tir's grip.

"That's fine," Hel said soothingly, resisting the urge to stab him through the heart and be done with it. They needed to find out what he knew. "We'll just go for a little walk to the elevators. Maybe sit in the garden for a bit."

"Hel! What are you doing here? You should be in bed." Bast's voice snapped from behind her, somehow carrying over the loud music.

Spinning in place, she saw Ra and Ryker flanked him on either side. What was *she* doing here? What was *he* doing here while it was Tir coming to comfort her in *his* bedroom? Fuck. She needed to calm down. Now was not the time.

"I'm just meeting a friend of Tir's," Hel said, hoping Bast would pick up on the need to play it cool through their connection. She did her best to project a sense of predatory focus to him.

"Oh shit. You know, don't you?" Marcus said from behind her, panic entering his voice.

Damn. This wasn't good.

46

Hel spun back to reassure him, but it was too late. It might've taken him this long to process Tir's accusation of betrayal, but now he was faced with three of the most powerful men in the city, the game was up. His face became dead pale and his eyes became just dead. He looked like he'd been thrown into a trance of some kind and she sensed an elemental power that shouldn't have been there—one that tasted of icy-cold winds that would strip your body of life. A moment later, his jaw clenched as if he was crunching down on something and another burst of elemental magic emanated from his body.

"Suicide spell!" Bast shouted in warning, as his hand shot out to encase the man in a sphere of his power.

Just in time.

Air magic blasted out from Marcus in spears of light crashing against Bast's shield. The man's body writhed in agony and the spell projected his tortured screams into the room, amplifying them louder than any airhorn. The suicide spell, although it was more like a murder spell, given humans had no magic to cast it, must've been encased in a tooth or his jaw because his face was slowly disassembling itself—magic pulling it apart piece by piece like someone tearing the legs off a bug one by one. Only it was tearing cartilage, tendons, and teeth. His eyeballs bulged, the optic nerve stretched beyond capacity as the very air he breathed tore him apart.

Hel felt the souls encasing the Tower pull closer at the threat and swayed on her feet.

Not again.

"Enough," Bast whispered, his voice somehow carrying over the noise as he made a sharp gesture that snapped Marcus' neck with soul magic, cutting off the screams.

Silence fell on the club.

"Tir, could you please portal him somewhere uninhabited? The death spell filled my containment sphere with toxic gas. I can't release it in here or everyone will die," Bast said, voice calm.

Hel swallowed hard and stood helplessly as Tir removed the remains of the body. As soon as it disappeared from view, the looming pressure of the souls receded.

"Who was he, Hellcat?" Ra asked.

"The traitor we were looking for," Hel replied.

"Then he got what he deserved," Bast said, already turning to leave.

His voice was calm. His show of strength reassuring to the club goers around them as the music started back up.

Only Hel could sense the regret beneath his seemingly ruthless exterior at the life he'd been forced to end. Well, Ra probably had an idea too with their connection, but no one else around them would've guessed. Shaking off the need to comfort him when he couldn't even bring himself to remain in her presence, she turned back to Tir.

"I should've seen through his deception. I could have saved him," Tir said, their eyes mournful.

"We all have to live with the choices we've made. Or die with them," Hel replied.

THE NEXT DAY, when Hel emerged in the penthouse lounge around lunchtime, it was strangely quiet. Ana must have taken Kaia out somewhere because their laughter would usually fill the space as the older woman took a break from managing the entire tower complex to make everyone a meal. Hel rolled her eyes at herself. A few months of company and someone else cooking for her and she felt the absence like a stone in her shoe on a long courier run.

Ridiculous.

As she toasted herself some bread, she searched her patchy memory for what had happened in the Earth Court before she'd collapsed. Tir and Marcus had distracted her the day before, but the unfamiliar sensation of her father's power that she'd sensed in Mica's land was worrying. In a lifetime of being hunted, she'd only ever sensed his portals—searing rifts between worlds. His hounds barely carried a hint of the taste of his power. What she'd sensed where she'd faced down the wraiths was different. Unknown. And nothing good ever came from that.

She could tell he'd erected some kind of shield to hide his hunters and whatever else he'd built there—that huge metallic shard of stone like a meteorite carved into some sort of strange dowel piercing the earth. With her power to see through the protections, the magical message hadn't been subtle. The construct may as well have been wrapped in barbed wire with a sign saying *trespassers will die by wraith*. But there had been a complexity to the feel of the magic, and it was that part that had her worried. Not the shield, but what was hiding beneath it. It felt like she'd been staring at a deceptively blank casing to an intricately engineered ... something. Bomb? Staging platform?

The more she thought about it, the more concerned she became. What if he was doing the same thing near the city here with that huge portal she'd sensed? Taking her toast and tea out to the terrace, she settled cross-legged on a sun lounger and closed her eyes. The shrieking call of a kākā in the distance, one of the native brown forest parrots with their inner wing feathers flashing red, distracted her briefly, but she let the noise sink into her awareness and then let it go. The magic infused in her tea blended with the chill energy of the city air and called her to *wake*. Wrapping the feeling around herself, she used it to help focus the propulsion of her power as she extended her magical awareness outward, searching.

A shudder wracked through her body as her mind passed the shield of souls that wreathed the tower. The now-familiar battering ram of deaths pressing into her mind, briefly threatened to derail her, but she wasn't in danger now and the souls had no reason to wrap her in their toxic protection. She took a breath. And then another. Then she let her magic sweep out over the City of Souls, imagining it riding the ubiquitous zephyrs of wind sweeping between the high-rise buildings. Ignoring the sickening sensation of the points of contagion that continued to multiply in the city, she moved past the city—over forested valleys and ridgelines and out further, faster. Her awareness stretched far past where she could usually safely venture. The mating bond with Bast had not just wended itself through her power, but had also made it more. Just as hers did the same for him.

Finally, on the very edge of her extended range, she felt a signature of power like the one she'd sensed in Mica's lands. Her mind brushed against the smooth surface of the shield that had the faintest taste like the ashes of conquered solar systems and felt like malignant innocence, coyly stroking her awareness to look *elsewhere*. The distraction didn't work now she knew what she was looking for. It was no wonder Mica had been oblivious to the incursion on the periphery of his city, though. Her father wasn't messing around with whatever this shielding was.

Straining, she tried to reach past the surface of the shield to feel what it might hide, but she was too far distant. Each time she tried to pierce its bounds, her power slipped away from her like it was being sucked into the structure she was trying to breach. All she was doing was reinforcing it. As her magic drained with her efforts, she could feel the protective souls who watched her hovering in concern. Cursing, she pulled back. If she overextended, they would feel compelled to 'save' her, probably killing her in the process.

Light seared into her eyes as she blinked them open and Hel groaned as fatigue swept through her. The sun was, reassuringly, in more or less the same place in the sky as it had been when she'd started searching. She hadn't lost too much time. But when she took a sip of the tea still sitting beside her, it was lukewarm. Her face twisted in a grimace as she took a bite of her breakfast and added chewy cold toast to the list of insults the world was throwing at her today. At least the walls of the terrace were blocking most of the wind.

Hel let her head hang back to stare up at the deep blue of the sky, feeling the sun's harsh warmth on her skin. She wished she could photosynthesise it into some energy to fight this dragging lethargy that threatened to drown her.

A plummeting flash of movement hidden by the sun's glare had her rolling out of her chair and drawing her baton, twisting it open to reveal its twin blades. She moved instinctively into offence, prepared to strike. Her attacker remained sheathed in sunlight that was too bright to look at even after they landed. It was only the stray hint of electric blue and cream reflecting in the steel of her blade that allowed Hel to pull the strike she'd already committed to. Just in time. Stumbling back inelegantly, she landed sprawled over another lounger as she redirected her momentum.

"Kaia! I could have killed you!" Hel shouted.

The twelve year old's tinkling laughter filled the terrace. "Nah. You're too good for that."

Hel growled at the girl's recklessness and sheathed her weapons. She'd have to check them later for damage. One had ricocheted off the terrace tiles in her fall. Kaia was dancing closer with her wings fluttering, as if it was a wonderful joke. Hel could feel the fading glow of the magic the girl had used to pull off her little hiding stunt, and it did nothing to improve her mood. At this rate, not only was the girl going to get herself stabbed, she was going to be shipped off to the Earth Court before they could get Mica to agree to take anyone else with her.

Hel surged to her feet and locked a hand around Kaia's arm. "You're going to explain to your mum what you did and see if she agrees."

"Auntie, no! You're too good for that, too," Kaia whined. "Auntie?"

Hel ignored the girl's pleas and pulled her inside the apartment. Ana and Ra had both returned while she was outside. Their heads were bent together, both looking serious as they discussed something. Kaia's protests cut off the second they were within sight, and both of them looked up with eyes narrowed in suspicion.

"What did you do this time, K-bear?" Ra asked.

Hel released the girl in front of her mother and stood with her arms crossed, glaring. As the poor thing realised she wasn't joking, she hunched in on herself, pulling her wings in tight to her spine and looking down at her feet.

"Tell her," Hel said, struggling to keep her voice stern in the face of the sad picture of dejection the girl made, which was probably how she got away with so much.

Kaia stayed silent, but she winced in discomfort.

"Kaia," Ana said, warning clear in her tone. "If even our reckless Hellcat thinks you've done something dangerous, you know it's true."

"Hey! We're not talking about my behaviour here!" Hel protested as Ra smothered a chuckle.

"She's not wrong," he chimed in.

"I'm an *adult*. Could we focus on the matter at hand?" Hel snapped. "Kaia. Explain yourself."

Kaia's jaw clenched in stubbornness, but she couldn't hold out against the disapproval in her mother's face. She was a good kid. She was just starting to test the boundaries, and that was a problem while she wasn't somewhere with teachers to train her in the power that was slowly growing to fill her young body.

"I just wanted to surprise Auntie Hel," Kaia muttered.

"Well, it worked," Hel said.

"You're always so serious," Kaia continued, finally looking up to meet Hel's gaze. "I thought it might make you smile."

Hel felt her heart twist a little in her chest and resisted the urge to draw the girl into a hug and let it go. She needed to understand she was playing with fire. "Focus a little more on what you did instead of the why."

Kaia swallowed hard. "I just used a little magic to sneak up on her."

Hel snorted. "You dive-bombed me and cast an illusion that completely screened your form in sunshine. I almost stabbed you through the heart. You're damn lucky I caught your true reflection in my blade."

Ana's face froze. "Kaia Selene Archer..." the woman couldn't even finish the sentence. She was that rigid with fear and anger.

Ra wrapped an arm around Ana's shoulders in support.

"Sorry, Mum. Sorry, Auntie." Kaia said, her feathers rustling softly as they trembled with tension.

"Even ignoring the risk of ambushing poor Hel, the more you use your power, the faster it's going to develop," Ra said.

Hel couldn't stand the morose expression on the girl's face any longer and pulled her into her arms, wings and all. "I forgive you," she said.

"I can't deal with this right now," Ana said and pushed away from Ra to walk towards the door.

The three of them shared a look of surprise as they watched the usually commanding woman retreat in silence. Ana had always been so strong, but this problem of Kaia's power was slowly breaking her. She didn't want to let her little girl go. But she would have to.

"I really didn't mean to make my power worse by using it," Kaia whispered.

Hel looked down at the girl's head nestled by her collarbone and stroked her white-blonde hair. "Are you sure about that? Sometimes when we're worried about something, we just want it done already."

Ra watched Hel from across the bench and raised an eyebrow. Yes. Alright. Some days it might feel easier to do something rash like go face off with the hounds and let the souls consume her rather than succumb slowly to the erosion of her sanity. But they were talking about Kaia. Why did everyone have to keep bringing her into it?

"I just need to know when they're going to take me away," Kaia said, as if she was facing a firing squad. She turned her face into Hel's shirt and starting to sob softly.

Ra was there in an instant, wrapping both of them up in

a group hug. Hel even let herself lean on his shoulder for a moment.

"Oh, sweetheart," he said. "No one's going to steal you away in the night. When it happens, you'll have time to pack and get ready. You'll have time to hug your mum and tease Auntie Hellkitten about how well you're going to be able to ambush her once you get back. And we'll make sure you have someone from home with you."

Hel wasn't sure Ra could really make that last promise. But Kaia's eyes had lit up at the talk of ambushing and Hel couldn't help but grin at the young woman cradled in her arms.

"I'm gonna get you so good when I've got all my magic under control," Kaia said.

"You sure will," Hel agreed.

"Now, go report to Morrigan for punishment duty," Ra said.

Kaia groaned, but her footsteps weren't dragging so much as she headed to the lifts.

Ra kept his arm where it was, loosely wrapped around Hel's shoulders. "You're a good Auntie to her."

"Shut up," Hel said, pushing him away. But she didn't really mean it.

She had to admit she kind of loved the way Kaia had adopted her right from the start, even when her relationship with Bast had been a sham. She scowled at that thought. Their relationship was still a sham, just a different kind. And the damn infuriating man had left her unconscious in his bed and hadn't even come back to check she was okay.

"Will punching me make it better?" Ra asked.

Hel snorted. "It's not you I want to punch."

CHAPTER 4
BAST

Bast sat in his office, staring vacantly out at the cityscape. He'd been ducking Mica's calls since they'd disappeared from his court, unsure what he could safely reveal to the Earth Lord without putting Hel in even more danger. Humans had no magic and elementals couldn't portal with theirs. If the courts discovered she wasn't what she appeared, they'd either try to use her or kill her. Maybe he could claim the portalling was a newly discovered aspect of his soulweaving?

That still wouldn't help with their other problem. Mica knew they were mates, which meant he knew they were on borrowed time. Of all the courts' rulers, the Earth Lord was least likely to exploit their weakness by attacking. He'd exploit it in other ways, though. Use the information to steer Bast in the direction he wanted.

Bast felt it the second Hel woke and sent a tendril of his awareness down their connection to check she was recovering. It was barely a minute later that the shifting surges of emotion started. He really needed to teach her how to keep her feelings more to herself. It was distracting as fuck to be sitting trying to concentrate, only to feel a sudden rush of anxiety or anger that wasn't even his. At least she wasn't suddenly appearing in The Crypt this time. He'd been terrified when he'd felt her presence disappear from above him for the split second before it reappeared below. The incident with Marcus could far too easily have been deadly. Why couldn't she just stay put until he figured out how to save her?

Far below his vantage point, elementals flew from place to place. Figures filled the roof gardens and terraces of the city, taking advantage of the warmer weather. The spring winds had brought with them an influx of tiny winged skinks that swirled in small murmurations, delighting their youngest citizens.

Bast shook his head and refocused *again*. It was the first time in weeks he hadn't been called away to deal with an emergency. He'd had a decent night's sleep, and he needed to use this time to figure out the structure of the shielding he'd subconsciously wrought as a baby to keep himself safe from his own power. He'd been trying to create a mental map of sorts since the morning after he and Hel had rashly, and more-or-less unintentionally, bonded themselves together. Even the stray thought of that night sent a surge of sexual frustration through him he quickly locked down. He needed to figure this out before it was too late. Hel deserved better.

Hours later, Bast sighed in frustration. He wasn't getting anywhere. The weaving fractals of power that anchored in his wings integrated with every part of his essence in ways he couldn't even perceive. It wasn't the kind of construct anyone with a solid understanding of the world could create. It had been born from a mind untainted by learning and unaware of the impossible, too complex to keep straight in his mind.

As if sensing his failure, the wellspring of souls that surrounded the tower surged in a wave of concern.

Can you help me? he asked them.

He waited as thousands of the dead pored over his body, sending wracking shivers through his muscles as they took the invitation to poke and prod at the power that was so deeply integrated in his form.

Maybe if we use an approach like your reality database, one of the more recently dead suggested, her voice evoking a sense of long hours in quiet libraries and a hint of bergamot tea.

Unlike Hel, he could keep his sense of her limited to these quieter observations and his protections automatically deflected the darker and more dangerous aspects. He could've felt her death if he chose to, but it wasn't a tide waiting to consume him.

Bast pondered the idea, hope growing inside him for the first time since he'd deciphered the complexity of the shielding he was dealing with. In the early days after the Melding, Ra had helped him set up a database to keep track of the groups of souls that held the city's reality together and let it function. Between Ra, Bast, and Zee—their magical engineer—they'd conceived a system that split the souls into sectors and allowed them to interact with the database directly. The souls could independently record reallocation of their resources, new threats, and any number of other small useful things that helped the city to run smoothly, reducing the drain on his time and energy.

A computer was far better placed to map the irrational geometry of this shielding than any single brain, and with thousands of souls feeding their measurements and observations into it, the mapping would be infinitely faster.

Genius, he thought back to the woman who'd suggested it.

Her fizzing joy at the compliment even had him smiling as he texted Ra and Zee to come and get started.

Finally, a way forward.

Now, if he could just figure out what Lady Aliya was planning, find a cure to the contagion, and send the fucking starhounds back to wherever they came from so they stopped hunting his damn mate and killing his people, he'd be all set.

Rubbing his temple, he slumped in his chair as the momentary sense of achievement succumbed to the avalanche of their other problems.

"WE WON'T GO any faster with you watching us," Zee snapped two days later as they coaxed copper conductors to bloom into metal pitcher plant shapes that thrummed with magic in the 'computer' they were constructing with Ra to accept the souls' inputs.

The engineer hadn't seemed all that surprised when Bast had revealed his mating with Hel. Zee was the only other powerful magic user in the area, so it wasn't unexpected that they'd sensed it before he'd been ready to tell them. Luckily, they were discreet. Zee had understood immediately the need to keep the information secret to avoid anyone panicking that the city's chief protector was about to die.

Ra glanced up from a more conventional computer and smiled tiredly at Bast. "We should be able to record observations soon and then we'll need you here to scan. Go and do something else while you can."

Bast frowned at the signs of fatigue in his friend—the slack muscles of his face and glassy eyes unfamiliar in a man who was usually so full of energy. They'd worked through nights and days. All of them were conscious that a delay could be the difference between life and death for Hel and, by extension, Bast.

"Go. We're fine," Ra repeated.

Zee had already forgotten Bast's existence and Ra was turning back to his screen. He clasped his friend's shoulder and slipped from the room.

They'd set up their project on the fourteenth floor where their servers were housed, the heart of the Tower. It was far enough from both the pool of power that sank into the foundations below them and from the metal spikes that crowned the building, anchoring its shield of souls, to avoid any disturbance. The space had evolved into a tech hub of sorts; the offices requisitioned by a mixture of surveillance and communications. Spies and marketers. It was Ra's domain, and he'd decorated it to match. Everywhere you looked was comfortable elegance with a twist that invited you to linger.

Bast thought about settling into one of the leather armchairs studded with metal rivets and catching up on his messages, but he couldn't shake the nervous tension riding him. He was grateful for the respite from their other problems that allowed them to focus on finding a way to shield Hel, but it had been suspiciously quiet. The hounds hadn't been spotted in the city since Hel sent them packing, and his spies had worryingly little to report on Lady Aliya's activities. Even the contagion seemed to be lying low with no recent outbreaks. Which all meant there was nothing to distract him from the woman he'd been avoiding. The woman he should continue to avoid for her own good.

The second he let himself think of her, his traitorous power brought their connection into focus, creating a pull on his soul down to wherever she was in the Tower. He still couldn't believe how entwined their magic had become so quickly, or how powerful the draw between them was. Mating bonds had been so rare during his lifetime that everything he knew about them was from reading history texts too dry to talk about the burning need for each other they were suffering. Mates weren't designed to avoid each other. The bonding made them like co-dependent symbiotes.

Bast looked up in surprise as he discovered his feet had led him into the elevator, instinct making him select the floor where the gym was. The sensations coming through their link were a juxtaposition of focused calm and aggression he associated with martial arts training, so it was a reasonable assumption. He knew he should steer clear even though it seemed the distance he'd forced between them hadn't slowed the progression of her decline. If nothing else, staying apart would make it easier if he had to resort to finding a way to sever their connection to save her. The thought stabbed through his heart where Hel's claiming mark sat on his skin.

He barely noticed he was still making his way to her until he entered the gym, his own subconscious sabotaging his better judgement. It was quiet at this time of the afternoon—only a few off-duty guards using the weight machines.

The tug on his soul drew him onward into one of the sparring rooms.

His eyes snapped to Hel's body the second he entered. She was the only one in there. For once, she wasn't in her ubiquitous black jeans and tank. Ana must have found her some workout clothes. Not that he'd seen her often enough to know what she'd been wearing. He was seeing her now, though. And he couldn't fucking look away. Those long, long legs of hers were on full display as they gripped tight to a punching bag she hung upside-down from. The ripple of the muscles in her thighs as she held herself aloft with nothing but sheer strength just about made him groan as he imagined them wrapped around his waist instead. She was doing upside down vertical sit-ups, and he could barely breathe as he watched the flex of her abdominals each time her head neared the ground.

Bast was stalking closer before he could think, focused on nothing but her. His steps were silent, but she must have felt the surge of his desire because she flipped upright as he neared, landing perfectly balanced as she spun to face him. He couldn't stop himself from dragging his gaze across every inch of soft skin she'd left exposed in her boy shorts and crop top.

"Did you need something?" she snapped.

Bast finally risked meeting her jade-green eyes and he cruelly let his need for her flare between them for a moment before tamping it down. If he had to suffer, then so should she. His mouth twitched as he watched her pupils blow wide with arousal. They were each as screwed as the other, even if neither of them would admit it. He really needed to stop with this game of chicken before one of them caved.

"Do I need a reason to visit my mate?"

Hel rolled her eyes. "You tell me. You're the one who's avoided me for months because you're killing me. You didn't even stick around to check I was okay last night."

If he didn't know better, he'd say she was feeling hurt by that. The stark reminder of her near death was the ice down his spine he needed to regain control.

"You're right. Sorry for disturbing you," he said, turning away and striding back towards the elevators and the safety of any floor that didn't house temptation incarnate.

"Wait! I actually needed to talk to you," Hel called, jogging to catch up with him.

Her intoxicating scent wrapped around him as she drew alongside, and he started breathing through his mouth to avoid it.

"So walk and talk," he replied, his words curt and tense as he clung to control.

"I sensed another concentration of power like the one we found at the Earth Court. It's somewhere north of the city, the Wairarapa I think."

"It's too dangerous. The minute you're in danger, the souls will swarm," Bast snapped, too frustrated to be polite.

"We need to go check it out," Hel insisted.

"You're not leaving the tower until we've figured out how to shield you from the souls."

"Excuse me? The minute you try and keep me prisoner here is the minute I'm getting the fuck out of this overgrown death stalagmite of a tower."

Bast slammed his finger on the call button for his personal lift and glared at the infuriating woman beside him. "You barely survived your last trip. You really want to see how much worse it can get?"

"And whose fucking fault is that?" Hel growled, striding into the elevator ahead of him.

Bast let his anger push back his guilt. "The mystery man who keeps trying to kill you. Who is that again?"

"Fuck you, Bast," Hel said, shoving his shoulder hard enough to slam him back and crush his wings against the controls.

Bast grabbed her wrist before she could pull away, his fingers tightening as she tested her strength against him. The skin-to-skin contact sent a lightning bolt of need through their connection. They both froze in place, gasping for breath as the sensation continued to amplify the months of aching desire they'd ignored.

Every muscle in Bast's body locked as he fought his craving for the woman in front of him. He watched, mesmerised, as her breasts rose and fell in a panting motion. His free hand dropped behind him, pushing the emergency stop. As the elevator car jerked to a halt, he lifted his eyes to meet Hel's. Her tongue darted out to lick her lips and he barely had time to groan before she was throwing herself into his arms, both legs wrapped around his waist as she slipped her tongue into his mouth, just like he'd been fantasising earlier.

Fuck. This woman. She was everything.

His brain shut down. All he could think about was worshipping her.

The light dimmed as his wings flared wide to fill the too small space, casting them in shadow. Hel was grinding herself against him as their mouths battled for supremacy. Every movement was delicious agony. As he pushed her back against the cold mirrored wall, she sucked in a sharp breath at the change in temperature, breaking their kiss. He immediately bent to trail kisses down her neck, nipping at her collarbone as he savoured the clean salty tang from her recent workout. Her moan vibrated against his mouth as she tilted her head to give him better access and his fingers slid from her thighs past the hem of her shorts.

"Fuck. Bast," she panted.

"Did you need something?" he teased, mirroring her earlier greeting to him.

He kept his touch light and not quite where she wanted it, needing to stretch this out and savour it before they came to their senses.

Hel growled in frustration, but before she could twist their passion into anger, he dropped to his knees and arched his wings high to keep the harsh artificial light from breaking the haze of lust between them. Slipping his hands behind her, he pulled her hips forward. He paused as he hooked his fingers in her waistband, looking up at her in question. Her fingers had wound tight through his hair sending sparks of pleasure-pain through him where she tugged. Her head was leaning back against the wall as if she'd lost the ability to hold it up.

"Still with me, Hellcat?" he asked, his voice husky with need as his nose brushed the fabric of her shorts and the sweet scent of her desire threatened to overwhelm him.

Hel tugged on his hair again to pull him closer, but it wasn't enough. He needed to see her eyes if he did this. Needed to hear her consent. Her anguished accusation after they mated, asking what *he'd* done to *her*, still burned like bitter acid in his memory. She had a habit of ignoring her part in their bond. As if her power wasn't stroking through his every nerve, clinging to him and drawing him closer even more than the fist in his hair. She might think it was elemental magic at fault but whatever the source of her power was, it had forged their connection impossibly stronger than anything he'd ever heard of.

Finally looking down at him, her green eyes flashed in frustration. He pressed his mouth gently to her as she watched, sending hot air sinking through the thin fabric of her shorts as he exhaled against her while refusing to give in to her unspoken need.

As she opened her mouth to speak, the elevator shuddered back into motion.

"Fuck," Hel moaned in complaint.

Bast leaned his forehead against her bare stomach and grasped for the control that had been slipping through his fingers. Ugh. Thinking about his fingers slipping through things was not helping. He needed to stand, but the soft pressure of Hel's hand on his head held him paralysed. He was still kneeling before her when the doors opened, and a burst of male laughter sounded from behind him.

"Oh, I'm sorry. Am I interrupting something?" Ra asked innocently.

Hel's grip finally relaxed and Bast rose to his feet to face his friend, running his hand through his mussed hair. He kept his wings flared out, screening Hel from view to give her a moment to collect herself.

"Like you don't fucking know that already."

"You did press the *emergency* stop button. The alarm system wouldn't shut up. And there was a reasonable chance one of you had done serious injury to the other in an enclosed space like that. My bet was on Hel stabbing you," Ra said.

Another spark of desire shot through him as Hel's hand closed around his sensitive wing edge to shift him aside. He gritted his teeth to keep his reaction hidden as he exited the elevator. It didn't work, of course. Ra might not have the same level of connection to him as he and Hel did, but they still had one. His smirk said he knew exactly how Bast was feeling. Bast glared in warning at his long-time friend as Hel stepped up next to him.

"What floor are we on?" Hel asked, looking around curiously.

"Why? Were you a little distracted?" Ra teased.

"Ra!" Bast and Hel both growled at the same time, and his grin only stretched wider.

"You two are too cute. We're on fourteen, Hellkitten. My slice of Bast's domain," Ra said, before turning to Bast. "We're ready to give this scan a go if you've got time."

"What scan?" Hel asked, suspicion surging through their connection.

"Calm down. They're scanning me, not you. We're mapping the way I shield myself from the effects of the souls so we can try and re-create it for you," Bast explained, exasperation clear in his voice at Hel assuming *again* that he had some nefarious purpose.

"Oh."

"Might be better if you left us to it, babe," Ra said, slinging an arm around her shoulders as he directed Hel back toward the elevator. "We'll need him to be using his power and calling souls to him to see what's happening. It's a small space. Wouldn't want you to be caught in the crossfire."

Hel twisted around to look back at Bast as she left, her green eyes meeting his.

"Thanks," she murmured, so quietly he almost didn't hear.

He'd expected another poisoned barb, not that quiet gratitude.

It took everything he had not to follow her into the lift, wrap her in his wings, and finish what they'd started.

It was another three days before they had a reasonable approximation of what his power was doing to protect him. Three days of sitting in a chair for hours, calling to the souls in different ways while Zee and Ra endlessly tweaked. Three days of distance from Hel that was simultaneously too much and not enough. When would the physical ache to be near her subside?

"I think we might've got it. Try again," Zee said.

Bast sighed and sunk his consciousness into the interface they'd designed for what felt like the hundredth time. Shards of light and power flashed before him as he shut out the rest of the world to focus only on the connection with the machine and the souls that were playing assistant. He would have blinked in surprise if his eyes had been open. His shielding that had been too complex to follow was now slowly resolving in his mind, the genius of Zee's magical engineering somehow translating the data into a form his brain could process.

Studying the whirls and eddies of protection, he noted the exact way they anchored through the structure of his wings. It wasn't surprising. An elemental's wings were more than blood and sinew, feathers and bone. That's why the feathers of those with enough power shifted colour as they brought their magic under control. Even for those without enough magic to need training, their colouring could reveal hints of their identity and how the power of the ley lines of their world had shaped them.

The more he focused on the protection, the more he realised why he'd struggled to follow it earlier. He'd thought it was like the shields he used to contain the contagion, but it wasn't. It was more like antibodies fighting off the dangerous parts of the souls. A magical vaccine. He wasn't sure how long he spent committing the structure that protected him from the souls to memory, but it was dark when he finally cracked open his eyes. Trepidation filled him as he disconnected his mind from the machine, wondering if his understanding would dissolve back into chaos without the computer's assistance.

"Welcome back. Did it work?" Ra asked as Bast stood and stretched muscles that had been immobile for too long.

Bast pondered the question, his brain still catching up with reality.

"It did," he said, relieved it was holding. "But I'm not certain it's replicable for Hel. It's so physically dependent on elemental anatomy to anchor it, like it's genetically coded or something. It occupies the hollow spaces in my wing bones and the shafts of each and every feather."

Ra winced. "Shit."

"Indeed. I'll attempt it, anyway. It's not like we have anything to lose."

"What's Plan B?" Ra asked.

"Find a way to sever the mating bond."

"Isn't that even more impossible?"

Bast banged his head back against the wall he was leaning on. "Yeah. We're into conspiracy theories and pseudo-magic at that point."

"Fuck."

When he made it back to the penthouse, Bast took a moment to stop and just drink in the picture Hel made sitting in the living room reading with a glass of whiskey. She was back to her usual jeans and tight shirt, her legs curled beneath her. She'd brushed out her hair and it traced a sleek path down her front, partly obscuring her breasts he was *not* looking at. Not even a little bit. They couldn't afford to slip up again.

"You know I can feel you watching, right?" his hellcat said.

"And you know I can feel how much you like it."

Yeah. That probably deserved the glare she was sending his way. He was breaking an unspoken rule by pointing it out, but fuck it. She started it.

"How'd your science project go?" she asked, her casual tone belied by the laser-focus she now had on him.

"Worse than I hoped. Better than I expected," he replied.

"What on the Earths does that mean?"

Bast shrugged. "Shall we try it out and see?"

He took Hel's head tilt as acquiescence and sat down on an ottoman near her, his wings draping behind him.

"What do I need to do?" she asked, putting her e-reader aside.

He resisted the urge to reach out and take hold of the hand resting loosely in her lap, clasping his own hands together so they didn't get away from him when he was distracted.

"Nothing. I just need you to hold still while I see if I can get the shield to anchor in you."

"Fine. Do your necromancer thing."

Bast grimaced at the rude description of his power, but it didn't enrage him like it used to. He knew it was a kneejerk reaction she only used when she was feeling vulnerable. It was his power's fault she was feeling that way, so he could hardly blame her.

Closing his eyes to reduce the distraction of her presence, he dropped all the barriers he was holding between them for the first time since they'd mated. Power flowed through their connection like the king-tides of spring, surging higher and further than it ever had. He could feel the way her essence had soaked into him unnoticed in the intervening months, exquisitely staining his soul in a way he knew could never be undone.

He wasn't there to sight-see, though.

Forcing himself to focus, he started crafting a replica of the multi-dimensional structure they'd mapped. He could feel Hel's power twining through his as he worked, reinforcing, transforming. The unknown factor of her magic made him pause, but it didn't feel like it was hindering their purpose. Fatigue washed through him as the days of testing and lack of sleep caught up with him, but he refused to succumb. His will was stronger than his weakness. Always.

As expected, it was not the intricate, draining, beautiful soulwoven creation that was the problem. It was how to graft it to his equally intricate, draining, beautiful mate. Time after time, he tried to connect it to her body, draping it over her soul, fastening it to her cells, embedding it in the marrow of her bones. Every time, it slid free from her body like he was grasping at a limb slick with oil and watching it slip through his fingers.

"It's not working," Hel said, what could have been hours later.

Bast opened his eyes and found he'd shifted to the couch while they worked. His hands were wrapped tight around her biceps.

"Sorry," he said, his voice cracking from his dry throat. When was the last time he'd drunk anything?

"Not your fault."

"It kind of is," he corrected.

Hel sighed but didn't contradict him. "As long as this is a bust, we should go check out the power signature over in the Wairarapa."

Bast's hands clutched tighter to her arms until he noticed he was leaving white marks on her skin. Fighting the possessive urge, he relaxed his hold.

"I told you. Not until you're safe."

"I might just get worse and worse, Bast. We should go now while I can still function. You need my power to see through the screening magic."

"No."

Hel growled in frustration. Her anger at him shouldn't have been as sexy as it was. Fuck, he was tired. He wondered if he could convince her to sleep in his bed tonight. Just sleep. He needed her scent wrapped around him. Needed to know she wasn't gone yet.

He immediately discarded the thought.

"Well. What's our next play then? What do we need to do for you to let me out of the tower?" Hel asked.

"I need to find a way to break the bond," Bast muttered, and his whole soul screamed in protest at the words.

A torrent of raw emotion flooded down their connection.

He couldn't separate out the strands to make sense of what his hellcat was feeling. Rage? Pain?

"Right," she said, her voice emotionless, her face expressionless. All while their bond continued to combust.

Bast watched as she pushed to her feet and walked away, every step begging him to call her back.

This fucking bond. This fucking woman. It was agony. And still every part of him rejected giving it up.

CHAPTER 5
HEL

Hel lay in bed, staring up at the ceiling. She seemed to be doing that a lot lately. Her body weakening every day. Bast's words the night before shouldn't have surprised her, let alone hurt. She'd been railing against the way he'd requisitioned her life since that first meeting in his office, so she should be grateful he wanted to set her free. Should be welcoming his new focus. She wasn't. Sighing in disgust at herself, she flipped over onto her stomach, trying and failing to find a more comfortable position.

Until a few months ago, all she needed was to pay off her debt and *leave*. Get away from everyone. Now, she had all these inconvenient connections she'd never sought. She enjoyed teaching Kaia and teasing Ana. Loved drinking whiskey and talking shit with Ra. She didn't want to leave. Didn't want to be alone again. Finding a family was an unexpected dream. Bonding a soul-mate was ... something else.

After two months of Bast avoiding her as much as possible, she'd hoped some of his unwelcome appeal might have worn off. Instead, she faced an infuriating montage of compelling memories. The way he jumped to her defence like no one else ever had. The way he cradled her close like she was precious when he carried her in flight. The glimpses of his outcast childhood and absent father that made her feel like he might actually understand her past. His steadfast dedication trying to save her.

And the man was a fucking saint for his work staunching the contagion in the other courts after they either actively tried to hunt him down and kill him, or passively stood by while it happened. Ugh. Why did he have to be so ... him?

She reinforced her crumbling emotional walls with a litany of reminders. If she stayed here, eventually her father would find her and hurt all those people she'd grown close to. Bast might be compelled to care for her by their bond, but he'd abandoned her over and over again these last two months. He'd left her alone to face the terror of a thousand deaths dragging her to her own.

Bast's presence in her awareness had receded sometime in the last hour. He was sleeping in his spare suite lower down in the tower. Again. Avoiding their proximity. Which suited her just fine tonight. She'd worried he might stick around to keep an eye on her.

Smirking at how he'd underestimated her again, she slipped out of bed fully clothed and bent to pull on her boots. He might have a direct connection to her emotions, but he still didn't *know* her. Not really. If he did, he would've realised she wasn't going to sit on her ass while that power signature loomed in the distance, threatening the city.

It would be a long run around the harbour and over the Remutaka Range to reach the dry and isolated ex-farmland of the Wairarapa. She wouldn't be able to make it before

Bast woke and realised she was gone, but at the speed she travelled she should be able to get far enough that by the time he caught up with her the only logical move would be to carry on. There were advantages to having more strength and less need to breathe than a human, and one of them was the ability to maintain a steady punishing pace over distances most wouldn't even attempt. It's what had made her such a successful courier.

Slipping on her leather jacket and an infinity scarf she could use to hide her face and the distinctive silver streak of her hair, she strapped a water canteen to one leg and her modified steel baton to the other. There was no reason to limit herself to concealed blades now Bast knew she could fight. She was a cautiously trusted member of his inner circle. Trusted not to kill him, anyway. She could have openly worn daggers, but the baton that twisted out into twin blades had been with her as long as she could remember. It was an extension of who she was. And sometimes you just wanted to crack someone's skull open, not bleed them out.

When she looked in the mirror, the only hint of her softly glinting skin that showed was a thin band around her eyes. She'd snuck out of the Tower once before, using the twisting elemental metal façade to climb down from the lowest balcony to the glass archway that covered the building's entrance five floors above the ground. There was no way that would work this time. The souls that seethed within the metal would drive her mad in no time. She'd probably lose consciousness and fall. And she doubted anyone checking the security feeds would stay quiet for long if they saw her sneaking downstairs in her current outfit. That wouldn't get her the head-start she needed.

Instead, she would take advantage of this one location where she could use her power without fear and portal down to just outside the quieter side entrance of the building. She'd still be within the bounds of the encasing protection of the Tower that would prevent her father from tracing her, but she wouldn't have to come into contact with the souls. Hopefully, the guards wouldn't look too closely given she'd be outside the security doors by the time she appeared. Hopefully being the operative word.

The trick would be making sure she didn't wake Bast with her activity. Ignoring the unwelcome guilt that roiled through her, she let her mind sink into their connection and used it to lull Bast into a deeper sleep. She projected calm and safety, letting her magic dance with his in a hypnotic pull that threatened to entrance her as much as it had his already unconscious mind.

Reassured that Bast was suitably sedated, she bit her lip hard to distract herself. The edge of pain and the metallic taste of blood in her mouth kept her from succumbing to her own trap as she spun her magic tighter still and formed the image of where she wanted to be in her mind. Perhaps he would have woken if she was portalling further. But the disturbance wasn't much when all she was doing was dropping herself twenty-nine storeys to the ground. The swirl of her power filled her vision and she stepped forward through the familiar sensation of her plasma blue sun flares like a calmer echo of her father's signature. She took more care than usual as she released her power. She couldn't risk waking Bast or drawing the attention of the surrounding souls. They would give her away eventually, but she was fairly certain they wouldn't wake Bast unless they thought she was in danger. So, she kept her energy calm and her movements fluid as she emerged into the shadows of the night and jogged clear of the Tower's looming protection.

Nothing to see here, souls.

Something that had been wound impossibly tight inside her released as she took off through the city she knew better than anyone. This was what she'd been missing. That small taste of freedom that came from running unseen, knowing every shadow and awning that would screen her from view. Even when she'd thought she was trapped by indenture, that momentary breath of control, pitting her body and strength against nature and the city alone, had kept her going. It was different now, though. Now she had an anchoring presence high above and behind her she could always feel. It was both reassuring and infuriating. Still, she revelled in her flight on foot along the roads out of the city. She tried not to think about how that joy in movement was another point of commonality with the man she'd left sleeping back at the Tower. It was exactly what she felt from him when he took to the air.

As she ran, she stretched every sense wide for any sign of attack, but the world was eerily quiet. The earth remained quiescent, with no signs of the wyrms that hunted along the land's fault lines. The giant winged spider arachdryn must have been hunting westward because nothing emerged from the bush-clad hills that overlooked the main road from the city as she passed the northern boundary of its safe zone.

She kept to the old human roads as she veered east. The pull of her father's magic would've taken her straight through the forests, but she wasn't brave or stupid enough to try and navigate them in the dark. Even in daylight, it would probably be faster to follow the road and double back. Of course, it would have been faster still if Bast had listened to her and just flown them there, but whatever. Hopefully she'd make it over the hills before he found her and she could at least get a ride home. There was that word again. Home. It kept sneaking in. She shook her head and sped up her pace, determined to outrun her thoughts.

The first blush of sunrise was touching the horizon when she reached the highest point of the Remutaka Hill road. As light snuck back into the world, all she could see around her was rolling forested hillsides. The eerie call of a dragon circling in the distance was answered by the mocking tones of tūī birds. As she carried on her steady pace down the winding cracked tar seal, a shiver of icy awareness spread across the black wings magically inked into her back by Bast. She grinned and put on a burst of speed as gravity helped pull her down the road faster.

He was awake. And he wasn't happy.

Her raging mate finally caught up to her as she made it to the deserted settlement nestled below the eastern edge of the ranges. Abandoned shops glared accusingly from either side of the road, betrayed by the Melding that had left the human town exposed to predators.

Bast landed in a vertical drop mere feet in front of her as she ran full-speed. There was no way to stop in time and she only bothered slowing to a more human speed, careening into his body in a fit of pique. Bast expelled a breath at the contact but didn't shift back even half a step. The damn man was made of muscle and had the balance of a born fighter. His black wings flared behind him, sucking in the morning light and giving nothing back.

Hel put both hands on his chest and tried to shove him away, only to find that he'd grasped both her biceps.

"What the fuck do you think you're doing?" Bast growled.

"I told you we needed to see what was going on with that power signature."

"And I told *you* it wasn't safe to venture out until we have a solution to your vulnerability to the souls. What are you planning to do if you come across more of those wraiths?"

"That's why you're here." Hel hid a smirk as Bast glared at her.

"I'm here to take you home!"

"Sure. Much appreciated. We just need to take a brief detour that way first," Hel said, pointing south to where the power she'd sensed was drawing her.

Bast looked like he wanted to shake her, but his firm grip on her arms remained gentle. His wings, on the other hand, were trembling in frustration.

"You're infuriating," he said, shifting his grip to swing her up into his arms. She could see the resignation in his eyes.

"It'll be fine," Hel said as she felt the controlled surge of his muscles and power propel them up into the air.

Three scouts caught up to them and dropped into a guard formation as Bast angled their flight in the direction she'd pointed. She felt a moment of guilt for pulling them away from whatever they were supposed to be doing. This was important, though.

"How far away is this power signature?" Bast grudgingly asked.

Hel focused on the sensation tugging her forward and pushed the feeling to Bast through their connection, letting him feel it for himself.

His hands jerked tighter around her in surprise before he adjusted to the sensory input.

"Clever trick," he murmured, his gaze going distant as he focused on assessing the information her power contained.

"Any idea where it's taking us?" Hel asked when she grew bored of waiting for him to say something. They were quickly approaching their target, but there were no obviously sinister buildings or landmarks ahead.

"Patuna Chasm. Mica and I dealt with a contagion outbreak there a few months back."

"I thought the contagion usually gravitated to human habitation."

"It seems to, but we really have no fucking clue. Maybe we're about to find out what led it here."

Hel wrapped her legs tighter around Bast's waist as he freed a hand to sign to the nearby scouts to land. Below them, trees hugged the curves of a river. As they descended, she realised the canopy was hiding a split in the landscape—the chasm.

They landed in the shadow of a rusted, roofless hay barn surrounded by dry golden grass stretching higher than her knees. Bast kept hold of her hand even after releasing her body, as if he didn't quite trust her to stay put and wait for the rest of their party. The three scouts accompanying them didn't so much as rustle a leaf when they dropped to the ground.

"Orders, sir?" a woman asked.

Her wings were mottled like a sunlit forest and would have been the perfect camouflage if they were in the shadow of the trees. As it was, the varied greens reflected in the sunshine like emerald and jade. They were shot through with a deep brown reminiscent of the trunk of a ponga tree-fern, complete with hints of the silver-white colour that graced the underside of its leaves. Not for the first time, Hel was envious of an elemental's wings. Not just their beauty, but the freedom they personified. The ability to just take off and fly.

"Hel and I will drop in near the waterfall. I want you spread along the top of the chasm, far enough away that you can get down to the stream without being seen from our position," Bast said as he relinquished Hel's hand and moved between the scouts touching each briefly just below their ear. The comforting taste of his magic seeped through the air, soothing her as it brushed against her own.

"What did you do to them?" Hel asked as Bast picked her up again, ready to fly.

"I just placed a drop of my power. It will heat if we need to call for help silently."

Hel resisted the urge to investigate the alarm-system further. She had no doubt she'd be able to use it with her access to Bast's power if she tried, right before she passed out when the souls came to investigate. The lure of his power was a constant temptation, begging her to play. She pushed it aside and focused on the barely discernible sensation of her father's screened power ahead.

Bast had used his magic to hide them as soon as they'd returned to the air. Her connection to him allowed her to see through the sphere of illusion surrounding them like peering out through a mirror ball. Adrenaline flooded her system as they approached the source of the power. Why had she thought this was a good idea? Too late now.

Bast pulled into a hover over the section of the limestone chasm coated in a cascading wall of moss where a thin stream of water that could barely be classed as a 'fall' dropped into the shallow river below. Hel pointed further along, not making a sound. The power signature was coming from just past a twist in the river that was partially blocked by a large boulder. Below them, the scales of a partially decomposed wyrm glinted in the sunlight. Its body was sunken in the centre forming a nest for the ball of Bast's power that was keeping the contagion inside it contained. The shield was still intact, anchored in the bones of the dead majestic creature whose body was permanently stuck half exposed to the air above and half nestled in the arms of the earth it had called home when it lived.

Bast dropped them down silently between the looming limestone walls, coming to rest near the point where the wyrm had emerged from the ground. Holding his wings arched high behind him to keep from dragging in the water, he waded into the shallow river. He drew his sword with one hand as he released Hel to draw her own weapon. She immediately twisted the baton to release the two hidden blades that were each as long as her forearm.

As they passed the bend in the river, the chasm walls opened up to a wider area. A huge spike of rock that looked like carved meteorite wavered in the air before them as her father's defences tried and failed to shift her gaze from the stiletto piercing deep into the earth. She'd barely processed what she was seeing when pain swept through her and her skin started crawling like she was covered in fire ants. Hel staggered to put her back to Bast's as wraiths descended on them, distantly aware he'd sent the call to the scouts for help. His shielding hid them from view, but its signature must've triggered a defensive response.

Bast solidified the ball of illusion around them as she sheathed her blades and fought to stay upright, infusing it with his power until it could hold their attackers at bay. The shadowy forms hissed as they reached its bounds. Tendrils of sickly grey smoke tested its limits. The voices of the souls channelling Bast's magic to him crescendoed in volume, threatening to take her under again as the threat grew. She stiffened as memories not her own crept into the corners of her vision. The frustration burning through her at her weakness not enough to hold them at bay.

"Stay with me, Hellcat," Bast said from behind her, spinning to tuck her into his chest. "The scouts will get a look at whatever that thing is while we distract the wraiths and then we can get clear, okay?"

Hel gritted her teeth and nodded. At least he was taking the threat seriously now.

"Why don't you just blast them?"

"That kind of energy blast would draw the souls like nothing else. You're barely holding on as it is," Bast said, his voice distracted as he wove targeted attacks of power from all angles to keep the wraiths focused elsewhere and distract the, thankfully few, souls surrounding them in the isolated chasm.

Hel whimpered instinctively and Bast's arm wrapped around her in comfort.

A flash of movement near the spike of star-rock soaked in her father's power drew Hel's attention away from her internal struggles. The two scouts who'd been above and ahead of them were closing in on it but seemed unaware of its presence. Their eyes were scanning their surroundings, unable to see through the illusion. As they approached, a figure materialised from within the dark metallic stone. He was humanish in shape, but even from as far away as she was, she could see that he looked akin to her father's hounds.

His double-hinged jaw dropped wide to reveal teeth dripping with venom like the starhounds. Bat-like wings stretched from his shoulders. His naked torso was ripped with muscle, the skin a deep red colour and the same texture as the leathery black of his wings. Blood-red eyes burning with inner fire flashed as she felt him gathering destructive power in a way that made her blood run cold.

Her eyes flicked to the scouts who remained oblivious to the giant stone structure and the monster now tracking their every movement. She opened her mouth to scream a warning. Too late. A surge of power akin to her father's but darker than she'd ever felt before snapped out from the spike of rock, called forth by the being who'd already turned away from the elementals as if they were no longer a threat.

Hel watched in horror as their bodies jerked in the air—stretched impossibly wide. Their wings strained away from their torsos until they tore from their backs like they were fragile as butterflies.

Time seemed to freeze and all she could see were droplets of ichor suspended mid-air framing the wingless elementals' faces contorted in agony. Then their bodies erupted as dark magic wrenched every remaining bone outward in the same way as their wings. Ribs pierced through their chests and flew like shrapnel through the air. Vertebrae and unidentifiable white shards still dripping blood rained down on the shield surrounding them with a gentle pattering noise like popcorn cooking on a stove.

Bast let out a strangled sound of despair she felt in the depths of her soul before raising a hand to shoot out a whirlwind of pure death. Wraiths scattered and howled in a way that vibrated her skull until her brain felt like it might leak out her ears.

The hand around her waist tightening was all the warning she got before they shot skyward, bursting through the residue of the soulwoven magic that had just poured from the man holding her. She clung to consciousness as Bast beat his wings so fast they became a blur in her vision. Her hair blowing in the back draft felt like tiny whips of glass on her face.

Death swirled through her and around her as they fled. She groaned as her vision doubled. Part of her was aware of the ground still dropping further away beneath them and the stoic grief and rage emanating in waves from the man carrying her. The larger part of her was re-living the deaths of those scouts. From the inside.

Their souls had ricocheted at her right along with their bodies and they couldn't help but bleed the agonising nightmare of their last moments into her mind.

CHAPTER 6
BAST

The temptation to turn back and obliterate the being that had killed his scouts pounded through Bast's veins like a call to war. The only thing holding him back was the terrifying vulnerability he'd caused in the woman he was cradling in his arms. He couldn't turn to fight and still keep her safe. The souls were riding them too hard.

Back off. I have her, he snarled at them, unable to maintain the polite control required to deal with the dead.

The soul magic they fed him cut off for a split-second in retaliation, slowing his flight before they relented and stopped strangling its supply. It was a reminder they could make his life much more difficult. He could overwhelm them if he chose and steal what he needed, but it would vastly reduce his potential and make every working take longer. A single second of delay in a situation like they'd just faced could mean their deaths. With the danger behind them, at least the souls could finally drag themselves away. He could feel how difficult it was for them, though.

Hel shifted in his hold and some of the tension in her

body relaxed as the souls withdrew. Her eyes that had been wide and vacant as she was trapped by the dead slipped closed, and she nuzzled into his neck as she succumbed to fatigue.

"Sir? What happened? The chasm was empty. How did they die?" the strained voice of the remaining scout called from behind him.

She'd caught up when the souls had slowed him down and he felt a stab of guilt for his single-minded focus on his mate that meant he'd left her behind.

Bast glanced across at her. "You didn't see anything? The structure? The wraiths? That thing that tore them apart?"

"Nothing."

"We'll debrief at the tower. Call Morrigan and have her gather everyone."

The scout nodded, her wings trembling with every beat as she fought back shock. Bast kept his speed down to match hers as they passed over the rolling hills, hiding the way it chafed him to delay. He had no words of comfort to offer, but he could make sure she wasn't alone. Why hadn't she been able to see what was right in front of them? He hadn't even noticed a screening spell this time, but it must've been there. With their powers so interwoven, he wasn't sure if it was Hel's magic or his soulweaving that had let them see through the illusion. It was impossible to guess when Hel still wouldn't tell him about her past or her power. Even having used that power himself, it was still foreign to him, a puzzle. One he assumed Hel had the answer to and kept refusing to tell him. He wasn't sure what he'd do if she kept clinging to those secrets when it was putting his people at risk.

When they landed back at the tower, he carried Hel with him to his office, the scout trailing behind them. Every instinct told him to tuck her into his bed and let her rest, but there wasn't time to indulge their weakness.

The leaders of the city, the other six members of his ruling partnership, were gathered waiting for them. Their faces were a study of grief or carefully staunch expressionlessness, depending on their nature. Ra frowned in concern and jumped to his feet as he caught sight of Hel's limp form in his arms.

"How bad is she? Want me to take her?" he offered.

Bast snarled and clutched her closer before forcing himself to strangle back the protective noise. Ra just smiled in sympathy and clasped his shoulder briefly before returning to his place.

Bast settled in a chair behind his desk with Hel draped over his lap and looked down at the slack face of the woman he was bound to. A fist of guilt shoved its way down his throat, but he didn't let any of that show. Instead, he reached along their connection and tugged hard, pulling her back to consciousness. True to form, Hel came to by lurching upward and reaching straight for her weapon. He tightened his grip on her, holding her still as he turned that mental tug that had called her back into a phantom caress of his relief that she was awake.

"I'm not a damn cat you need to pet," she complained, pulling away from his body as if she could escape the touch of their connection. It had worked, though. He could feel a hint of calm sneaking into her, balanced with a healthy dose of annoyance at his high-handedness.

"What happened? How did my people die?" Morrigan snapped from his left, impatience ringing in her voice.

Bast ran them through the events of the morning, not glossing over the horrifying deaths of the scouts.

"So, what you're saying is that your woman took off by herself like an idiot and got my people killed," Morrigan said.

Bast felt a surge of regret through his connection with Hel, but her voice was nothing but sharp defensiveness when she answered. "We needed to know what was out there and I didn't ask anyone to follow me."

"And if you'd died? What then?" Ra asked, leaving silent the part of the equation the others in his circle were missing. The fact that if Hel died, Bast would've followed.

The guilt from Hel intensified, but still none of it showed to the others. How had he ever thought she was selfish and uncaring? It didn't mean he could go any easier on her, though.

"What were you thinking?" he asked, keeping his voice neutral.

"I was thinking you have a hostile force that only I can sense building fuck knows what on the edge of multiple courts and, despite asking you twice, you refused to *allow* me to investigate. I'm not sworn to you. You don't own me and I don't owe you my obedience," Hel said, pushing out of his arms to stand with her feet braced apart and her back to the window as if every person there was a threat to her.

Zee's dry voice filled the silent space. "I'm not saying she went about it the right way, but the woman's got a point," they said.

"I didn't allow it because it was too dangerous. And I think we can all agree I was right on that point," Bast growled.

"Can you tell us anything more about the power behind it, Hel?" Ra asked.

Bast watched the minute movement of Hel's body as she shifted in response to the question. He couldn't feel her thoughts, but he could tell they must be frantic by the surge of adrenaline the question sparked. He could also see the calculation hidden in her eyes and knew she was choosing her words carefully, always preserving her damn secrets.

"The magic that killed them was related to portalling. Sort of like a half-formed gateway where you tear the world open on one side, but with no destination. The tears were located with surgical accuracy on a moving target. I hadn't even imagined something like that was possible."

"And who would be capable of doing that?" Bast asked.

Hel stared at him, lips tightening. "Tir's 'Emperor of Suns', I assume," she said.

"The guy who made the Melding happen?"

"That's what the label on the tin said," Hel replied, the snark returning to her voice.

"And that was him today who killed my people?" Morrigan asked.

Hel's eyes dropped to her feet. "No. That wasn't him," she said, softly.

"And who is he to you that you know that?" Bast said, jealousy surging through him as he tried to imagine why someone so powerful would hunt *his* mate so obsessively.

Hel looked up at him in surprise. "Not that," she said, answering the silent accusation.

"What then?"

"Irrelevant. This had nothing to do with the hounds hunting me. There weren't even any there," Hel said, but there was a shiftiness to her energy that said she was skirting the truth if not outright lying.

And then his endlessly frustrating hellcat left the fucking room, head held high as she turned her back on everyone and strode out. Bast's hands clenched tight on his desk as he fought to control his temper.

"She could be right. It could be unrelated," Ana said, joining the conversation for the first time.

"It felt connected," Bast growled.

"Do you think she's a traitor?" Niko asked, his old voice gentle as if he hadn't just voiced the bombshell everyone had been pointedly avoiding.

"Can't be a traitor if you haven't sworn loyalty. She said it herself. She owes us nothing," Morrigan said, pure threat in her eyes. Whatever friendship had been building between his scout captain and his mate had been rocked by these deaths.

"She's not a fucking traitor," Bast growled.

"You can't know that," Niko said, his old voice almost gentle.

Bast bared his teeth and breathed deep as he dealt with the overwhelming need to lash out and defend his mate from their threats.

"It's time to tell them, bro. It was a security risk before. If she's going to go off half-cocked like this, it's even more so," Ra said.

"Tell us what?" Morrigan asked, eyes narrowing.

Bast glared at Ra, but his usually relaxed friend wasn't backing down. His head dropped and he looked down at his hands, focusing on releasing each of his fingers from their white-locked grip instead of letting loose the protective rage still flooding through him. Ra took it as the surrender it was.

"That she couldn't betray him even if she wanted because she's his mate," Zee chimed in.

If he'd thought the silence that had fallen after Hel's

outburst before was awkward, it was nothing compared to the deathly quiet that followed Zee's words.

"Well, that explains more than it doesn't. How?" Morrigan asked.

"Come on. You must have suspected she wasn't human," Zee said. "The woman can sense portals. That's not something human or elemental can do."

"She can make them, too," Bast admitted, ignoring his instincts screaming at him to keep his mate's secrets.

They couldn't afford to keep information from his inner circle any longer. He'd hoped to be able to cure the soul taint in his mate before they found out and avoid causing them extra stress, especially if they started trying to figure out succession plans. He didn't think he could sit through a discussion about what would happen if his mate was dead.

Zee's eyes lit up. "Ooo ... do you think I could engineer a doorframe that would hold a portal? That'd be cool."

"That would be a giant fucking security risk," Morrigan snapped, but the distraction had faded the murderous gleam in her eyes.

She was just plain grouchy now. At least his revelation had made her realise Hel hadn't meant to put the scouts in danger.

"None of this is helping me avenge my people," Morrigan added.

Bast nodded, dragging his focus back to where it needed to be. "This guy with the bat wings is the first creature of this emperor we've seen that was more than a rabid animal," he said.

The wraiths had a cunning and pack mentality that made them dangerous, but they were foot soldiers at best. The hounds were the same if they were part of it, and the taste of the power that had killed his people was familiar enough that he would bet they were.

"They're clearly not from this world. They might be used to hiding from other magic-users, but I'm betting they're not used to dealing with human technology. Maybe we can find something to counter his shielding. Morrigan, hook up your scouts with thermal imaging cameras and whatever else you think might help you see behind the illusion and see if he's still at the chasm. Ra, get your people on the satellite imagery in support and see if you can track that bat guy. I want to know if he's been in the city. Fuck, I want to know if he's been anywhere in the world. The chances they're only hitting us and the Earth Court with whatever this is are slim. Zee, I want you partnering on the tech. Whatever you can do to stop us operating blind."

They took another twenty minutes to cover the essentials of managing the city before dispersing to get to the tasks Bast had assigned. Even with the contagion blooming and the new unknown threat of this power, his people still needed to stay fed and safe. Niko reported human separatist graffiti had tripled in the last month, a quiet echo of the turmoil that had been spreading through the other continents. It saddened him that even here in the City of Souls where humans like Niko, Ra, and Ana were a vital part of their leading partnership and the elemental scouts and architecture helped keep everyone safe, there were still those who wanted to live apart so badly they would put themselves at risk. Only time would tell if Niko and Ra's efforts would help boost the morale of the city and keep everyone working together.

News of his temporary death at Aliya's hands had spread despite their best efforts, and even the staunchest of their human supporters were taking a dim view of the elemental courts because of it. Their elemental citizens were almost as bad because it was the nature of the free city that had existed here before the Melding for their people to be anti-establishment. Not that he wanted them to be pro-courts, he just needed them to be pro-peace. There was enough going on in the world without adding more conflict. Sighing, he rubbed his aching head as they agreed to divert scarce resources into making this right. There was no point pouring all their people into fighting off threats, only to discover the very thing they were defending, the peace of their home, had collapsed behind them.

He remained seated when they finished, staring at his computer screen until Ana's hand fell on his shoulder.

"I'll go check on your girl for you," she said.

"Make sure she eats something?" Bast requested, reaching up to touch her fingers in thanks.

"Of course. Don't forget to take your own advice."

BY THE NEXT MORNING, they were confident the creature who'd murdered the scouts had left the area. Zee and Ra had tweaked the satellite feed until they found a combination of magical and thermal imaging that revealed the structure in the chasm. They had Lady Aliya to thank for the advanced satellite spying above them, which Ra's people had hacked to get the images. It was ex-military from the American continent and had locked onto them shortly after she'd pinned Bast's dead body to her wall. That was a mixed blessing, given it meant she was watching them. The spine of meteoric rock itself was invisible, but the hole it made in the earth glowed like a pin-prick lantern in the imaging. With an extra filter of Zee's design, they could just see a swirling mist surrounding it that must be the wraiths.

The adjusted night-vision goggles that Morrigan and her small team had worn to get a closer look had worked just as well. While the elementals still found their eyes refusing to stay focused on the target, as long as their cameras were pointed in the right direction, the video feed back to the comms centre ensured Ra's people could provide a running commentary of what they couldn't see before them. They stayed well clear of the boundary where Bast and Hel had triggered the defensive attack by the wraiths, and between them mapped out the area in enough detail to be confident the bat-winged threat was elsewhere.

Bast hovered in the control room, shirt untucked and hair dishevelled from a long night running his hands through it while Ra's team attempted to hack every other military satellite they could around the Earths to see where else the structures might be. His communications people were trawling the internet for any sign of someone matching the guy's description. He had bat wings, for fuck's sake. Someone must have noticed him.

A hot mug of tea pressing into his hand jerked him from his thoughts and he smiled over at Ana in thanks.

"You should get some sleep. You're no good to anyone if you collapse," she said.

Ra looked up from the screen he was peering at over someone's shoulder. "She's right. Go take a nap and make sure your hellcat isn't going to run off again."

Bast winced, kicking himself for being so distracted he hadn't checked, and focused on his connection to Hel. He sighed in relief when he felt her presence upstairs, still safe in the tower. Ra was right, though. He needed to make sure she was going to stay put.

Ra followed him out as he made his way to the lifts. "How you holding up?" he asked quietly.

"I've been better."

"Anything I can do?" his friend asked.

Bast pushed the call button and leaned against the wall, watching his friend. "Have you had any luck researching something to break the mating bond?"

"Not yet. But I've still got people on it. Will you really give her up?"

"Call me as soon as you find anything. On the bond or that bat-winged-bastard," he said, ignoring the question that he honestly didn't know the answer to.

Hel was in his blood, wrapped through his soul. He wasn't sure what would be left if he ripped her out. The damage would tear him to shreds. Like he had so many times before, he forced himself to stop thinking about it. He'd deal with it when the time came. There was no point dwelling on it.

His muscles were aching from so long standing tense and he leaned his head back on the cool metal of the elevator while he made his way back up to the penthouse. Reaching up to rub his stiff neck, the rough stubble on his jaw scratched at his hand. He needed a shower. And clean clothes. And to wrap himself around Hel in bed so he could sleep without worrying she was going to sneak out.

He did a double-take when he walked into their home to find the woman who wouldn't leave his thoughts cooking pancakes in the kitchen. Hel was the antithesis of domestic. As if hearing his thoughts, she glared at him where he stood just keeping the surprise from his face. He frowned as he noticed the signs of strain around her eyes and a weird pallor to her skin. She was deteriorating.

"What? I needed to do something to take my mind off ... everything," she growled. "And I can't work out on the balcony anymore. The souls in the surrounding walls are too much."

Bast cautiously dropped onto a stool at the breakfast bar, wary of what this new and unexpected mood in his mate might herald. She felt more passive than she ever had before, subdued. He sat in silence as she carried on pouring batter and flipping.

She didn't speak again until she was putting a plate piled high with pancakes between them. She was so quiet he almost didn't hear her when she spoke, voice laden with guilt.

"I'm sorry."

Bast sighed and stood to walk around to where she waited, shoulders hunched forward and staring down at the food she'd made. He reached out and touched her chin gently, silently asking her to look up at him. The pain in her jade-coloured eyes almost broke him when she did.

"It wasn't your fault they died," he said.

"It was reckless."

Bast shrugged uncomfortably. His own guilt was just as thick as hers. He'd had to call the families of the scouts last night. Hearing their grief made the dull ache of their loss return to searing pain.

"It was. But I should have listened to you in the first place. We could have gone in more prepared."

Hel's surprise at his admission seemed to shock her out of her melancholy, and her mouth twitched as she watched him.

"Yes. You should've," she said finally, grabbing a pancake and folding it in half to take a bite. "But if you'd brought a larger force, we may well have lost even more."

As she was chewing, he bent forward and grabbed her wrist gently to take a bite of the piece still in her hand.

"Hey! Get your own!" she said, shoving his shoulder ineffectually.

"But yours tastes better," he teased, too tired to hide his need for this woman like he usually would, as his affection flowed down the bond between them.

Hel rolled her eyes and shoved the plate toward him.

"Ra and I used to make late-night pancakes when we first converted the Tower. The hydroponic floors were still being finished and some weeks our diet was incredibly bland as we ran out of supplies. Once a month, we'd get a delivery of whiskey and they'd include a few bags of flour. You should've seen my face the first time he made them."

"Not a lot of pancakes in your childhood?" Hel asked.

Bast scoffed. "No. My foster parents were terrified of me."

"I never had them before joining the couriers, either. We were always running to the next hiding place. I hid in the hallway to watch Ryker making them so I could learn how."

Bast laughed at the image filling his mind of a younger and even more feisty Hellkitten using all her stealth to learn something his old friend would've been thrilled to teach her. "I bet he knew you were there."

Hel smiled ruefully. "Yeah. It didn't occur to me until years later that he probably didn't need to read the recipe aloud while he cooked."

"I wouldn't ever betray your secrets. You don't always have to face everything alone, you know," Bast said.

"It's part of my charm," Hel said. "How's the search going?"

"We're making progress. The tech's working how we need it to. It's just a matter of time."

"Did you get any sleep last night?"

Bast felt warmth fill some of the numbness in his soul at the concern that drifted from her. "No. You?"

"Couldn't. I kept remembering..." her voice trailed off. "I just couldn't," she finally finished.

"Come lie down with me?" he whispered, not able to look at her as he waited for her rejection.

Deceptively delicate fingers twined through his as she took his hand in a firm grip.

"This doesn't mean anything," she said as she pulled him to his feet and led the way to his room.

He fell onto his bed fully clothed, pulling her after him until he'd wrapped her body in his wings and her head was resting on his chest, tucked right under his chin.

"Nothing at all," he agreed, his eyelids already closing as her steel and jasmine scent filled his nose and his body relaxed into the feeling of home.

A PERSISTENT KNOCKING WOKE Bast from dreams of trailing his fingers over soft skin. He jerked upright before he remembered he was sharing a bed. Hel's curses filled the air as she rolled off the bed into a fighting stance before realising there was no imminent threat.

"Shit. Sorry," he mumbled.

"Bro! Are you decent? Actually, scratch that, I don't care

about you. Is Hel decent?" Ra's voice sounded from the other side of the door.

Bast pressed his fingers to his aching eyes and then checked his phone. They'd slept six hours, and he'd somehow missed the vibration of multiple notifications of texts Ra had been sending.

Hel stalked to the door and yanked it open. "We're both decent. And we have been the whole time," she growled, and Bast could swear she seemed as annoyed about being decent as she was about the question.

The same thought must have occurred to Ra, because he was smirking.

"What's up?" Bast asked, not bothering to do more than pull himself up to lean on the headboard.

"We've got two more suspected structures in the Fire and Water Courts. And there are reports on social media of sightings of 'the real batman' in the American continent, within the shadow of the Air Court stronghold even. He was seen at a cemetery in Nashville."

"You think Aliya's working with him?"

"Could be. Or her guards aren't any better at seeing him than our scouts were. We can't get a good satellite image of the area because her floating monstrosity is in the way. If she's working with a foreign power, the other courts might take her to task."

"If she's working with him, we can't guarantee any of the other courts aren't as well," Hel said.

"Is there a structure there? Is he actually making contact with her? Everyone knows she's preparing for a fight with us. They won't take sides unless it's undeniably clear she's betrayed them," Bast said.

"That's if we can even convince the other courts they're

under threat at all," Ra said. "They can't see the damn things, remember?"

"We need more information," Bast concluded.

"If only we had someone who could both see him and had the ability to travel long distances in a single step," Hel said drily.

CHAPTER 7
HEL

"No," Bast said, voice flat and any sign of the softness they'd briefly indulged in gone.

"How'd that approach work out for you last time?" Hel shot back, which was admittedly a low blow.

"The souls would need to screen you. Even if they didn't kill you, you wouldn't be able to move around once you get there without the screen failing and giving up your location to your hunters. And what even happens to your portal if you collapse unconscious from the souls protecting you at the other end? Does it close and trap you there? Does it remain open and let Aliya's army straight into my fucking tower?"

"I assumed your overprotective self would come with me and we'd figure it out," Hel said, keeping the fear of the soul taint from her voice even though she knew Bast would have sensed it.

"Could you use her power to go alone?" Ra asked Bast, sitting down at the foot of the bed like they were having a gentle morning chat.

Bast looked at her thoughtfully. "What do you think, Hellcat? I suspect I probably need to be fairly close to you to channel your power. Once I was through, it might be too far."

"The hunters would still find you if you moved away from it. They're chasing any portal signature and it would taste of my power."

"We could send drones," Ra suggested.

"Hard to shield and likely to draw attention. Aliya's not much of a one for technology, so they wouldn't be common there. People would notice. She's all about the old-school biblical aesthetic," Bast said.

"You said it was a cemetery, right? There must be plenty of souls there. What if we close it as soon as we're through, and you ask the local souls to shield that location until we're gone? Then we should be able to move," Hel said.

"Plenty of souls means plenty of risk to you," Bast said.

"Only if I'm under attack. Which I won't be if no one knows we're there. Look, if this soul taint keeps getting worse, this might be our only chance to get the intel we need to protect the city. We know Aliya's been building an attacking force. If she's working with that monster too, then we need to make sure the other courts know. Let me do this. I may be dying, but I'm not weak."

Both of them knew what she wasn't saying out loud. They might be desperate for vengeance on the monster who'd killed their people, but that wasn't the only reason this trip was so urgent. If they died, the city would be all but defenceless against anyone powerful unless the courts stepped in. No way in hell would they leave their people vulnerable to Aliya, so they had to be able to prove what they suspected about her. If these were her last weeks, Hel was asking to use them for something meaningful instead of hiding in the Tower. She felt a moment of guilt for appealing to both his protectiveness of the city and the mating bond that would make it hard for him to resist the plea in her voice. Regardless, it worked. She could feel his resistance evaporate.

"We'd need to be quick. It's so close to her stronghold. It will notice our presence even if her guards don't," Bast said.

"Great. It's decided then. I'll just have a shower and some tea and we can get going."

Bast looked like he'd swallowed something unpleasant and Ra was laughing softly at his capitulation.

"I'll get a back-up team ready and grab you some body cameras," Ra said.

Bast intercepted Hel as she headed to the door on her way to her own room, grasping her forearm. "You don't have to do this," he growled, their bond thrumming with his fear for her.

Hel looked up at him and raised an eyebrow. He was the one who was always telling her not to be so selfish. "I know. But I'm the best person for the job. Or *we* are. We need that intel."

"If it gets too much, we leave immediately. No heroics."

"Yes, Sir," Hel said, letting her sarcasm at his overbearing direction push back the pit of anxiety that felt like it was swallowing her stomach whole.

It backfired. She could feel her words sparking a surge of dominance in Bast. Which was ridiculous because that wasn't even really him. Nor was the reciprocal craving his response sparked in her. Stupid magical mate bonds weren't designed to be ignored. They were both turning a little unstable. That might also have something to do with the risk-taking behaviour they were about to embark on. Oh well.

Bast's eyes dropped to her lips and the concern she'd been feeling through their bond morphed to something else, something that left her wavering closer to the muscled form of the man standing next to her. She reached out without thinking, stroking a finger down the soft inner feathers of his wing. The silver of his magic danced around the path where she'd touched like motes of sparkling diamond dust in sunshine made of shadow.

"Don't tempt me," Bast said, his voice rough with need.

Hel pulled away from his grip and paused in the doorway as she walked away.

"Would it really be that bad?" she asked quietly, with her back still to him.

Bast let out an explosive breath and she resisted the urge to turn around.

"Yes. Breaking this bond is the only way to save you and I won't be able to do that if we get any closer than we already are. Fuck. I'm not even sure I could do it now. That's if I can even find a way to break it. I can't watch you slip away, Hel. I won't."

The defeat in his voice and the guilt down their connection was enough to override Hel's usual anger. She knew that kind of guilt personally. Had felt it every day since she watched her guardian slaughtered and her only friend dragged into her father's portal to keep her hidden. To keep her safe. Her existence caused their deaths. She ached to comfort this man whose hidden pain echoed her own in so many ways.

"So, what you're saying is no quickie?" Hel asked, somehow injecting a teasing tone into her voice despite the heaviness of her thoughts as she stared back over her shoulder at him.

Bast's jaw dropped in surprise and then his laugh rang out. A bitter laugh, sure. But a laugh nonetheless. She gifted him a quick grin and then sauntered down the hallway to her room, warmth filling her chest at the lightening she sensed down their connection. She'd helped. And if she'd felt the souls in the tower's shield bowing toward her and threatening to break through as the emotions flowed between them, that wasn't something Bast needed to know.

It was the next day before everything was ready for their spying mission. They'd decided it was safest to portal from the roof, close to the weaponised crown of the building if anyone pursued them back home and clearly visible to their scouts who could hover above in case of an ambush.

"You want to do the honours?" Bast asked as he turned to face her on the windswept tiles.

Ra had secured them detailed photos of the cemetery they were aiming for. Hel had never tried to target a destination by image before, but she thought she could probably make it work in combination with her memory of portalling to the general area last time. Bast was no help because he'd been dead the only time he'd been in Aliya's territory. She knew she could land them *in* Aliya's stronghold. She just needed to make sure that this time they landed below it instead.

Holding the image and the memory in her mind, she stretched out her power, skipping across the connections between worlds that were rife in their melded earths like a stone across a lake or a train passing by stations. Range was different when she was actively using her power than when she was passively sensing and searching. On the plane in which her portals formed, distance was almost meaningless. Other than her short, simple portal to the ground, she hadn't used her magic like this since they'd mated.

The difference was immeasurable between then and now that she had such a deeper awareness of the dead. The souls chased behind her consciousness, their instincts telling them her presence in this plane was dangerous and compelling them to swarm closer to her. Their silver forms were uncannily similar to the wraiths her father had set to guard his structures. They might not have teeth, but Hel could feel the danger of their memories snapping at her soul as she fled before them. The line of her magic that connected her body to her consciousness was hidden by their passage, and Hel fought back a chill of foreboding as she checked back the way she'd come. She knew in that second that if they caught up to her before the portal formed, she'd be lost.

She didn't have time to make sure their destination was correct. As soon as she felt the tug of awareness that suggested her power had found the location matching her will, she let loose a flood of power to burn open the gateway between cities.

"Hurry," she gasped to Bast as she threw her body through the shimmering veil.

Her vision darkened and she fell to her knees as soon as she was through, a symphony of screams tearing through her soul. Bast cursed and she felt the sweep of soft wings over her body as he lurched to the side to avoid stepping on her. She let the rift unravel as soon as she felt his touch against her skin. A surge of his power nearby, redirecting the souls to protect her by swarming her portal to hide it instead of her body, preceded gentle hands scooping her up from the ground. He carried her well clear of the cluster of the dead now writhing around the point they'd entered. At least the souls could still pull back when the danger to her faded, although she could tell that was getting more difficult each time.

They'd aimed to land in the deeper shadow of a mausoleum on the far edge of the graveyard. The pressure threatening to crack open her skull reduced a little as they left the souls screening their entry point behind them, but their screams persisted in the background. It was like she had her own personal horror theme playing on an endless loop inside her skull as they slunk between shadows through the trees and tombstones.

The rocky foundation of Aliya's flying stronghold loomed above them, free-floating three hundred feet in the air. The yellow tinge to the surrounding vegetation suggested she hadn't moved it for a while. The cemetery was clearly one of those locations where the synchronicity between the realities that had melded together to form their world was uncanny. Both humans and elementals had laid their departed to rest there, the miniature glades of the elemental resting places softening the concrete and marble human memorials scattered between them. She would've known both were here even without that visual, because she could *feel* them all pressing in on her soul, human and elemental alike.

The sensation that she was caught in a horror movie only intensified as she spied a vandalised memorial tree. Its thin trunk was splintered in half and blackened with char that was just visible as it poked out from the partially decomposed human body impaled on it. Vacant eye sockets stared at them as they passed and it was impossible to tell if the poor person had lost their eyes before or after they died. Someone had carved letters into their stomach, the raised scars and dried blood still visible against the discoloured skin of the corpse.

Hel paused to make sense of the word—Defiler. She sighed. The underground of human separatists who wanted to live free of elemental control were a spectrum from relatively peaceful activists to terrorists. They didn't get many of the extremists in the City of Souls, but even there they had the occasional crime like this man had been labelled with—the damaging of elemental graves. In the City of Souls, they were usually made to pay reparations, clean up their mess, and face the families of those they'd harmed. The stupidity of trying it in the shadow of the Air Court's stronghold was mind-boggling. Lady Aliya was renowned for her ruthless punishments, as this tortured body proved. Pain stabbed through her torso in sympathy, and she couldn't tell if it was psychosomatic or caused by the body's soul looming close. Wincing, she rubbed at her stomach.

"You okay?" Bast whispered, pulling her away from the gruesome scene and beneath the branches of a tree thick with leaves as a winged elemental form flitted in the distance.

"In hindsight, a cemetery may not have been the best destination for someone succumbing to death by soul magic," Hel said, biting back a groan as another flashback that wasn't hers pushed through her mind.

Searing pain shot through her, and this time she was certain it wasn't psychosomatic as she felt every bone in her body crack while a dozen stakes impaled her. The only silver lining was that it threw her so far out of her mind she couldn't have given them away with a scream if she tried. Bast growled and she was distantly aware of his mind-voice pleading with the souls in the area, reassuring them she was in no danger while he was beside her. Eventually, the sensation faded to an uncomfortable itch crawling through her muscles along the lines the pointed steel had taken.

"She sure likes poking holes in people," Hel said weakly, gritting her teeth as she took short, sharp breaths.

"Do we need to leave?"

"We're here now. We just need to hurry," Hel whispered, forcing her mind away from the deaths swirling around her to focus on scanning the area for her father's power. "That way. Not far," she said, pointing.

Bast slipped an arm around her waist as they crept between the silent graves, the touch helping to anchor her to what was real and present. She could feel his communication with the dead around them like the distant buzz of a radio station tuned to the wrong channel. Warning them away. Begging them to leave her be. Promising he could protect her alone. His thumb snuck beneath the hem of her shirt, stroking circles against her skin like he was trying to reassure himself she was still there. Still warm with life.

When a huge shard of dagger-like sculpted meteoric rock like the one they'd seen at Patuna Chasm appeared before them, Hel drew in a sharp breath. This one wasn't hidden away on the outskirts of a court. It was right beneath Aliya's floating stronghold. Although perhaps it hadn't always been, given the Air Court floated around to its lady's whims.

She could feel the same shielding on it the others had, making it invisible to the casual observer as their eyes skipped away. To her sight unaffected by her father's shields, it was brazenly obvious. Although it only stood out from the more fantastic pyramids and catacombs of the cemetery because of its size and the alien material it was formed from. They paused just outside the radius at which they'd triggered the shard in Patuna Chasm's defences and stared at the alien rock spire.

"Surely someone's noticed this," Bast murmured against her ear, his breath stroking across her cheek.

They both flinched as a susurration of shadow twisted down from the edge of the stronghold far ahead of them, crouching down lower behind the concrete of the crying angel they were sheltering behind. Aliya had centred her floating city above the cemetery, which meant anyone coming from the stronghold would emerge a decent distance away. It also meant they'd be totally exposed to any elemental flying overhead given how low they'd have to fly to the ground.

"Elemental squadron training?" Hel whispered as she focused on the figures swirling in the distance who were sweeping closer.

Bast nodded. "They're using the stronghold to screen their training from any satellites. We knew she'd stepped up recruitment. This is what she's doing instead of helping deal with the contagion," he said, his low voice dripping with disgust.

"I've never seen a squadron that size," Ra said through their comms, and Hel jumped a little.

She'd almost forgotten they had camera feeds streaming back home. Elemental squadrons were generally quite small given their population wasn't as numerous. They basically only grouped together to protect the battle mages in their ranks who did the real damage. Ostensibly, a squadron should be only large enough to deal with the predator outbreaks that were their usual focus—a rabid griffin or a clutch of dragons that grew too bold. Usually a handful of elementals was enough, and the council had rules about how many squadrons a court could marshal day-to-day to avoid a magical arms race.

"That's because you only need that kind of force to invade. I'll need to talk to the other courts. Even if it's us she has in her sights, surely the others won't want her to have this kind of advantage over them," Bast said.

"We need to move," Hel said, as the winged squadron drifted closer.

"Can you sense any portals nearby? Do we know if that bat-winged bastard's been in the stronghold?" Bast asked, as they hunched low to the ground to retreat further from the spine of rock and the incoming fighters.

Bast stretched a wing over her as they moved, and she could feel the brush of his magic as he wove a tight illusion around them. Hel took a moment to stretch her magical senses out wide, realising she'd drawn them in instinctively as a protection from the dead surrounding them. She frowned in confusion at what she felt. Other than the structure they'd been spying on, there was nothing that suggested her father's people had portalled to the area. The grainy social media image that had brought them here was recent, only a day before. There should've been something.

"I've got nothing. Could the sighting have been faked?"

"No. We're confident he was there at the time of the post," Ra replied through her earpiece.

"He must have flown in, though I can't imagine why he'd waste the time," Hel said as Bast used a touch of his power to break the lock on a crypt and pulled them both inside the cramped and cold interior.

This particular crypt was a circular room with urns of ashes resting in a dozen wall cavities scattered around them. A stained glass window on one side should've left them with a dim light to see by but with the door closed and the constant looming shadow of the stronghold above them, it was only the silvery glow of Bast's magic on his inner wing surface glinting off the metal capsules that made them visible.

"How're you holding up?" Bast checked in again, reaching a hand out to smooth the furrow from her forehead.

Hel gave in to the wariness dragging at her body and leaned forward to rest her head on his chest. A moment later, soft feathers enveloped her as he wrapped her in his wings. Some of the pressure of the dead pushing against her dropped away as she stood motionless in his embrace and she breathed a sigh of relief at the temporary respite. It was short-lived. As if it had been waiting for her to relax, a sentience that was vast compared to the souls of the dead brushed across her mind.

She'd been careful to keep her mind shielded from the curiosity of the stronghold above them, making herself seem human from long practice. Something must have made the crystal city suspicious though, because she could feel its focus narrowing onto her—a feral animal drawn by the scent of prey. There was something disturbing about the Air Stronghold she couldn't quite put her finger on, as if the facets of its crystal planes had fractured its personality as much as they did the golden light Aliya flooded through the space. She tried to soften her mind, reinforcing the veneer of obliviousness she'd draped like a cloak over herself. It didn't work. A thump of rock nearby sent the ground trembling and several urns crashing to the ground.

"Shit. The stronghold found me," Hel gasped, choking on the ash scattering in the air and trying not to imagine who she might be breathing in.

"Portal. Now. Ra, be ready in case we're followed," Bast snapped.

Hel grasped for her power and would have sunk to her knees if Bast hadn't caught her in his arms. She wasn't sure if it was the cemetery, the ashes of the dead literally coating her lungs, or the increased threat of the stronghold, but it felt like every soul nearby was converging on her. Chills wracked her body as the deluge soaked into every point of vulnerability like she was a drain through which their floodwaters had no choice but to pass. It was lucky she didn't need to breathe as frequently as a human, because she could no longer make her chest rise or fall. She wasn't drowning in their memories anymore; she was just flat out drowning.

Bast's voice growled from so very, very far away. "Dammit, Hellcat. Don't stop fighting."

A tug that barely registered compared to the sensory overload of the deaths rushing through her was followed by a burst of warmth against her power as a portal formed.

Oh good, she thought. *As long as only one of us dies.*

"Neither of us is fucking dying," Bast growled, slightly closer now. Not because she'd come back from wherever this tidal wave of souls was taking her, but because he'd dived in after her and was attempting to use his power to hold her head above water.

Her lungs were aching from lack of air, but maybe also from the way he was grasping her so tight. She was dimly aware of the light changing as they emerged from the portal, but the concentration of souls only got worse as they hit the Tower; the vast pool of the dead swirling close. That was okay. Bast was home safe, now. She could just drift on the ice-cold torturous tide for a bit.

A slap of power across her soul jolted through her like a shock from a defibrillator, and a dark, desperate voice sounded in her mind. *I said don't stop fighting!*

Hush. I'm tired, Hel thought back.

Blessed silence reigned for a moment. Then the comforting sensation of ghost feathers draped over her soul. That was wrong, though. She would've frowned if she could still feel her face. *Why are you here? You should go back.*

I can't go back without you, sweetheart. And I wouldn't want to.

The words sunk into her consciousness like warm tears trailing down her ice-cold cheeks. He wasn't yelling or pleading. Instead, he was wrapping her in affection, an unanswered call and response.

The danger to him finally broke through her forced apathy. Desperately grasping for an anchor with her mind, anything to hold her steady, what she found was the promise of home and a man who ached to save her. As oxygen rushed into her lungs, something even more essential rushed into her heart. The last thing she felt before comforting darkness was the sensation of real corporeal feathers brushing against her too sensitive skin.

CHAPTER 8
BAST

"You've been ignoring my calls," Mica said in lieu of a greeting.

The acoustics of the limestone cave he was calling from dulled any background noise leaving solely his rich tenor to emerge from the speakers of Bast's computer. If he hadn't been so worried about Hel still lying unconscious two levels above him, Bast might've smirked at Ra subconsciously wetting his lips across from him as he listened in.

"My apologies. I've been busy."

"With your mate? The one who has the unique ability to portal you forgot to mention?" Mica asked, and Bast had to ignore Ra again, who was now mouthing *Oh, shit* across from him.

"With figuring out why Aliya's mustering an invading force and what the fuck that emperor guy is building on the edge of all our courts," Bast said.

Mica didn't respond immediately, his face giving nothing away as Bast waited to see if he would let the change of topic stand. "I didn't see a building. Just those strange shadows attacking your mate."

"She has a name," Bast growled. "And you didn't see a structure because it has shielding that makes you look away."

"Let me guess. *Helaine* can see the structures," Mica said.

"We both can. Don't shoot the messenger. Would you rather I leave you unaware of the threat?" Bast asked, trying to rein in his frustration. He needed to keep on good terms with Mica. Kaia's future depended on it.

Mica inclined his head. "I appreciate the information. I would appreciate it even more if you had not been keeping secrets from the council."

"As if you all don't keep secrets from each other constantly. You had the information you needed. Hel's abilities are irrelevant," Bast said.

"And what is she, then? Clearly she is not human if she can form a mate bond with you and portal. Is she immune to the soul taint?"

"Also, irrelevant," Bast said, relieved that Mica's discovery of Hel's power meant he wasn't assuming she was dying. At least they could keep their weakness under wraps for now.

Mica stared at him in surprise. "You don't even know what your own mate is, do you? This is a major security risk, Bastion. I'm not sure how comfortable I am working with you, or hosting anyone from your household, when I know nothing about the motivations of this person who has such an intimate ability to coerce you."

Bast ground his teeth and swallowed the growl that had formed at the insult to his mate and the sly implication Mica would refuse Kaia training over this. How many times had he dropped everything to save Mica's ungrateful ass from the contagion? And now that it was all safely contained, he wasn't sure if he wanted to work together anymore? Fucking typical lord bullshit. He was just as bad as all the rest. Bast shook with rage, already on edge from Hel's vulnerability and trying to suppress his instinctive reaction to threaten the Earth Lord right back.

Ra stood up and came into the camera view, placing a firm hand on Bast's shoulder. "Perhaps we should continue this conversation later when tempers have cooled," he said, and even his usual easy-going voice was tight with anger. Ra was loyal to a fault and had no tolerance for anyone threatening his family, which included both Kaia and Hel regardless of whether he actually trusted Bast's mate.

Bast had the satisfaction of watching the usually poker-faced Mica swallow hard and look almost chagrined as he realised Ra had been listening in to his posturing.

"That might be best," he said.

"We would appreciate any insight you gain into Aliya's armed forces and we respectfully suggest you monitor the cave system near your stronghold where Hel was attacked. We've found similar structures here and beneath the Air Court, and satellite footage suggests they are likely near the Water and Fire Courts as well," Ra said, his voice so professional it was almost painful.

It didn't go unnoticed if the strain on Mica's face was any indication. The two of them had only just begun to show an interest in each other on his last visit, but clearly Ra's opinion meant something to Mica. Bast felt a grim satisfaction at his friend's willingness to use that to their advantage.

"That went well," Ra said when the call ended, voice

dripping sarcasm as he perched on the edge of Bast's desk beside him.

Bast ran a hand down his face and stretched his wings and neck where he sat. "Any news on a fix for the mating bond?" he asked.

Ra frowned. "Tir's been searching their memory for whether there was anything relevant in the Archives about it. They said there was mention of an elemental artificer forging a pair of pendants that blocked the effects a few centuries back. He's still alive."

"Your expression says there's a catch," Bast replied.

"He's living on Murano."

Bast pressed his fingers hard to his temples, feeling the stress headache that had been threatening all morning take hold. "Of course he had to be in Ty's territory. I guess he might let us in if he thinks severing the bond will hurt me."

"That's not all. The pendant has to be made from a piece of the stronghold associated with each mate and within its bounds. Something about the residual sentience is essential to the process," Ra said, wincing.

"What does that mean? Neither of us is associated with a stronghold."

"Tir said they thought there was a fifty/fifty chance it could work with a piece of your father's stronghold, given you were born there. That would be the pendant Hel would wear to block the bond with you. We've got no clue how to make one that would work in reverse."

"So, not only does Ty need to let me enter his territory, but he needs to let me do this in the heart of his stronghold and take a piece away with me? All for a fifty percent chance of success, where success is defined as Hel being free of the bond, but I'm still subject to it?"

"Ah, yeah. That's pretty much it," Ra said.

"Fucking great."

"Are you going to do it?"

"Of course I'm going to do it. The alternative is her dying."

"And *you* dying," Ra reminded him.

Bast shrugged. He'd die whenever it was time. He'd spent a lifetime talking to the dead and navigating their plane. It didn't scare him. Not like the idea of Hel's beautiful fire being extinguished because of him. That fucking terrified him.

Ra looked unhappy at whatever he saw in his face, but carried on regardless. "I've spoken to the artificer already. He's agreed to give it a shot so long as it doesn't put him in Ty's firing line."

"I guess we'd better talk to my dick of a brother then," Bast said, pulling up Ty's number on his phone. He was feeling too raw to videoconference and risk giving away more than he wanted with his expressions.

The call rang for so long he thought Ty was going to ignore it, but finally his chill voice sounded through the speaker.

"Bastion," he said, though it couldn't have been construed as a greeting.

"I'm coming to visit," Bast said, getting straight to the point.

Before Ty could jump in with some scathing commentary, he gave a short, clipped explanation of what he needed. He couldn't risk revealing Hel's weakness, so instead he spun a line about her refusing the bond and demanding to be released. It wasn't that farfetched after all. The line went silent as the brother who'd spent thirty years trying to kill him considered his request. Technically, as a blood relative of the ruling family, Ty couldn't refuse Bast access to the Stronghold, and he was perfectly within his rights to take a memento. Many elementals who called one of the sentient strongholds home took a living piece with them for comfort when they travelled. In reality, they both knew Ty could make things very difficult for him and the Stronghold itself could reject him if his brother wasn't on board.

Finally, a dry laugh sounded. "That's quite the mess you've made yourself, *brother*," he said, the last word dripping with scorn. "Just to be clear. If this works, you will still be pining for your irritating mate and she will walk away from you?"

Bast ground his teeth. "In all likelihood, yes."

"Count me in," Ty said, hanging up before he could say anything else.

"That ... was not how I expected that call to go," Ra said, frowning in concern.

"Yes. He agreed far too easily," Bast said.

"I know he's spent a lifetime hating you, but he should at least be pretending to get along better now he knows you didn't kill your father. He still sounds..."

"Venomous? Obnoxious? Irrational?" Bast offered.

"Yeah. That. I'm worried about what he might be planning. It feels like a trap."

Bast sighed. "It's not like we have much choice. And as long as Mica doesn't rat us out, he won't know we can portal out if needed."

"Can you risk that? It seems to set off the souls."

"I almost lost her this time," Bast admitted in a low whisper. "But if the pendant works, it should be fine."

"And if it doesn't?"

"Then we'd better hope my brother isn't cunning enough to pull off whatever he's thinking."

THE EERIE FLATNESS of the mating connection while Hel was unconscious just about killed Bast with guilt. How many times would he have to stare down at her slack, unresponsive body? How many times would they have to pierce her soft skin with an intravenous drip to keep her healthy? It had happened enough now that he could recognise when she was coming back to him through their bond. The first blips of consciousness registered like a heart monitor recording the seconds after a defibrillator finally dragged a pulse back from flatline.

He made sure to be there when she woke this time, perching on the side of his bed like he was a visitor in his own room. Her beautiful jade-green eyes fluttered open, and she immediately winced them closed again with a groan. Bast smoothed her hair back from her face and kept stroking as the tension left her at his touch, running his fingers through her hair.

"How long?" she croaked. The same question she asked every time.

Bast slipped an arm under her shoulders to support her head while he offered her sips of chilled water. "Two days. No more portalling to the Tower. It's getting worse each time."

He expected Hel to rebel against the words but she didn't, and that only made him more concerned. Exhaustion was sapping her into uncharacteristic compliance. Hel's hands were clumsy when she finally pushed away the cup he was holding, her muscles still uncoordinated so soon after waking.

Bast replaced the cup on the side table but kept his arm around her, lifting her so he could stretch his wing along the headboard and resettle her against his chest. Her head rested over her mating mark that he still hadn't shown her. It sent tingles through his skin despite the clothes he wished weren't between them. Returning to stroking her hair, he felt her body relax into his on her next breath.

"I thought this was against the rules," she murmured just as his own eyes were slipping closed in contentment after the restless nights worrying if she was going to recover.

"I won't tell anyone if you don't," Bast said.

This might be the last chance he had to hold her like this, and he wouldn't give it up until he had to.

When he woke hours later, the bed was empty but his body felt better than it had in weeks. He almost skipped taking a shower in favour of preserving her fading scent on his skin, but he needed the driving hot water to get his head back in the game.

By the time he entered the open plan living space of the penthouse, he had most of his instincts under control. He managed not to wrap himself around Hel's tempting back. She was sitting at the breakfast bar, the stylised wings of his mark on her clearly visible through the strappy singlet she wore despite the chill breeze blowing in through the sliding doors to the patio. She was like an elemental with the way she didn't seem to feel the cold even when they were flying at altitude. Another indication that her appearance of humanity was misleading. Bast busied himself making tea to distract his hands from the compulsion to touch her.

"So, what's the plan? Ra said something about the Fire Court?" Hel asked.

Bast's fingers slipped on the jug before he recovered. He really could've used the energy boost from the tea before having this conversation. Turning around to face the woman who featured in his every obsession, he leaned back against the counter and indulged himself in watching her.

"Yeah. There's someone there who can make a pendant that might block our bond."

Hel's brow furrowed briefly before she caught herself, but he could feel the spike of hurt through their connection before she recovered.

"I'm not rejecting y—"

"I know!" Hel cut across him, not letting him finish. "Just ignore whatever you're feeling from the bond. If I've got a problem, I'll tell you."

Bast frowned. "I'm not going to ignore it when I can feel I've hurt you."

"Look. I don't want to die. You don't want to die. This is what we need to do. End of story."

Bast kept watching her and she shifted a little on her barstool, breaking eye contact to stare down at her tea intently like it might hold the answer to all their problems. He sighed. That kernel of hurt was tainting their bond, twisting it. He *needed* her to understand. Because if they succeeded, there would be nothing else holding her to him.

"Life is greyer than that, Hellcat. If you weren't dying, I wouldn't even be considering this. I can't say that I meant to mate you, but I *can* say that breaking this thing we have between us now will be like cutting off a piece of my soul. You understand my past like no one else because you know what it is to have no one and to be hunted. Even when you hated me, you saved me, and you have no idea what it means to me that you'd do anything to protect our family, our city, and *me*. You challenge me. Excite me. Accept me. You fill a hole in my life, in myself, that I didn't even know was there. I don't want to go back to who I was without you."

He'd crossed the room while he was speaking. By the time the last words left his lips he was standing next to her, gently tipping up her chin so he could see what was going through her beautiful eyes. For once, she was speechless. Her reply was spoken instead through the surge of affection along their bond and the press of her lips to his as she stood to pull him closer. It was a bitter-sweet moment. Each deepening of their connection would make it that much harder when the time came to end it.

"Dance with me?" he whispered in her ear, not ready to step away. He could be strong later.

She didn't resist as he pulled her gently into the living area and used his phone to turn on soft music that filled the space. Her body nestled in close to his as delicate rhythmic strings filled the air backed with a throbbing drumbeat his Hellcat couldn't help but move to.

She let out a soft snort and arched an eyebrow at him as the words of the female vocalist started. He'd put on the same *Wicked Game* cover Ra had played for them in The Crypt nightclub just after their first kiss.

Like he had that night in the club, he leaned down and pressed his lips to her soft neck as they moved together, her shivers as he kissed her eliciting the same from him. Even before their bond, they'd fit—their bodies having their own fluid, grinding, perfectly synchronised conversation. Now, they moved as one; their bond a drugging electric connection that stole the world away and left nothing but the two of them, enraptured. If only everything else was as simple as losing themselves together this way.

Hel reached up and wrapped her arms around his neck, pulling him into a kiss as the lyrics they both ignored in the background spoke of falling in love before falling into silence.

"We should get going," Bast said, breaking their kiss to rest his forehead against Hel's.

He could tell things had gotten too real for his Hellcat, but for once she channelled it into brusque organisation instead of lashing out. It was an aching reminder of the partnership they could've been if this mating wasn't fatal.

"You need to eat something first. And Ra said there's some city stuff that's getting urgent. Something about scout patrols to discourage the separatist vandalism. Plus, someone's in a coma from trying to cut through the metal vines on the tower, and Zee needs you to re-brief one of your soul sectors so they can shift some infrastructure for one of the building projects."

"He told you all that?" Bast asked as Hel pushed him onto a stool and dished him out a bowl of porridge still warm from the stove, covering it with berries and cream. He knew Ra had been befriending her, but he'd also been the one warning Bast not to trust her when she still held so many secrets. Was Ra trying to include her so she'd stick around once they blocked the bond? He'd have to remember to thank him.

"Don't sound so surprised," Hel said, her voice teasing for once.

Bast took a moment to just exist in this piece of domesticity. Hel glanced up at him and smiled tentatively, no doubt sensing his contentment through the bond. He wished he could pull her into his lap, kiss that smile until it shone, and then drag her back to a bedroom for the rest of the day. That couldn't happen, though. Probably wouldn't ever happen.

His food became a lump in his stomach and he hardly tasted his final mouthfuls.

"I'll be back soon. Be ready to go," he said, hating the deadness that had entered his tone. He left before she could reply, not trusting himself to hold the distance he needed to stay sane.

BAST WASN'T BACK SOON. Darkness had fallen by the time he'd finished up with his tasks and the city's leaders. Plates of food had quietly appeared on his desk from Ana as he worked, and little Kaia had come and curled up on one of his chairs for a while. But his Hellcat hadn't hunted him down to see what had kept him.

"She spent the day with Tir and Kaia," Ra said, taking pity on him when he checked his phone for the ninth time and told himself it was good she hadn't reached out. Even though he'd bled his feelings into words for her before he'd shut her out. Words she hadn't returned.

"Any news from Mica?" he asked, ignoring his friend's smirk at his obvious deflection.

"No."

"Have you been in touch with him since that call?"

"No."

Bast looked up at Ra, momentarily distracted from his own aching heart by the uncharacteristic neutrality in his friend's voice.

"Everything OK?" he asked softly.

"He's the consummate politician. He knew exactly what he was doing when he said what he did. It was a threat. And Kaia was the leverage. Children are *not* fucking leverage," Ra said, emotion finally returning to his voice as his words became clipped with anger.

"Mica was just playing the game," Bast said carefully, tidying his desk as he stood to leave.

He was still furious at the Earth Lord, but it had been years since Ra had shown a genuine interest in anyone after they'd left his immediate orbit. He wasn't going to encourage his friend to make a rash decision to end whatever potential they had going based on one conversation.

"And if that's how he wants to play it, he can find someone else to play with. You need to get going. The artificer will bail if you're late," Ra said.

Bast sighed and dropped the subject. He'd tried, at least. Pausing by Ra on his way out, he offered his raised hand at heart-height—the handclasp ironically reserved for one's closest friends and the enemies against whom you needed to prove your strength. People who made you feel, be it good or bad. When Ra returned the grip, he pulled his friend into a hug.

"Thanks for having my back on this."

"Always, brother," Ra said. "I just wish it wasn't necessary."

Bast flicked Hel a text as he made his way to the elevator —*On my way. Flying out in fifteen.*

She hadn't replied by the time he reached the dark penthouse. The only illumination in the living space was the dim light from the entryway and what little moonlight made it through the windows.

"Hel!" he called, irritated that she wasn't ready even though he'd kept her waiting for the better part of a day.

There was no response. Nor was there when he knocked softly on her bedroom door. He knew she was in there, their bond thrumming with proximity. Was she asleep? He stepped into her room and glanced around. Still no sign of her, but the tug in his soul was drawing him to the en-suite door. He knocked softly again and pushed it open so he didn't have to yell. The sound of water sloshing didn't quite cover her sharp intake of breath. She was in the fucking bath.

"We need to go," he snapped, fighting the urge to open the door further.

Arousal shot down his spine as his mind formed the picture of her naked body reclined in the water that he refused to look at for real. Would she have filled the tub high and hidden all that beautiful skin beneath bubbles as her midnight hair floated on the water's surface? Or was she sitting only partially submerged, her body on display, her nipples hardening in the cooler air? Groaning softly, he pressed his forehead to the doorframe.

"That's not helping *at all*," Hel said, slightly breathless. "I'll be out in a minute."

He felt a surge of excitement shortly after and his groan became a growled order. "Don't even think about it! Not unless you want me in there replacing your fingers with mine."

"Can't I get any privacy?" Hel snapped, irritation replacing arousal along their connection.

"That's the whole point of this trip. And if we don't leave in ten minutes, we're going to be too late," he said.

"And whose fault is that? You didn't even tell me when

we needed to leave and you've been out all day. I said I was coming!"

"And *I* said no coming without me," Bast shot back before he could stop himself, masochistically revelling in the fury his amusement ignited.

Anger was familiar between them. Solid ground. A foundation to keep them from crumbling under these damn feelings that kept slipping under his guard.

A dripping wet Hel, barely wrapped in a towel, yanked the door the rest of the way open and glared at him.

"Out!"

Bast smirked and backed away, hands raised in surrender and wings held tight to his back to hide their telltale tremble as he drank in every inch of exposed skin.

When she was finally ready and he could wrap his arms around her to take off into the night, it was all he could do to keep his hands from digging beneath her shirt to touch that skin. With the two of them, there was never much distance between fury and lust, and Hel was trembling with both. The tension between them pulsed in time with his surging wingbeats as he took them higher, weaving his power to speed their passage and shield them from the driving rain carried on the city's winds.

Drawing in a deep breath in an attempt to calm himself, the scent of the woman wrapped around him filled his lungs. This was going to be a long fucking flight. Hel exhaled against his neck as if she'd read his thoughts and agreed.

"I don't suppose you could fly in a less suggestive manner?" she muttered, lips brushing against his neck. He could hear the wry smile in her voice.

He grinned, grasping her tighter and shifting his weight to tumble them into a barrel roll before snapping out his wings to catch the ocean winds. As he'd suspected, the surge of adrenaline had his fearless hellcat riding on a high that left him feeling almost drunk.

She threw her head back and *laughed*. Laughed like he'd never heard her before. Carefree. Joyous. He needed to hear it again. Strengthening his wingbeats, he dragged them higher again as his magic and strength shot them forward. He took them above the clouds, out of sight of the shadowy stretch of ocean below them. The air thinned and a chill snuck into the sphere of his power. Neither of them cared. Looking down at Hel's face, he was rewarded with a wide grin and sparkling eyes.

"Again," she whispered, her eyes dropping to his lips.

His mouth stretched in a matching reckless grin. Then he captured her lips in a kiss and flipped them so she was sitting astride his horizontal form. His back muscles ached as he held them steady, gravity and the ridiculous aerodynamics of this position fighting him for control he refused to cede. Using his power to shape the wind as he needed, he flew like that for one beat, then another, caught in the taste of Hel's mouth against his own. Then he held her tight and spun downward, abandoning forward momentum to let them fall like the human performers did with their silks. They spun and unravelled until he flared his wings just above the cloud-cover to send them skimming along the top of clouds softly lit by the silver of the moon and the reflective glow of the soul magic dancing across his wings.

Another addictive laugh like music drifted from his mate.

"Show-off," she teased.

"You wanted less suggestive," he said, still smiling as he

returned their flight to something he could maintain over the long distance ahead.

"Uh. That was like swapping from flirting to foreplay, Bast."

He groaned as he felt her shift against him where her legs wrapped around his waist. His hands drifted lower without him meaning to. One stroked the skin of her hip, exposed by their acrobatics, and the other skirted just below the waistband of her jeans.

"Have you ever..." Hel started to ask before trailing off.

Bast gritted his teeth and forced himself not to imagine what she was asking, carefully rearranging them to remove the temptation pushed tight against his steel-hard arousal. Fuck. Who was he kidding? Nothing was going to remove the temptation. All he could do was try and pull them back from what was a terrible idea. There was no telling what would happen if they... And if she lost consciousness now, there was nowhere to land.

"I shouldn't have kissed you. I'm sorry," he said, when he had himself marginally more under control.

"That's not an answer," Hel said, stubbornness underpinning her rising annoyance.

"You never finished your question."

"Have you ever fucked someone while flying?" she snapped.

Bast glanced down at her in surprise. Was that jealousy? Hel's frown deepened as he failed to hide his satisfaction when he realised it was.

"No, Hellcat. But if we sort out this bond, I'd be happy to try."

A red flush flared up Hel's neck and he resisted the urge to trace its path with his tongue.

"If we sort out this bond, we won't need to," Hel snapped back.

Bast's hands tightened around her as possessiveness roared inside him, and then he shut everything down. No anger. No pain. She didn't know that only her side of the bond would be blocked if this trip succeeded. And if he stayed unfeeling, she wouldn't know how he was bleeding out from that blow, either.

CHAPTER 9
HEL

"You're late," said the Elemental artificer who flew out to greet them over the Tyrrhenian Sea.

His wings were a fiery red-orange that told the world he was a loyal Fire Court vassal with enough magic to have trained within the volcano stronghold they were about to enter. True to his calling, they were also a work of art. Unlike the Fire Lord, his wings didn't evoke the roiling lava that was the earth's lifeblood flowing beneath them. Instead, at their tips, his feathers faded to the almost white-hot heat of the glassblowing forges he no doubt worked at in his Murano home. His face was stern, unyielding, as if he drained all his beauty into his creations and what was left was only harsh angles and disdain. Hel wondered how much Bast had to pay this dick to help them.

"Thomas, I assume?" Bast asked.

Hel could hear the fatigue in his voice, but only because she had an inside look through their connection. The vagaries of flight time and time zones meant the sun was setting over the horizon here, just like it had been when they'd left. She'd had some rest when she drifted off for the latter part of the flight, at least. The awkwardness between them at the purpose of this trip jarred against her mind in Bast's too careful neutrality.

The artificer barely tilted his head in confirmation. "Come. Before my Lord rethinks his welcome."

Their descent took them to the main entrance of the Fire Court, a shining obsidian terrace suspended over lava cascading like waterfalls. Hel felt the stronghold's sentience recognise them as they swept within the shadow of its walls. Last time they'd been on the island, it had welcomed them right until Ty realised they were there. Then it tried to bury them in a pile of molten rock.

She was hyper-aware of their vulnerability as they landed inside what may as well have been its jaws. If it decided it was sick of them, all it would need to do was drop part of the ceiling on them or burrow a hole in its walls to shower them in fresh lava. The stronghold wasn't homicidal right then, though. Not yet. Instead, it twined around her mind, nipping gently at the places where her magic bonded with Bast's. It could sense she was the key to overcoming the communication barrier between it and the man who felt like its family but was deaf to its approaches.

"Bastion," Ty's voice echoed in the entry chamber as he approached, and the reverberation of sound drew Hel out of her introspection.

The stronghold had made its entry walls from sheets of lava that fed the cascading falls beneath. The shining black obsidian tiles of the floor reflected the burnt orange light of the glowing liquid flame casting everyone in the colours of the Fire Court. It also threw Bast's obsidian desk back home into a new light. She hadn't noticed before how he'd snuck those little reminders of where he'd come from into his surrounds, although who knew if it was nostalgia or a reminder not to drop his guard against his murderous family.

Ostentatious glass chandeliers of twisting perfectly blown reds, oranges, and yellows hung from the ceiling of the entry chamber above a strip of lush carpet that led them toward the elemental lord waiting for them. The courts never missed a branding opportunity, and this space was no different in the way it screamed obscene wealth in the colour palette of the Fire Court. Hel almost rolled her eyes.

Bast hadn't let go of her when they landed and she felt his fingers grip on her waist almost tight enough to bruise at the tension in his brother's greeting.

"Ty," he replied, and she knew he'd omitted the honorific of his title on purpose.

She hid a smile as the beautiful Fire Lord's jaw tightened in anger. It looked so similar to Bast when she was riling him up, their shared heritage clear to see.

"You can do whatever you need here. Don't come any further into my home. You have one hour. If you're not out by then, I will consider it an attack and the stronghold will respond accordingly." Ty was already turning away before he'd finished his speech.

Hel felt the stronghold's uncertainty at the situation and reached out without thinking to reassure it, brushing her mind across its vast presence around them. It felt like ageless patience and volcanic pressure all in one. Even aside from the fact it recognised Bast's power twining through her as part of the family it centred its symbiotic nature on, there was a kinship between the heat and flame of its essence and her own magic that was reminiscent of the banked plasma core of a tiny sun. She let a little of her power's heat stroke the sentience, like a scratch behind its non-existent ears. The lava on the wall nearest them surged in twisting patterns of light in response, becoming a woven tapestry of autumnal fire.

"What are you doing?" Bast whispered in her ear as Thomas headed purposefully toward the over-excited fiery wall.

"Making nice with the stronghold," Hel whispered back. "It's sad that you can't say hi, and it doesn't get why Ty thinks we're intruders."

Bast looked like he wanted to ask more about the sentience, but Thomas had turned toward them and was not so subtly tapping his foot. He'd unrolled the leather satchel he'd been wearing and spread it on the ground. On it sat a heavy cube with a hole in the top and a long metal grasping tool, presumably to keep his fingers clear of the lava that was heating the air enough to make Hel sweat despite whatever magic shielding was in place to protect the inhabitants.

"Right. This is fairly simple. Each of you puts a drop of your blood in the mould and imbues it with your power, if you have any. I'll top up the rest with a piece of the stronghold, in this case the lava. Then you communicate what you need from the stronghold and I'll take care of weaving the magic into the form and making it stick. Questions?"

"Give us a moment?" Bast asked, pulling Hel out of Thomas's hearing. "Can you handle talking to the stronghold?" he whispered.

"Sure. But it might draw Ty's attention," Hel said.

"He knows you're my mate. If we're lucky, he'll assume your link to the stronghold is related to that. I'm concerned he hasn't made a bigger deal of it already, though. He's planning something."

"I can't talk in words to the stronghold. It's more concepts and sensations. What do I need to convey?" Hel asked.

"Show it the bond and a visualisation of blocking or severing it. A wall. A knife. Whatever works for you."

Bast's voice sounded strained, and Hel rubbed at the ache in her chest. As if sensing the imminent threat to their bond, her power seemed to weave tighter around Bast's. Clinging.

"Are you sure this is a good idea?" she asked.

"It's the only idea."

Turning back to Thomas, they found him holding out a knife and the mould. Bast grabbed the second and ignored the first, drawing his own dagger from a sheath at his waist. His movements were economical and his face unreadable as he made a shallow cut on the edge of his palm and let a trickle of blood run into the mould before passing the blade to Hel.

Thomas's eyes were glowing golden and Hel could feel the stronghold's awareness coalescing around them as he started doing whatever magic it was that would make this work. She hesitated as she looked down at the blade in her hand. It was still tinged red with Bast's blood, but she didn't bother wiping it clean. Some perverse part of her wanted to see their essences mix even while they worked to tear themselves apart. She didn't want to break the stupid bond, but she didn't want to die either because it would kill Bast. That thought was enough to get her moving. She barely felt the knife as it split her hand open. It was nothing compared to the pain building inside her soul.

Hel reached out for the sentience of the stronghold as Thomas clamped the mould and carried it towards the flowing wall of lava. Just as Bast had suggested, she focused on her magical sight and showed the stronghold their bond. She was distantly aware of the mould breaking the flow of molten rock, but she was thoroughly stumped by how to communicate what she needed to the sentience. Bast had suggested a wall or a knife, but their bond was a nervous system of their power woven together throughout every part of them—body, mind and soul. It wasn't something you could wall off or sever like that.

She tried to imagine Bast's silver power that flowed through her darkening until it disappeared. All she felt back from the stronghold sentience was confusion. She visualised their power unravelling and separating, but the weave was so complex she couldn't hold the image in her mind with enough detail. Finally, she just showed the sentience an image of her in Bast's arms, and then an image of a wall between them.

A responding image and raw emotion flashed back in response—both of their ribs being cracked open and their hearts being torn from their chests still beating as they pumped their lifeblood out onto the obsidian floor, accompanied by a firm sense of stubborn refusal. Then the image shifted and not only was it their dead bodies she saw, but thousands of others. Millions, even. All she could see was the world as a charnel house; piles of bones as far as the eye could see. Was it a premonition? Whatever it was, it was a warning. And a refusal. Dragging herself from the vision with a muffled gasp, she locked every muscle in her legs to stay standing.

The strongholds were a contradictory mix of complexity and simplicity. In some ways, their understanding was so much larger than humanity's or elemental's. But in others, they were reductionist loyalists. The scent of danger filled the air as the deep warmth of the Fire Court's sentience wrapped itself around Bast like a guard-dog pressed tight against him as it bared its teeth at a threat—the woman who was trying to sever the bond with him. The only thing keeping her safe right now was that it understood what killing her would do to the family member it was protecting.

Hel stepped closer to Bast, pressing close so she could whisper in his ear and keep the conversation private from the artificer. "It's no use. Something's wrong and it won't take the order from me. It's trying to protect you," Hel said.

She felt Bast's growl of frustration in her bones. "Thomas!" he snapped. "The stronghold is refusing me. Can you speak to it?"

Thomas looked back at him with a frown. "It won't sever a mating bond on anyone else's request. It probably doesn't trust you as a stranger. Let me see if I can give it a nudge," he said.

His eyes went vacant as he tipped his head to the side. His eyes snapped open barely two breaths later. Dropping the metal tool he was still holding, he dived to the side. Fiery light streamed from his fingers as he formed a shield around the mould just in time before it exploded in a spectacular display of white hot splashing magma.

When the after-image burned across her retina finally faded, there was nothing left within the shield Thomas had erected—his tools, the mould, the half-formed pendant—all gone. She should've felt despair, grief, and frustration at their failure. The only hope they had to fix her had just literally gone up in smoke.

All she felt was relief.

Looking up, she met the familiar darkness of Bast's eyes

and saw the mirror of her feelings in him. They were so screwed. Even with his guilt, even with her anger, even with both their lives on the line, neither of them actually wanted to sever this stupid bond. They'd both been lonely too long. Like he'd said before, they each filled a missing piece in the other.

Dammit. She hadn't asked for this. She didn't want it. And she couldn't fucking live without it.

Thomas had taken out his phone while they were distracted and walked away to make a call, no doubt to tell Ty they'd failed. His body screamed with tension where he stood with his back to them. Hel narrowed her eyes and was about to say something to Bast when her awareness of the surrounding sentience suddenly dropped away like it had been severed. Her eyes widened in fear and Bast was moving before she'd even said anything, sweeping her into his arms and sprinting to the entrance.

"The stronghold's blocking me out. They're going to attack," she gasped out.

Ty would've known they wouldn't stick around and Thomas' call had triggered whatever he'd been planning. The familiar shimmer of Bast's shield formed around them just as the lava walls stretched to cover the nearby entrance-way, blocking them in. Bast ignored it and sped up as they drew near, wings spreading wide as he took them airborne. Drops of flame scattered like sparks from an angle-grinder as he pushed through the barrier, their progress slowing as Ty's magic and the power of the stronghold fought to keep them contained.

When they finally burst through, the air beyond was suspiciously empty. No elemental scouts taking aim. No dragons swooping to attack. This was not Hel's first rodeo with the Fire Lord and if there was one constant, it was that he wasn't shy about attempting to kill them. Something was different this time.

Darkness had fallen while they'd been inside the stronghold and Bast shot them due west, chasing the now disappeared sun. The black absence of light that was his wings disappeared into the night sky as they flew. If it wasn't for the air buffeting across her face and the tensing of his muscles straining in flight, she would almost think they were floating rather than flying. Even the sparks of his power on his inner wing surface looked more like impossibly close falling stars than magic infused into the feathers keeping them aloft.

"This doesn't feel right," Bast said, right before a surge of power flared to their right and he froze mid-flight—suspended in the air like his scouts had been only days before.

For a terrifying moment, Hel thought the magic would tear him to shreds and hurtle their bodies to the ocean far below. Then she felt a tug inside her as Bast drew deep on her magic to shake off the foreign power with a roar that vibrated through her everywhere their bodies touched. They dropped in freefall for a breath before Bast forced his wings to function again, twisting them toward their attacker.

Red glowing eyes shone in the darkness, but Hel strained to make out the rest of the man's form. When squinting didn't work, she focused on sound instead. There it was. Just underneath the familiar music of Bast's feathers cutting through the air was something raspier, discordant. The man's bat-like wings displaced the air differently, but were just as invisible in the darkness as Bast's.

"What do you want?" Bast growled, hovering in the night sky.

Glowing eyes disappeared briefly, a blink, but grew no closer.

"The girl," he said. Cold. Calm. Decipherable despite those long hinged fangs that reminded her so much of her father's hounds making him trip over the 'th' sound.

"I'm not a fucking child," Hel snapped, as if that was the most important thing to take from that statement.

"Only because I didn't find you in time," the man replied.

"How did you find me this time?" Hel asked.

But she knew the answer already. The stronghold's efforts to hold them said it all. It would only have done so at Ty's request.

"Some people of this world are smart enough to know not to challenge Him," the man said, directing his words more to Bast than her.

"Who is she to him?" Bast asked, and Hel jerked in his arms, letting him feel the full brunt of the fury he'd sparked by trying to find out her secrets from one of her father's damn hunters.

"She is the atonement your council searches for," he replied, and Hel flinched.

After all they'd been through, the only remaining reason she'd never told Bast that Sol was her father was to keep him from realising she was the atonement from Amira's message —that she'd been meant as a sacrifice to her father. The secret of who Sol was to her was one of the last things she'd held between them to keep their distance. Could she let him in that final step? Now was not the time.

She knew in her bones Bast wouldn't, couldn't, betray

her. She told herself she'd kept the secret out of habit, but deep down she knew she'd done it to protect him from the pain of knowing he might have to give her up. The only way that would happen would be if they both knew there was no other way to save the Earths.

"Enough stalling. Give her to me and I will let you live," their attacker said.

Bast's arms tightened around her. "I won't let you take her."

"It's her power that stopped me, not yours. You're not strong enough to fight me."

"But I am, dickhead," Hel snarled, and then she reached for her magic in a way she never had before, finding the place between worlds he'd used to cause so much damage to the scouts and tearing open with her mind the space he occupied.

It was a clumsy attempt at mimicry, the unfamiliar use threatening to tear from her control, but it was enough to distract him. His curses filled the air as Bast added a wave of death magic to the attack, weaving it through the tears in her magic. He didn't stick around to see how the creature would respond. They both knew they'd be in trouble if reinforcements came. Bast flew high and hard to the west, wreathing them in shadow and illusion.

"We need to portal," Hel said, but the words came out as a whimper.

The souls who'd been quiescent while they'd tried to break the bond had now returned with a vengeance in response to the growing threat behind them. At least they were moving away from civilisation, so there weren't so many.

The bat-winged man was the only one of her father's

hunters she'd come across here who was capable of flight, but that didn't mean they could assume he wouldn't send more now he knew where she was. Bast was funnelling raw power into their shielding in an attempt to keep her hidden, drawing desperately through the souls while they were still near. Each one that answered his call brushed against her awareness like poisoned spines, the darkness of their deaths seeping into the myriad points where Bast's power connected with her own. So many weak points now. So many places where memories and pain washed into her soul, the essence of who she was, until it threatened to wash her way.

"You barely made it last time you had to portal. I'm not risking you like that," Bast said, replying to the statement she'd already forgotten she'd made.

Hel clung a little harder to him as he shifted her to a one-handed hold and fixed an earbud in place. She jerked in surprise when his fingers brushed her ear gently to put its pair in her own ear. The touch sent a shiver through her that was definitely *not* appropriate when they were on the run, but at least it distracted her a little from the souls.

"Ra, Ty betrayed us to Hel's hunters. I need whatever surveillance you can give us on our location and I need to know whether the other courts are involved," Bast said.

"On it." Ra's voice drifted into her brain like her mind was full of static.

Hel whimpered as another soul brushed against her. This one had fallen from the sky as a teen, lost to a surge in untrained power. The world faded away as she relived the joy of flight turned to terror, the dizzying pull of the earths calling her to break upon it, the final despair as her wings failed her again and again while the power that had been pure temptation burned out just beyond her reach.

A surge of Bast's power pushed them further and faster as he sought to outrun the souls and then his mouth pressed to hers, biting down hard. The pleasure-pain broke through the memory just as she would have felt the moment the dead teen hit the ground. She gasped into Bast's mouth.

"Stay with me, sweetheart," he murmured.

"You've got one tailing you. Not gaining, but not dropping away either. He must be damn fast," Ra said over their comms.

Bast's body tensed as he somehow put on even more speed, but Hel could feel his deep fatigue. He wouldn't be able to keep this up for long.

"What about the rest of the council? This guy was claiming Hel is the atonement and they want her," he said.

"I haven't heard anything like that, but they could be keeping it quiet. Mica's called a council meeting to discuss the structures. He wouldn't tell me when or where. I think he knew you'd show up and he's still arguing you could be compromised."

Hel glanced up at Bast's face in confusion. Wasn't Mica more or less an ally? Bast gave no sign the news was surprising, though. "Not as compromised as Ty actively tipping off a foreign power," he gritted out.

"It's possible Aliya's in on this too, given how close they were working last time," Ra said.

Bast swore. "Which means this emperor could already have half the council in his pocket. We need to find out what he's promised them. There's no way they'd choose to let a powerful unknown player into their territory unless there was something in it for them."

"Ah, shit," Ra said a moment later.

"What now?"

"I just widened the surveillance radius around the city. Nerida's deployed scouts off the coast here. They're outside our territory, but if you approach by sea, she'll know as soon as you return."

"And I can't even complain because it's her damn territory she's patrolling. Fuck," Bast said. "Where's her stronghold at the moment? Is she there?"

"Out on the open water. In the North Pacific just south of Mexico. Mica hadn't left for the council meeting when he called, so she's probably still home as well. What're you thinking?"

"I won't make it back in one shot with the amount of power I just used, and I can't land in Ty's territory. Nerida's usually a neutral party and if she's got her stronghold as close to Aliya's territory as ours, then she might just be keeping an eye on both sides. Even if she's not, I need to at least try to talk her and Mica around before the council meeting. Where do we think the enemy structure is in her territory?"

"Isla Pinta. Not too far from where her stronghold's floating. It's the northernmost island of the Galapagos. Uninhabited. Well, apart from the winged version of giant tortoises, which I still can't get my ahead around. How does something that size find enough to eat on such a tiny island?"

Hel smiled despite everything at Ra's attempt to distract Bast from his worry. It was so very him. The smile was gone as quickly as it formed when she noticed Bast's flight slowing and becoming laboured.

"We'll land on the island on the way. If we stay clear of the structure, we should be able to rest undisturbed and there won't be any souls there to bother Hel. I can heal my wings, and we can check it out to give Nerida a report later."

"You're not going to make it that far," Hel said, her mouth close to the speaker in his ear.

"I can make it," Bast said at the same time as Ra swore again.

"Is bat-man gaining on us?" Hel asked.

"Holy shit, it's that guy following you? I thought it was one of Ty's people," Ra shouted, making both Bast and Hel wince at the volume.

"Less volume, more intel," Bast snapped.

"Sorry. You were making ground. But yeah, he's gaining on you now. Are you injured or just tired?" Ra asked.

"I think I might have a hairline fracture or two in my wings from that last attack," Bast said.

Hel's mouth dropped open and she just about hit him for hiding that from her. "What the fuck, Bast? Why haven't you landed already?"

"For the record, I agree with the Hellcat. But given I know what a stubborn bastard you are, I'm gonna get our people on the African continent to release a drone swarm at him. I assume however he's tracking you will stop working with enough distance. We just need to distract him long enough for you to get clear," Ra said.

Hel missed the rest of whatever came next, her heart dropping as she realised she hadn't even checked to see if she could sense any power searching for them. Sweeping her awareness out into the night, she breathed a small sigh of relief. She couldn't feel anything nearby, but she could sense the hunter's power signature in the distance. He was probably using his magic to aid in flight like Bast did.

"What's up?" Bast asked, and she realised he'd ended the call while she was distracted.

"Just checking if I could feel him magically tracking us. I don't think he can sense us as long as we don't actively use my power."

Bast nodded and now that she knew what to look for, she could feel the sharpness of his pain down their bond that he'd been hiding.

"How did I not notice you were injured? Can you block our bond?"

Bast sighed. "No. But if I concentrate very hard on something, it takes precedence in what you feel through our connection."

"What were you concentrating on that could possibly distract you from flying with broken fucking wings?" Hel asked.

"I can take most of the load with my power. It's not as bad as it sounds."

"Until you burn out. And you didn't answer the question."

He was silent so long she thought he wouldn't answer.

"You," he said, finally. "I'm always concentrating on you."

CHAPTER 10
BAST

Hel's body pressed so close to Bast he could feel her swallow hard when he answered her question. Every wingbeat was agony, but he forced his focus to her warm breath on his neck and her legs wrapped tight around his waist. Instead of letting himself feel the pain in his wings, he felt the brush of her hands where they pushed into his shoulders. She'd clenched them tight into fists the moment she realised he was hurt and he could feel her knuckles skimming the sensitive feathers where his wings emerged from his back. It didn't make his suffering any less, but at least he could avoid subjecting her to his pain.

"Can I do something to help?" she asked.

He should be asking her about why she was the 'atonement' and what it meant, but he couldn't face that conversation in his current state. "Just stay with me. Don't let the souls take you."

Letting go of the little control he safely could, he stroked his fingers across the bare skin of her waist under her shirt,

151

tracing endless circles that made both their hearts race. He forced his aching back muscles to pump his wings in time to her pulse, losing himself to the rhythm of her body.

He almost didn't notice when she started softly singing, her voice husky and pure in the cold night air. The tune was melancholy and as unfamiliar as the words that made up its lyrics. When she sang the last note, it hung between them like a whispered secret.

"What song is that?" he asked long after she finished, reluctant to break the spell she'd cast around them.

"One my guardian sung when I was little."

"What do the words mean?"

"I never learned the language. She called it a breath of home."

"Where was home?" he asked, almost holding his breath as he waited for her to shut him out like always.

"A long, long way from here."

"Was it your home, too?"

"I was born here on the Melded Earths, and she never claimed me as her own. I have no home."

Bast ran his hand up her spine as if he could hold her any closer than he already was. Both of them sucked in a breath as his fingers crossed the marks he'd left on her back, sending shockwaves of sensation along their bond.

"*I* claimed you. My home is your home. Always. All you have to do is choose it," he said.

She didn't reply, but she nuzzled into his neck and he felt her draw in his scent as she laid her head on his shoulder.

They'd been in the air for three hours when they heard from Ra again.

"You lost him. Your shielding was working, after all. He must've assumed you'd head straight for Panama. He's well south of your position, now. Of course, you also added an hour or more to your flight time. You need to change course before you hit Aliya's east coast patrols," Ra said.

Bast swore silently. He'd meant to head straight for Panama. The pain and Hel's singing had distracted him. He was losing his edge. Fast. At least they'd lost the hunter as well.

"ETA at the island?" he asked.

"You've been slowing for the last half hour. If you can maintain your current speed, maybe four hours?"

It was the longest four hours of his life.

Hel started tensing and whimpering as the souls surged around them in response to his failing body and how much power he had to sink into staying aloft. When she finally fell asleep, the drag on his arms as she stopped doing half the work of keeping herself attached to him was agony, but he was so relieved she hadn't succumbed that he couldn't make himself wake her to face them again.

Ra called back as he was flying high above the Panama Canal to navigate him away from the scouts in the area. Bast pressed gently on Hel's earpiece to turn it off so his voice wouldn't wake her.

"You hanging in there?" Ra asked once they were past the danger.

"I've been better. How much longer?"

"Almost there."

Bast laughed silently. Ra was so full of shit. He'd slowed further and it was at least another half hour until they'd make land. Then he'd still have to make it to the Water Court and back across Nerida's territory to home without being ambushed.

"One wingbeat at a time, bro," Ra said, as if he could sense his thoughts.

And that's what he did. Losing altitude. Sinking closer and closer to the ocean. The souls feeding him power shearing away from him one by one as they responded to his desperate need to keep Hel safe and leave, even though it reduced the power available to him. Beat after painful beat. By the time the shore was visible in the distance, his wingtips were hitting the salt-spray with each downward stroke and his toes were wet.

Sunset was approaching. Again. This whole fucking trip had been endless sunsets, as if the world was sending an ominous message about what he and Hel had to look forward to. At least the darkness would help hide them while they slept.

He tried to put on a final burst of speed that would take them high enough to stay clear of the water. It was a mistake. He'd left the last of the souls behind and he didn't have enough energy to even channel the modest amount of power he usually could without them. His abused wings couldn't take the pressure without magical support. It was all he could do to keep them stretched wide as they failed in the hope they would catch the breeze and he could coast the rest of the way in. He had just enough time to wake Hel before they tumbled into the shallows. Chest-high waves surged against him as he staggered against their pressure and tried to balance them both with his hands clenched tight around his mate. His wings hung worse than useless behind him as the water left them sodden and dragging him backward.

"Let me go," Hel said, pushing away from him.

He finally, blissfully, let her weight release from his arms and sank to his knees. Warm water swallowed his face as he relaxed and let the ocean claim him.

Before he could do more than shut his eyes against the gentle salt sting, a grip like steel wrapped around his waist and hauled him back up above the water. Looking down, he blinked slowly and watched as Hel braced herself under his arm and started dragging him and the deadweight of his wings to shore. She was stronger than she looked. She was also just short enough that supporting him left her almost fully submerged. That was enough to overcome his shock and get him moving. Step after halting step. Until they both collapsed at the first hint of dry sand beneath their sodden boots.

The noise of Hel getting back to her feet barely registered as he lay on his back, eyes closed, breathing through the deep ache in his wing bones. He must've fallen asleep like that, because when he next opened his eyes, night had fully fallen and Hel was shaking his shoulder. He hadn't noticed at first because the rest of him was shaking almost as hard despite the temperate night air.

"Shit. You're either in shock or hypothermic," Hel muttered. She pressed her water canteen to his lips and let him finish what little was left.

"'mfine," Bast said, slurring his words.

"C'mon. We need to get you warmed up," Hel said.

Bast's eyes slipped closed again.

"That was code for getting naked, mate. Thought you'd be more into this."

Bast cracked an eye open and struggled to bring Hel into focus. Naked was good. Wasn't it? He vaguely remembered he'd been avoiding that, but he couldn't think why. Groaning, he tensed his muscles and tried to sit up. Stars burst across his vision, his back screamed in agony and he slumped back again.

Gentle hands slipped under his neck, finding the seam that would trigger the light magic on his shirt to unravel. As she pulled the still wet fabric from his chest, his shivers increased.

"We doing this on the beach?" he asked, trying and failing to pretend it was innuendo.

"It's all scrub and volcanic rock nearby. Would you rather lie on sand or a cactus?"

"Sand's good," Bast mumbled as Hel hauled off his boots and went to work on his pants.

It was a measure of how shit he was feeling that he didn't even look up as she stripped him and draped his clothes on the nearby rocks to dry. The world drifted on without him. There were no souls here to refuel the magic to revive him, and he'd drained everything he could access just to get them here.

A sliver of desire not his own pulled him a little closer to reality as a warm weight settled on his chest and those gentle fingers touched the silver-blue mark over his heart that had formed the day they'd mated. It was the first time Hel had ever seen it and he could feel the awe and possessiveness it sparked in his mate. His hands that had been lying slack beside him instinctively grasped at the naked body pressed against him and sensation overwhelmed him as his fingers found his mark that covered Hel's back. Heat flared from their connection, stilling his shivers. Every nerve sang as he stroked the physical manifestation of their bond.

"Fuck, you feel good," he groaned, still not with it enough to hold anything back.

Hel dropped her head to his chest and her tongue traced

the path of her fingers across his mark until her mouth brushed against his nipple. He groaned again and raised his hand to grip her hair weakly and hold her to him. He could feel her smile against his skin and the wicked playfulness along their bond right before she bit him.

The sharp pleasure finally snapped him back to full awareness and he'd flipped her onto her back before he even realised what he was doing. Still too fatigued and injured to shift his wing out from underneath her, she ended up totally wrapped up in him. The weight of her body resting on his sensitive inner feathers forced their chests tight together as he braced his arms on either side of her head.

"Your wing," she said, trying to shift from beneath him.

He settled his weight more firmly on her and his hips twitched forward. Hel moaned as he ground against her. There was nothing but his boxers and whatever she was wearing between them. His power that resided in Hel responded to their contact and he felt some seeping back into him where they connected like the first drops of liquid from an intravenous drip, shoring up his energy.

Dropping his head to taste her lips again, his tongue traced their sweetness until they opened enough for him to sink into the warmth of her mouth and devour her. Her legs wrapped tight around his waist just like she did when they were flying, only this time it was her body that was surging as she used the leverage to rock against him. Breaking their kiss, he trailed his mouth down her jaw and neck, tongue laving everywhere he could reach with the awkward constraints of their position. He growled in frustration as his trapped wing pulled him up short from dropping lower down her body. Hel's breathless low laugh broke the spell of recklessness that had woven between them, making him look up.

"You seem to be feeling better," she said.

Bast took inventory and realised the ache in his wing lying beneath her had completely faded, likely from the effects of pressing close to the concentration of his magic in the black-winged tattoo that stretched across her skin. Now that he was less distracted, he could feel the bones on his right wing knitting back together as well.

"You're like a portable charger," he joked, smiling as she whacked him lightly at the banal comparison.

"And you're like my personal steed. You gonna be able to fly us out of here? There's not a lot around."

Bast sighed as her words let reality intrude and lifted his body so she could roll out from under him. Pushing himself to his feet, he stretched his wings out wide and shook the itching sand free from his feathers. The movement still hurt, but it was getting better. The fractures had been small and had been healing en route. They probably would have healed already if he hadn't been straining his wings so hard.

"I think I'll be okay by morning. But not to fly far. The Water Court leaves their dead behind them in the ocean, but there should be enough souls lingering with their family there for me to get a decent power boost and rebuild my reserves."

"So long as they don't attack us," Hel said, getting to her feet as well.

"Yeah," Bast said, unable to look away from the swell of her breasts visible in the soft moonlight.

Hel raised an eyebrow at him and stooped to grab her abandoned clothes.

"How're you doing?" Bast asked, stepping closer to tilt her chin up and search her face for any sign of how much the souls had affected her this time.

"It's not as bad here," Hel said, tucking a lock of the silver hair dyed by his power behind her ear.

He wished he could wrap his fist in the strands and pull her back to his mouth, but the moment had passed. He needed to stop letting the hooks of their bond sink any deeper. The thought made him pause. He'd failed at breaking the bond as much as he'd failed at shielding her. Was there any reason to still avoid her? There must be, but his exhausted brain couldn't think of it.

"We're so isolated from any souls that this is probably the safest you'll ever be," Bast said.

Sand shifted beneath his toes as he took a step away from her and tried to disentangle himself from the driving temptation of their power that flowed between them, pulsing and twining through and around each other until the tastes of their magic melded into one.

Hel tilted her head and wet her lips, looking thoughtful. Bast frowned in confusion as she dropped the shirt she was holding.

"So, this is the calm before the storm?" she asked, reaching out to stroke a finger down his feathers.

When had he flared his wings out again?

"Yeah," he said, voice catching as she continued her exploration of his wing. "What are you doing?"

Hel's hand shifted to his chest. He shivered as she traced the lines of his muscles so softly he would've thought it was the wind if her touch hadn't left a trail of heat that had him tensing like he was about to take flight.

"Make me feel good?" she asked, but it wasn't her quiet plea that just about broke him. It was the reckless desperation he could feel behind her words. Like they might not have another chance like this. Ever. And she was right.

Bast sank to his knees before her, black wings spread wide behind him on the golden sand, and pressed a soft kiss to her hipbone. His hands wrapped behind her legs, stroking from knee to thigh as he trailed more kisses across her stomach. He groaned against her as she spread her feet wider for balance and he finally caught the scent of her arousal. When her hands fisted in his hair, he pulled away to look up at her.

"You sure about this?" he asked.

He could barely make out her expression in the darkness, but he didn't need to because her answer was to hook her thumbs through the waistband of her lingerie and drag them down until they dropped to her feet.

"Hellcat. Baby. I'm not gonna be able to control myself if you—" His babbling words cut off on another groan as Hel's hands tugged at his hair until his scalp stung.

His face was inches away from every dirty dream his frustrated mind had forced on him the last few months and he wasn't going to hold back any more. Couldn't hold back any more. He let his mate pull him closer, sunk his tongue between her legs, and fucking devoured her. More than devoured. He worshipped her. Every sense overwhelmed.

He was an addict the second her sweet taste passed his lips. Every whimper she let loose into the night made his cock throb. When her trembling legs collapsed and the only thing holding her upright was the grip of his hands on her body, he was so far gone that all he could do was growl in satisfaction. Either the vibration or the brush of his teeth turned her whimpers to a string of desperate curses.

"Fuck. Bast. Please," Hel moaned.

Shifted his hands to keep her balanced, he pushed two fingers inside her. Her body's response and the intoxicating thrill of second-hand arousal through the bond guided him until he was touching her just right. Every penetrating stroke had her clenching even tighter around him.

"Yes. Just like that. Don't stop," she panted.

She was so fucking wet, so fucking perfect. He couldn't have stopped if he'd tried. His cock was hard as steel and it was agony, but he wouldn't give this up for anything. Wouldn't give *her* up for anything. Her pleasure was everything. It was *his*. His to give her until every shard of loneliness and fear and despair that had cut into her disappeared.

Pushing another finger inside her, he sucked her clit into his mouth, biting just enough to feel the tension in her spike until she was screaming his name as she ground herself against him. He didn't let up until he'd coaxed her through wave after shuddering wave of release and her body hung limp in his arms. He just about came himself untouched as he remembered what it had felt like when she'd done that while he was buried inside her.

Letting her body slide down his, he collapsed back onto the beach and settled her on top of him, wrapping his wings around her now naked body to keep the light breeze from chilling her. He'd thought they couldn't get any closer, any more tightly bonded. He'd been wrong.

This drive to be near each other that they'd both been avoiding clearly wasn't just about needing his mate. It was a deep biological craving, a compulsion, to deepen their entanglement. And every time they increased the points of connection between their souls and their power, they created another weak spot for the souls to seep into her. His guilt surged as he realised he had no idea what this reckless interlude would do to Hel's susceptibility.

Sensing his turmoil, Hel nuzzled into his neck and he stroked a hand up and down her spine. His mate's proximity was short-circuiting his reason again. He couldn't help but revel in the feel of her curves pressed tight against him even while he clenched his teeth against the need to shift his hips and increase the teasing inadequate friction of her thigh brushing against his erection.

As if reading his thoughts, which she almost could, Hel slipped her hand into his boxers and wrapped her fingers around him. Bast groaned as she gripped him firmly and started working him. Fuck. He needed to stop this before their connection grew any stronger. He'd already gone too far, but he could justify it when it was about her because he couldn't deny her a damn thing. But if what they were doing now—taking his own pleasure—left her vulnerable, he would never forgive himself. Not that he would outlive her for long if she succumbed to the souls, anyway.

Reaching down, he gripped her wrist and pulled her hand away. "We need to rest. Another time, sweetheart," he murmured against her hair, but what he meant was another lifetime. Unless they found a way to block their bond and save her, there wouldn't be another time.

Hel pushed herself up onto her hands and glared down at him. He could feel the anger building in her. When she opened her mouth to start a fight, he surged up and caught her lips in a kiss, wrapping his hand behind her neck to hold her close and pull her back down to his chest.

He sighed in relief when he felt her relax into him despite the surge of annoyance down the bond. Tucking her head into his shoulder, he went back to stroking his hand up and down her spine over and over until she drifted into sleep, neither of them breaking their silence. There was no way he would risk resting while she lay exposed on the beach like that. Instead, he lay on the sand, staring up at the stars, and memorised the exquisite feel of her nakedness against his body and the terrifying new depth of their intangible connection.

Despite his resolve, Bast must have succumbed to sleep because he was woken by Hel's body jerking in his arms. Late morning sunlight whispered through the low cloud and mist hung over them. His body ached from the night on the beach rather than any injury, and his wings itched like sand had worked its way between every feather, which it may well have. He was on his feet an instant after Hel, eyes scanning the horizon for the threat that the thrill of her fear suggested was imminent.

"What's up?" he murmured, reaching for his pants that lay abandoned on the beach as Hel dropped her guard position and started yanking on her clothes.

"We've got company. A portal not far away. Feels like that bat-winged asshole."

Bast pulled on his shirt and looked along the coast where she was pointing. Elementals had sharp eyes made for hunting at height. In the far distance, he could just make out a glinting spire of rock in the shallows. He swore under his breath. They'd fallen asleep within sight of the damn thing. They were lucky they hadn't been ambushed by wraiths or worse while they slept, or while they'd ... Bast shook his head and focused on pulling on his boots. Better not to think about the previous night. It wasn't something they could repeat.

"We need to find out what he's up to, what those structures are. We'll need all the information we can get to convince Nerida not to turn against us. I can fly us there, but

I'm still drained dry. My power's a bust until we get back to civilisation," Bast said.

"Good thing it's my power that holds him off, then. Let's do it," Hel replied, shrugging on her leather jacket and hiding more of her beautiful skin from his view.

Not the time to be thinking about that, he reminded himself. He needed to focus.

When they were both as ready as they were going to be, he turned to Hel and held out his arms. "Your chariot awaits, Lady Soul."

The corner of Hel's mouth kicked up in a smile, but she was frowning too. "You can't say shit like that."

"Like what?"

"Calling me a lady. That's not what I am."

Bast studied the woman in front of him, frustrated at the discomfort his words had sparked in her and knowing he had no business trying to make her comfortable with him, anyway. What they needed was distance.

"You're my mate. I'm the Lord of the Soul Court. Or at least I will be once the council acknowledges I have just as much power as any of them. What did you think that meant? Get used to it."

He almost laughed at the wide-eyed shock she gave him in response, quickly followed by her familiar raging anger. She shoved hard at his chest and he couldn't hold his smirk back as he caught her wrists and spun her up into his arms. If there was one thing he knew after their months together, it was how to get a rise from her. They couldn't linger in that vulnerable place they'd been last night. This was far safer.

"Ready?" he growled, resisting the urge to kiss the elegant curve of her neck as he felt her shiver in response to his voice. This would be a whole lot easier if they could hide what they were feeling from each other.

He launched himself into the air the second Hel dipped her head in a nod, his strong wingbeats taking them into the grey cloud-cover until the world around them faded and blurred.

Hel's body was tense in his arms as she wove a shield of her power around them. It was the first time he'd felt her use her magic that way and he could tell she was modelling it off her knowledge of how he used his own.

"You ever tried that before?" Bast whispered, his mouth close enough to brush her ear. Sound travelled strangely in clouds like the ones they were flying through and he wasn't sure if her shielding was blocking it like his would have. That was his excuse, anyway.

Hel twisted up to look at him. "Never tried anything with it before I met you. Couldn't risk leaving a trace behind."

Bast frowned. He knew better than anyone how long it took to master a magic that no one around you could teach and how dangerous a mistake could be. Facing a threat like the creature they were stalking was not the place to experiment. "We'll attack the old-fashioned way, then. With steel."

Hel's face actually lit up at his words and her hand brushed the baton with its sneaky concealed double-blades strapped to her thigh. She was lethal elegance with a weapon, and she never seemed more at peace than when one was in her hands. He should know because he'd spent more time than he should have watching her train through the tower's surveillance cameras. He loved that juxtaposition of calm and violence in her. Loved that it matched his own training obsession born from years of fending off his brother's assassins. Loved that she'd shown over and over that she was strong enough to hold her own. He'd never been able to risk a relationship while Ty was hunting him. Hadn't been able to bring himself to risk someone's safety. With Hel, she was just as likely to come to his rescue as she was to need his help.

He swore under his breath. Focus. This was not what he should be thinking about. The bond was like a constant distraction, refusing to be ignored while they were still resisting it.

They were approaching the giant shard of alien rock now —a spire breaking out of the ocean's shallows—and he could feel the remnants of the portal ahead to their right by borrowing Hel's magical senses. Straining his ears for any sound that was out of place, all he could hear was the noises of the ocean and the island's birds below. The scents of brine and aromatic palo santo drifted on the still air.

There wasn't a lot of cover around. Just beach and volcanic rock. It was reckless to approach like this with no plan, but at least their quarry couldn't sneak up on them either. Bast dropped them down out of the clouds onto the narrow stretch of beach a little north of both the structure and the fading portal signature. His only weapons were his dagger and a short sword. Anything else got in the way on long flights, especially when he was carrying Hel. They both drew their weapons as they moved closer to their target, not wanting to be caught unawares. Hel was ahead of him to his right, already twisting her modified baton to turn it into two long-handled blades.

The only movement around them was the flitting of finches searching for food among the volcanic rock and the lapping of the waves to his left.

"Stop," he called to Hel when they reached the point where they might trigger the structure's defences.

She kept moving.

He'd kept his voice low and it was possible she didn't hear, but the grim determination and suppressed fear he was sensing from her suggested she was just ignoring him. Swearing, he strode to catch up with her. He would've grabbed her arm, but she was holding an unsheathed blade and he wasn't totally confident she wouldn't turn it on him in her current state.

He almost didn't hear the wind displaced behind him. Almost missed the flicker of shadow to his left in his distraction. Instinct had him shoving Hel to the right as he dived forward and carried on into a roll he hoped wouldn't re-injure his wings on a stray rock. He was still moving as he spun back to his feet to face the threat. Their attacker thumped into the sand, knees bending to cushion the impact of his high-speed descent as his broad batlike wings spread for balance before collapsing against his back to keep them clear of any strikes. He looked unarmed and there wasn't anywhere he could conceal a weapon between his shirtless dark red torso and the loose black pants he was wearing. The material was so thin that the wind shaped the fabric against his muscled legs, leaving nothing to the imagination. He was pure strength.

Bast's move had separated him from Hel, leaving their attacker uncertain of which threat to face first, his eyes skipping between them. To make a grab for Hel, he'd have to turn his back on Bast. Unless she ran right at him, which was exactly what she fucking did. Of course. Bast blinked as the man reached sideways. A tiny flare of power he sensed through Hel's magic was all the warning they got before he pulled a damn glaive out of thin air. If something could be said to glow black, then the polearm would be. The air around its length blurred like it was heated and the wickedly curving blade on its end was easily as long as his forearm and about as wide. Combined with the staff, the weapon was over a foot taller than Bast's considerable height. The man wielding it was somewhere in between, and he loomed over Hel.

Bast lunged forward as their winged assailant used the non-bladed end of the glaive to sweep Hel's feet out from under her before sliding into a strike that would have impaled Bast on its blade's sharp tip if he hadn't dodged aside. Bast was quick, but their attacker was clearly used to maximising the advantage of his longer reach. He was forced to abandon his return attack as that damn staff came sweeping at him again.

Keeping the pressure on, Bast launched strike after strike, forcing the man to focus on him instead of Hel, who was back on her feet but poised unmoving nearby. He couldn't tell if she was waiting for an opening or just fully engaged in blocking the magic their attacker was trying to throw at them. Possibly both. The burn of her power was thick in the air as she wrapped it around the creature to keep his own contained. It wasn't subtle or elegant, but it was effective. She'd basically smothered him in raw magic.

Bast cursed as he moved too slowly and the blunt end of the staff glanced off his shin. This was getting really tiresome. If he'd had any of his own power, he could've ended it by now. The guy was good, but with his magic neutralised, they were pretty evenly matched.

"Hel. A little help," he growled through gritted teeth as they clashed together.

His muscles strained as his next strike embedded in the glaive's shaft and lodged there. The face of his attacker stretched into a feral grin, dripping with venom. Shit. He'd forgotten about the venom. And now that black glow was creeping up the length of his sword, tainting it with oily shadow.

He tried to tug his blade free, but the glow seemed to weld their weapons together. His fingers started burning where they touched the hilt of his sword. Bast cursed and kicked out as he abandoned the blade just before the spreading darkness would have reached his hand.

As if they'd co-ordinated it, Hel moved in as he rolled to the side, her blades whirling in a double attack that compensated for her shorter reach. She'd reversed one of her blades so that it ran along her forearm, letting her block his strikes with her arm without risking breaking it or coming into contact with that black fire.

Bast drew his dagger and closed in behind the man while Hel's blade slashing at his face distracted him. As the bat-winged man tried to twist toward him, Hel flicked out the dagger she'd been using to block and tore a long gash down his chest. Bat wings flared toward him as the creature realised he'd let them in too close and he no longer had room to manoeuvre the long weapon. The hooked claws that lined the edges of his wings caught on Bast's hands as he gripped the muscled membranes beating at his body and tore outward. Grim satisfaction filled him as he wrenched out a wing and used his dagger to half sever it from the guy's body. He'd had to watch his scouts torn to pieces by this man's magic. It was only fitting he return the favour.

A screeching cry of pain filled the air and Bast could feel the desperation in the air as their attacker's magic flailed against Hel's containment, trying to punch a way out to call for help. The sickening crack of her baton against the creature's arm sent the glaive thudding into the sand.

It took all Bast's self-control to sheathe his own dagger and wrap the man into a submission hold instead of finishing him. They needed information. Hel backed off a step as soon as he was safely restrained, her chest rising and falling as she panted with exertion. He'd never seen her puffed like that.

"You ok?" he asked, biceps straining as their attacker struggled to free himself. He wouldn't have been able to hold him if he hadn't twisted the creature's joints to breaking point.

"Yeah. Just a little bruised. It's the magic that's the problem," she said, voice sounding strained as she kept her smothering power draped around all of them.

"You shouldn't be able to block me like this," the man in Bast's arms hissed.

Hel smirked as Bast kicked behind his knees and forced him to kneel. Even then, it only put the monstrous creature at eye height with his mate. "You're going to answer some questions for us," he growled.

The man stilled and stopped testing his strength against him. "No. I'm not," he said.

Hel's eyes widened in horror. "Bast. Move!" she screamed, already diving backward.

Bast's hands tightened on his captive until that same burning sensation he'd had from the glaive rushed around him. Cursing, he jumped into the air, using his momentum to land a hard kick to the kneeling man's temple. Even as their attacker toppled sideways toward the sand unconscious, he knew he'd been too late. Bast had just enough time to throw his body over Hel where she'd landed in the sand,

and then black fire exploded from the glaive, incinerating the man's body in a single breath.

Hel's power wrapped tight across his feathers where they spread to protect her from any shrapnel and he knew it was only her efforts that kept them from joining the man in death.

"Fuck," Hel breathed from underneath him.

Bast rolled off her and stared at the starburst of black glass that had formed on the golden sand beach. Stretching out his own over-taxed power, he took grim satisfaction in using the creature's fading soul to drag enough power to himself to entrap it. He wove gossamer threads of soul-magic into a web and caught the thrashing coil of the dead man's violence in its strands. They wouldn't hold for long.

What are the structures you're guarding? he demanded, and even with his power so low, the soul was powerless to resist him. He was too new to death.

Shards of stasis. Identical points between two realities, the reply came back slowly, every word dragged out against the speaker's will.

What do they do?

Anchor the magic that will meld the realities together.

Bast's vision narrowed. The strain of holding the soul quiescent without his well of power became a thud of pressure in his brain and he knew he was at risk of giving himself an aneurism if he kept this up much longer.

Why meld the realities?

This time, the answer came willingly, as if the soul was taking one last opportunity to achieve his ruler's aim. *Without Helaine, it is the only way to keep the contagion from spreading. Give her to Him or face another melding. The choice is yours.*

CHAPTER 11
HEL

Hel scrambled further away from Bast as she felt the surge of a soul near her. The last thing she needed was to lose consciousness again. Even with distance, she still had to grit her teeth against the pressure of their death. Thankfully, whatever he was doing didn't take long. The glassy-eyed, distant look on his face turned to something else as she watched. Fear? Frustration?

"What did you do?" she asked.

"Questioned our dead assailant. We need to move. I don't know if your power is going to draw more hunters."

Hel let Bast sweep her up into his arms, but there was something off about the way he felt through the bond. She waited until his familiar surging wingbeats had taken them high above the cloud-cover before questioning him again.

"What did he say?"

"That the structures are 'shards of stasis' that will anchor the magic for a second melding."

Hel's body stiffened. She'd guessed it would be something like that from the note her guardian had left, but she'd hoped there was some other explanation. Something simpler. Like, you know, gates for conquest or something they could actually fight against.

"Why?"

"Apparently, it's the only way to stop the contagion spreading unless he can get his hands on you."

Hel winced. Bast's voice was neutral. Toneless. He was waiting for her to volunteer an explanation.

"I don't know what he needs me for, but I know whatever it is would kill me."

"How do you know that?"

"My guardian made it very clear. And when I was younger, I heard her talking to a hunter like the one we faced. He said I was 'born to be sacrificed' and she should never have let me grow up."

"She got you away from him?"

"She killed him. She's the one who taught me everything I know about fighting with a blade, and she was only in my life until I was thirteen. I'll never be as good as she was."

"I can keep the contagion contained. We don't need to hand you over. I *won't* hand you over."

"What if it's the only way to stop another reality melding? So many people would die," Hel whispered.

"We just need to figure out how to take out those structures. Even destroying one might do it. A magical working of that magnitude needs to be perfectly executed. We only need to disrupt it just enough."

"The other courts won't go for that, will they? They'll want to hand me over. That creature will have told Ty the same thing he told you."

"They don't get a fucking say in it. You're *mine*," Bast growled.

For the first time, that sentiment didn't spark any anger in her. Something had changed last night. Their dynamic had shifted. Maybe it was just the way their connection had grown deeper and more complex. But she suspected it was more than that. In a moment of weakness, she'd asked for what she needed. She'd done it because she knew with utter certainty he would be there for her. He always was when it mattered. And when he wasn't, it was because he thought he was saving her. Trust like that wasn't something she'd ever experienced before.

Hel reached up a hand to cup his jaw and when he looked down at her, she pressed a kiss to his lips. "Thank you."

His hands tightened around her, but he didn't deepen the kiss. He just brushed her lips back gently and rested his forehead on hers for a breath before returning his focus to their surroundings.

"The Water Stronghold isn't far. We should be able to see it soon."

As they flew, Bast called Ra to update him and get the latest intel on what they were walking into. He didn't offer Hel an earpiece this time, or maybe he'd lost it in the fight. She didn't really mind. It meant fewer distractions from their surroundings when they had no idea what they'd be flying into here. The low cloud had dispersed as they left the islands behind them and Hel scanned the glittering ocean below them, searching the horizon for any sign of the floating city she'd only ever seen in photos. Sure enough, it was only another ten minutes before the first hint of the elemental habitat emerged in the distance.

As they flew closer, she could make out a series of connected islands that twisted like a nautilus shell constructed of glass and greenery. Tiers of lush, edible gardens filled the floating spaces. At each of the four compass points, towers stretched up five storeys above the waves.

"Huh. I thought it would be bigger," Hel said.

"The main living quarters are beneath the surface where it's more defensible. We're probably already flying over some of the more remote detachable pods."

Winged forms fluttered above the floating stronghold as elementals went about their business and she could see pairs of scouts scattered in the distance. None had approached them, though. Hel glanced back over Bast's shoulder after his comment and tensed as she saw pods breaching the waves behind them.

"What're the chances they're not trying to block our exit with those?" Hel whispered.

Bast twisted to follow her gaze and swore softly. "Slim to none. Hopefully Nerida's just being cautious."

He didn't sound very convinced.

As if her name had summoned her, the Lady herself launched out from the nearest tower and headed toward them. Her uniquely translucent blue-green wings shone bright in the sunlight, casting a ray of aquamarine light onto the whitecaps below. She'd probably enhanced it with her magic. All the rulers were peacocks that way, flaunting their power. Her long, deep red hair was flying free in the breeze.

Bastion pulled up into a hover and waited for the Lady of the Water Court to approach.

"Welcome. This is unexpected. Why are you here?" Nerida said when she was close enough not to yell. The Water Lady was renowned for her dislike of visitors. Her stronghold was her sanctuary. As a ruler of a court, she was expected to entertain visitors, but they never stayed long.

"Do you really not know?" Bast replied and Nerida laughed softly, her ageless eyes crinkling with amusement.

"Come. This is not the place to discuss such matters," Nerida said, spinning in the air and heading back toward her floating stronghold, so certain they would follow she didn't even look back to check.

They landed on a hardy green ground-cover that sank beneath Hel's feet and wafted the scent of citrus up to her as Bast lowered her to the platform. She might've gawked around her like a tourist but for the sudden pressure of deaths against her awareness as Bast drew deeply on the wellspring of his power through the lingering souls to restore his reserves. Taking two steps away from Bast, her body stiffened as she fought the drive to fall to her knees. The distance barely helped. This was not good. She wasn't even facing an active threat. Her lungs burned and breathing became an exercise of willpower as she re-lived what felt like a dozen drownings. Had Nerida's stronghold sprung a leak sometime recently? She'd have to discuss it with Bast once they were alone and she felt less like she was dying.

A playful brush against her mind followed by a surge of grieving guilt snapped her free of the trap her mind had been twisting into. Each stronghold had its own personality and the Water Court was one she'd never visited before. It felt a little like one of the ocean creatures it floated above, a dolphin perhaps, or an orca. The kind of friendly that was endearing even though you knew it was just as likely to kill you for fun as it was to play with you, that it could take pleasure in beating a smaller animal to death or tearing it to shreds. It had sensed the drowning sensations she was experiencing and it felt bad about them, though. Interesting. The stronghold's power should've been enough to protect its inhabitants from that kind of death.

Usually, she kept a low profile with the strongholds, hiding her true nature behind a veneer of boring humanity. With this one, she let a little of the predator in her show through. She didn't want to be confused with someone weak and defenceless it could toy with.

Hel's eyes had dropped to her feet while she was dealing with the psychic overwhelm. When she looked up, Nerida was watching her with curiosity.

"My stronghold likes you," she said, sounding surprised.

Hel shrugged and took the opportunity to fire a warning shot. "I think it senses a kindred hidden violence in me."

Bast shifted closer and put a hand to her back as Nerida's mouth twitched up in a smile. He could only sense the stronghold second-hand, and she could feel his concern through the bond as he tried to determine the level of threat to them. She pushed a silent wave of reassurance through their connection. She didn't feel threatened. Yet.

"Fair enough," the Water Lady responded. "You must be tired from your journey. We can talk after you've eaten and rested."

"You will honour guest law?" Bast asked.

"Of course," Nerida said, inclining her head.

They didn't have the time to spare, and they sure as fuck couldn't trust her not to betray them, but they had little choice but to follow one of her people into the depths of the stronghold. Bast still didn't feel like his usual concentration of raw power and they both desperately needed sleep. They were faded versions of themselves.

Despite the fact they were floating on the ocean, the

structure they walked across didn't rock beneath their feet. Hel suspected the stronghold absorbed all that energy from the waves to use for itself rather than letting it release in movement.

The guide who led them down into the passageways beneath the ocean's surface had wings of deep cyan shot through with white like the whitecaps breaking on the nearby waves. The rich colours of the water court were a sure sign he was a powerful magic user.

They entered the guest quarters through one of the transparent walls that arched in fluid gentle curves supporting the edible gardens visible from the air. Her mind flashed back to pushing through the heat of Ty's lava as they stepped through the thin layer of cold salty water that formed the entrance. Somehow she emerged dry on the other side of the barrier despite feeling the ocean on every inch of her skin.

Her hand brushed her hair, finding it still dry when it should be sodden, and their guide smirked back at them. She wished she could punch the superior look off his face, but they were in a precarious enough position as it was. The stairwell down was enclosed in similar water walls to the entrance, making it feel like they were submerged in a stormy sea, which she guessed they were except she knew there must be living spaces and other rooms around them. She had to remind herself it was only the psychic games of the sentience surrounding them that made it feel like the depths of the ocean were pressing in against them and if she reached out a hand to touch the water it might spring a leak and drown her. She knew it was well within the stronghold's ability to make the illusion real.

The suffocating sensation remained until they reached

the guest suite Nerida had allocated them. As they stepped inside, the illusory view of the corridors paled in comparison to the curved central main wall of the suite, which was genuinely translucent, giving them a view of a school of fish passing nearby. The filtered light of the sun barely reached down to their depth, which must be at least two storeys beneath the surface. Whatever the walls were made of let off a soft glow to reduce what could have easily been oppressive darkness.

The space was generous and open. Couches and a dining table to their left were balanced by the large king-sized bed on the right. Opaque walls concealed them from the hallway they'd traversed to get there and kept the en-suite bathroom private. Hel wondered how many people could see them through the transparent wall looking out into the ocean where there must be many more such structures suspended out of sight. As if sensing the turn of her thoughts, their guide showed them the switch to turn the glass wall opaque and then left them to it.

Hel made a bee-line for the delicious scents rising from the meal set out on a table that looked like a fountain had been frozen in time to form a crystal pedestal. Bast wasn't far behind. Neither spoke as they devoured the delicate flesh of the succulent fish and perfectly sautéed and flavoured greens from one of the gardens floating somewhere above them. Despite the window stretching up to the curved ceiling over-head, she couldn't make out the structures their pod was hanging from. Perhaps they were on the outer edge of the stronghold? Or perhaps everything here was designed to hide Nerida's strength from them.

"How are we playing this?" Hel asked as she leaned back, finally sated after two days of gnawing hunger.

Bast looked around him and shook his head slightly, tugging on his ear. Hel sighed as she realised what he was communicating. He was right. Nerida didn't even need complicated technology to bug their room. The stronghold itself would report back any conversations it heard because they were literally standing inside it.

"We should shower and get some rest," Bast said, and Hel couldn't help the shiver that went through her at the rasp in his voice.

Looking up at him, she met his gaze and raised one eyebrow as she tested where they were at after that night on the beach. The thrill of anticipation quickly faded as his eyes flicked away from her and she felt him shut down. The man was infuriating. If she was going to die from his magic, he could damn well make her last weeks or days enjoyable.

"You can go first," he said, voice now calm and steady.

"It would be quicker together," Hel snapped back.

If she hadn't been watching him so carefully, she would have missed his reaction—the slight flare of his nostrils, the clenching of his hand where it rested on the table. The tells were gone almost as soon as they appeared.

"We can take turns watching the door," Bast said, pretending she hadn't just offered to get naked with him.

Hel sighed. "Fine."

NERIDA WAS as good as her word and no one disturbed them before they had a chance to sleep. The stronghold must have alerted her as soon as they were ready, because the knock on their door came just as Hel put down her spoon from breakfast.

"The Lady will see you now," the young guard at their door said.

Hel subconsciously leaned into Bast's touch when he put a hand on the small of her back to keep her close as they walked. She rolled her eyes as his smug reaction rolled down their bond and their magic flared against each other briefly. At least his power was mostly back to normal. Not the levels he would have had at home, but plenty strong enough to raise havoc here if they needed. Even with the danger it represented to her, she hadn't realised how much she'd missed the way it flirted with her own until it ran dry.

Their escort led them even deeper into the stronghold, deep enough that Hel had to equalise her ears from the changing pressure beneath the ocean's surface. She felt Bast's hand stiffen on her back as they stepped into what must be a formal reception space. Obviously, the pretence this was a social visit was over.

A trick of power and the sentience that resided in the surrounding walls made the space seem like an entirely translucent sphere. None of the tunnels or rooms that must surround them were visible. Their feet sent splashes of saltwater spraying outward as they stepped onto a clear causeway that stretched across its bottom third. Below them was darkness lit only by the stray lights of sea creatures from the depths, angler fish and who knew what else. There was no way to tell whether magic had attracted the animals to swim so close or if the stronghold was merely projecting an image onto its walls. It looked realistic regardless. The ocean view grew lighter the higher up the sphere she looked and at its highest point had a quality to it like it was only a hand-width below a tropical sea's surface. That section was definitely artificial. Even as large as this space was, they were deep enough that the surface wasn't anywhere near that close.

The space was lit by irregular bubbles of water floating mid-air filled with a mix of bioluminescent creatures twisted together into bizarre shapes. Without looking closer, all she caught were seething tentacles, sharper angles that must be coral, and the glint of too many eyes.

The Lady of Water waited ahead of them, seated on a throne that seemed made of the dark depths that stretched below them. She was backlit, of course, so the full effect of her uniquely transparent wings was apparent where they flared out behind her. She would have been beautiful if any expression had breached her cool visage. Instead, she appeared as cold as the ocean surrounding them. Her body draped there like a siren, deep red hair tumbling to the side to expose her undercut and matching red collared coat hanging open to reveal a teasing hint of the swell of her breasts and heavily tattooed skin. One combat-booted foot was slung over the low arm of her throne. All the elemental rulers were unique, but she was more so.

Bast's arm wound around Hel's waist, holding her close as they paused just short of the throne. There was no seating for them, of course. They were the supplicants in this charade.

"Ty tells me you've mated," Nerida said, addressing Bast and skipping any of the pleasantries the formal setting would usually have engendered.

Hel felt Bast shrug beside her, but she didn't take her eyes off the woman in front of them. She was by far the biggest threat in the room, even counting the dozen guards she'd now noticed encircling the space on a second causeway that circumnavigated the sphere's edge above them.

"That seems unwise given your necromancy," the Lady pressed.

Her tone pissed off Hel. The air of superiority and judgement palpable. An intense desire to irritate the woman filled her. "And your provocation seems unwise given his ability to save you from the contagion," she snapped.

Nerida's eyes flicked to her and then away again. "Is it true she isn't human?" she asked, continuing to exclude Hel from the conversation.

Hel's blood chilled. How much did Ty know? What had her father's people told him and what had he passed on?

"It's true she's my mate. Anything else is none of your concern," Bast growled.

"I disagree. Ty tells me that whoever is responsible for these creatures that have been invading our territories is doing so only to find her. If we hand her over, our troubles end. Just like Tir's letter told us."

"Did he tell you that same person caused the Melding? And that he's building magical structures to do it again? There's one on the island we flew from just south of here—a giant shard of metallic rock that will anchor the destruction," Bast said.

Finally Hel caught a hint of expression cross Nerida's face—surprised concern. "No. He didn't mention that."

"And did you ask him what he would get for helping hunt us down? You know him. He's not the altruistic sort. If he went out of his way to trap us, then he's expecting something in exchange," Bast pressed.

Nerida sighed and swung her leg off the throne, leaning forward with her forearms on both knees. "He's been struggling with a separatist uprising. Yesterday, someone took out an entire block in one of his cities. Every human inside was asphyxiated. It has Aliya's signature all over it. He couldn't risk turning his people against him and I suspect her taking care of them like that in a way that preserved his deniability was the price. Although I'm surprised she still paid out when he didn't secure you."

"I imagine she has to work a little harder for his co-operation, what with having murdered his father and all," Hel interjected drily.

"Apparently, that was an accident," Nerida said, finally deigning to acknowledge Hel's presence. "But, yes. I imagine there is a little tension to overcome. So, the real question is, what has Aliya been promised?"

A wave of bitterness had shot through her from Bast at Nerida's words. She could guess what caused it. His brother had hunted him for years thinking he'd killed their father, and now he was working with the man's actual killer so soon after discovering she was the true guilty party. She wondered if they were sharing a bed. It wouldn't be the first or even the second time Aliya had seduced a lord for her own purposes. So, what was the Lady of Air getting from Hel's father?

"I imagine power of some sort," Bast said as if he'd read her mind and it took her a moment to realise she'd echoed Aliya's question in her thoughts. "It's the only thing that drives her."

"Likely," Nerida agreed, frowning in thought. "She has more than enough already, though."

"Agreed."

"Give me another option here, Bastion."

"The contagion is under control for now. Let us have a go at destroying the shard near here for you. If we succeed, you back us with the council and stop them hunting my mate."

Nerida tilted her head as if listening to someone, her eyes going distant. "The stronghold says you have power of some sort that could make this possible," she said, finally addressing Hel.

Hel snorted. "Thanks for letting me know. I never would have noticed if you hadn't told me."

Nerida's distant expression snapped to a glare. "Don't push me. I'm going against the council directive to deliver you to Ty right now."

Hel suppressed a flinch at that revelation. There would only be a directive if they had a majority, which meant Mica had agreed to hand her over. They were lucky Nerida was more fiercely independent than anyone else on the council and had her own morality, even if it wasn't always in alignment with theirs.

Somehow, Bast kept the immense anger she could feel radiating from him out of his voice when he replied. "And you have our appreciation for that."

"I'll give you one shot at destroying the structure. My people will accompany you," Nerida said.

"And if we fail?" Hel asked.

The Water Lady's grim smile was as predatory as the sharks whose silhouettes were visible flitting past the sphere above them. "Then I will deliver you to Ty myself."

"That's not going to happen," Bast growled.

"You're in my territory, Bastion. Whatever I want is what will happen."

THE TRIP back to the island was far quicker than the trip to the Water Court had been, thanks to Bast's recovery. Before she knew it, Hel was standing on the beach she could have done without returning to and staring at the familiar visage of the dagger of meteoric rock piercing the Earths.

"Do you feel that?" Hel asked as the sickening taint of contagion brushed against her senses from somewhere nearby.

"Yeah," Bast said, frowning as he looked inland towards the island's peak. "Feels like it's coming from where our attacker opened his portal. That's too much of a coincidence not to be related. The contagion must be coming through them, whether by design or accident. Which suggests your hunters have been even more widespread than we thought, if it's their portals that have been spreading the contagion. I'll take care of it when you're done. I don't want to risk setting you off with my power before we've taken care of that structure."

Hel swallowed hard, thinking back to Tir's note: *the contagion's darkness slipped in behind us through the gate.* They should've made the link between her father's portals and the contagion's outbreaks earlier. It was something that had been playing on her mind for a while, but in the chaos that was their lives, she hadn't had a chance to process it. In her defence, she hadn't been accompanying Bast as he dealt with most of the outbreaks and he wouldn't have felt the portal signatures, especially if they'd faded with time. It was only now they had enough data to see the pattern instead of coincidence.

"Think there'll be any wraiths here?" she asked, returning her attention to the purpose of their visit.

A gust of air brushed against her skin as Bast's wings flared out briefly before he snapped them in tight to his back. "I don't think so. They registered a little to my power the other times. Like a discordant note among the dead. I don't get that sense here. It's all just absence."

"I guess they thought the isolation and the wards would be enough protection," Hel said.

A glance at the sky showed a ring of silently dubious elemental guards. They would be unable to sense the wards shoving their attention away from the structure to keep it hidden, and probably thought this was some elaborate hoax to get away from their lady.

"They won't give us long," Hel said.

"I can hold them off if it comes down to it," Bast said, curling a muscled arm around her shoulders protectively.

"There's twenty of them," Hel said.

"Well. Maybe I'll let you deal with a couple," he teased and Hel hid her smile in response. "And we can always use them as a shield if we need to use your power and your hunters come running," he added, killing her smile.

Hel sighed and took a careful step closer to the section of volcanic scree the structure was lodged in. She wasn't sure if these rocks had always split the beach in half to trail into the water or if the structure itself had displaced the golden sand in favour of the black igneous rock.

They both knew it was her power that meant they could see the shard of stasis looming above them, so it was Hel who'd have the best chance at assessing how to destroy it. Bast's presence was a reassuring weight at her back, guarding against the ambush that was likely to come from either Nerida's people or her father's hounds. At least they stood a better chance of escape out on the beach with only a portion of Nerida's guards to deal with than in the heart of her stronghold. The biggest problem was how on the Earths they were going to destroy something as powerful and complex as this structure felt?

"One step at a time," Bast said, responding to her silent moment of doubt. "Just touch it and see what you feel."

When she stepped into the shadow of the structure, it was like the sound of the world around them deadened. It soared three times higher than either of them—if she and Bast both stretched their arms wide, fingertip to fingertip, they would only just brush the edges of its width. Taking a steadying breath, she reached a hand out to touch its surface. She'd expected the jagged metallic rock to feel cool and smooth, or perhaps to feel the searing heat of her father's power. Instead, her hand sunk through the shard like it was an illusion and disappeared from her view. Bast stepped up next to her, placing his hand next to hers, and she watched in confusion as his palm flattened on the rock like she'd expected her own to.

"Well, fuck," she said. "Looks like I need to go inside."

"I don't think that's a good idea," Bast said.

Hel glanced up at him, surprised to see his expression matched the emotions she was getting through the bond for once. He was worried for her and he wasn't trying to hide it. Reaching out, he cupped a hand around her neck, stroking his thumb down her cheek.

"There could be anything in there. What if there are people? I'm not destroying something when we don't know what it is," she said.

She held her breath as Bast sighed and bent down to brush his lips over hers before nipping her lower lip lightly. "Don't try anything while you're in there. Just look and come back. I won't be able to get you out if you collapse again."

Hel rolled her eyes. "I'm not stupid."

"No. You're reckless," Bast shot back. His mouth twisted up in a grin at the words, but his eyes still silently pleaded for her to be careful.

Hel pulled away and, perversely proving him right, immediately strode into the rock before she could chicken out. The sensation on her body as she passed the façade of the structure felt like the very edge of a portal—the curved meniscus of power where it bent reality. Her father's power, which had been so quiescent from the outside of the elaborate shielding that kept the structure hidden, now surrounded her. Its blistering torridity pressed against her skin until she wondered how she hadn't combusted into flame.

She'd instinctively squeezed her eyes closed as she stepped through, and when she opened them, she found herself in a place between realities. Hazy grey nothingness filled every space around and below her. The air she breathed in too fast was tinged with drifting rainbows of light despite there being no obvious source for the glow. She was standing on a narrow ribbon of path made of the same rock as the structure but impossibly thin. That thinness was visible because the path literally twisted into a loop ahead of her, forming some kind of Möbius strip that meant she could see her own silhouette in the distance. Taking a step along the path, she watched as the figure in the distance took one as well. Was she staring at her actual self or an alternate reality? The bat-winged man had called this a stasis point between the realities her father would meld. Either or both options could be true. Regardless, she'd confirmed there was nothing else alive here and she wasn't going to try and destroy it from within. She needed to get back to Bast.

Spinning back the way she'd come, she blinked in confusion. The view was exactly the same as the one she'd just turned away from—a twisting ribbon of road and another her visible in the distance. Where the fuck was the exit?

Peering down and to the side, she wondered if she was brave enough to step off the path. Vertigo and disorientation washed over her as she saw the same twisting path stretching below her now, along with the same silhouette of herself, although this time, she appeared to be hanging upside down. Her eyes squeezed shut and she forced herself to take a breath to fend off the panic rising inside her. Was this all just an elaborate trap she'd walked right into? Was she going to be stuck here forever? Or at least until her father came to collect his wayward daughter at last?

A surge of concern skittered across her awareness through her bond with Bast. At least that was still intact, although it felt like he was far more than a couple of paces away. Forcing another deep breath, she focused on the connection with him, the draw of his soul to hers. Without opening her eyes, she turned until she could feel the warmth of his presence against her face.

Stretching a hand out in front of her, she leaned forward as far as she dared and let her fear communicate her need to her mate standing back in her own reality. She had no doubt she'd stepped outside of time and space into somewhere between. Without the bond, she wouldn't have a hope of getting back. She stretched her arm further, fingers trembling as they grasped for anything real. Just as she thought she'd tumble into the grey abyss around her, familiar warm fingers brushed against the tips of her own. Already falling, she used the last of her leverage against the strange ribbon of path to leap toward the promise of safety.

It should have been an easy jump into Bast's arms. She

only needed to make it past the edge of the structure after all. Just as far as her fingers had stretched. Physics or gravity or whatever it was didn't work the same there, though. She could feel the world drop and twist, feel the distance between them stretching instead of closing. There was nowhere physical to brace herself. Instead, her flailing mind held tight to the mating bond and pulled as Bast's power clutched back at her just as desperately.

It was enough. Barely.

Strong hands wrapped so tight around her wrists she was sure she'd be wearing bruises for days as Bast dragged her step by painful step back into the world. The place between places clung tight like a birth canal convulsing around her, crushing her body.

As her head breached the walls of the structure and returned to her own Earths, the few souls that had followed them to the island returned with a vengeance, swarming around her body like bees in response to the threat. Still sunk deep into the bond with Bast, she could sense their concern that her father would find her from the disturbance she'd made. They had to keep her hidden and safe.

Hel voiced a silent scream as death skittered across her skin, unwittingly dragging her into endless suffering.

CHAPTER 12
BAST

Fear filled Bast when only Hel's fingertips emerged from the blank façade of the meteoric rock, but that was nothing compared to the terror of her hand suddenly dropping toward the beach like she was on an elevator and the cable had been cut. Only his reaction speed, born of years of evading his brother's assassins, had allowed him to drop to the ground fast enough to grasp at her disappearing hand. He knew if he didn't catch her before that sliver of her body disappeared, she'd be lost to him. It was only thanks to the brush of her skin against his own that he could grasp enough of her power to reach into the rock and hold tight.

Bast's heart raced as he pulled Hel's body from the structure. Despite how easily she had stepped through the shard, the weight on his arms was so great it felt like he was literally dragging her through meteoric rock.

He could sense Nerida's infuriating guards dropping closer as he dragged Hel's body from the shard, but there was nothing he could do as it took everything he had to save his mate. He just had to hope they would give them a bit more time. If he let go of Hel's wrists, she'd fall into the depths of the structure. With his muscles straining to pull her clear and his power focused on screaming at the souls that had swarmed at the threat to leave her the fuck alone, he had no attention left for the vulturous elementals circling them.

When the structure finally released its hold on his mate, it was like releasing the tension on a tightly wound rubber band. Hel's body came flying at him, knocking him onto his back. Pain radiated through his jaw where her head connected with his chin and his hands spasmed as they finally released their death-grip on her. Hel's limp form draped across his chest as he lay in the sand shutting his eyes against the bright sunlight and fought with sheer willpower to hold Hel's soul safe from the danger of his power.

So focused on the internal battle, it took him a second to register the removal of her weight from his body. He lost vital moments to the disorientation of operating in both the plane of souls where he was desperately anchoring her consciousness and the physical world around them. It was the crushing weight of booted feet standing on each of his fucking wings that finally snapped him back to the world. Rage burned through him as he almost lost the thread he was holding tight to Hel. He prised open his eyes to the view of two guards looming over him, about to press their sword-tips to his throat.

Amateurs.

The courts liked to pretend he was no more powerful than any competent mage among their people. These two, with the deep tanzanite and lapis coloured wings of the highest levels of training in the Water Court, thought their power was a match for his.

They were wrong.

There was a reason his people called him the Lord of the Soul Court despite the fact no one else would acknowledge his claim to power, and it wasn't vanity. Bast didn't give any warning beyond the opening of his eyes. His expression didn't change. He didn't gesture with his hands and he doubted the guards noticed the flare of silver beneath their feet as his power surged across his inner wing surface. The souls that followed him drew close at his call, eager to help him even though he'd tried to hold them back from Hel. She was like a drug to them. A growing addiction they were increasingly unable to resist. They didn't hold his actions against him and they welcomed the distraction of the call to violence every bit as much as he did, channelling power to him in a cascading rush.

It took less than a breath to gather that magic and send it spiralling up the guards' bodies. He drew on the dull ache of their weight resting on his sensitive wings to focus the silver strands into speeding channels of light that went unnoticed until they wrapped around the faces of his attackers and *pulled*. A prick of pain against his throat said their swords had finally reached their target. The sensation barely registered as he focused on their eyes now registering fear before their bodies locked in place and shot back in a burst of magic and searing agony.

He was done playing nice.

He held back from killing them. Barely. Their broken bones would heal, but he could feel his power scoring into their wings in a way that would leave them permanently scarred with lines of feathers burned black. It wasn't the black of his own wings. But anyone looking at them would know who they'd angered.

His eyes were scanning the sky for Hel before their bodies had even hit the volcanic rock. He growled in frustration as he saw her still limp form suspended between another two magic users flying as fast as their power could accelerate them towards the Water Court. The remaining sixteen guards hung in formation in the air between him and his mate, more wary than they had been but willing to face death for their lady.

They were still underestimating him. Still treating him like a normal magic user instead of a lord. Bast wrapped a shield around himself as the first magical attack speared towards him and shot into the air. None of them could match him for speed. Nerida could have if she'd come herself, but there was no way they could keep him contained here on their own. It would be a different story once he had Hel back in his arms and he had to focus on holding her soul to her body, but right now he could finally let loose.

Barrelling straight through the middle of their ridiculous blockade, he relied on his shielding to protect his body as elemental guards careened away from him, either hit directly or caught in the swirling currents of wind he'd wrapped around himself.

He barely spared them a thought as he threw a net of power behind him that would slow them down and took off after the three figures in the distance. They had a head start and with two of them to share Hel's weight, they were almost fast enough that he'd struggle to catch them before they reached the reinforcements they'd undoubtedly have called for. He didn't have enough time to punish the rest of them.

Every part of him focused on the draw of his mate ahead of him. His wing muscles ached and his still recovering reserves of power flickered in warning at the punishing speed he forced his body to reach. He'd never flown so fast. Not even when he'd been running for his own life. Saving Hel was more important than saving himself. The beat of his wings was a hummingbird blur in his peripheral vision that sent wisps of silver power drifting into the air and trailing behind him like twin magical contrails. He would pay for the vast energy expenditure at some point, but that didn't matter as long as it was *after* he got Hel to safety.

The two guards carrying his mate had noticed him incoming. Each time they turned to check his progress, they lost a little speed. A grim smile spread across Bast's face as he drew closer. They knew they were prey now.

He waited until he was close enough to make out the individual strands of Hel's hair drifting in the wind before he reached for his power to slow them. The soul-power snare was ready to shoot out from him when a missile of power smashed into his shields from above, sending him hurtling towards the ocean and destroying his momentum. He had just enough time to glance upwards and see the familiar transparent wings of Nerida hovering above before a second attack was speeding at him.

Using his power to put on a burst of speed, he managed to dodge her magic this time. His shields were already ragged from taking the direct hit. He'd been so focused on Hel and watching the horizon beyond her for scouts, he hadn't noticed Nerida hiding her approach by staying at high altitude.

The Water Lady didn't stick around. By the time he'd stabilised his flight, she'd already caught up to where Hel was being carried far ahead. The rest of her guards he'd left behind were closing in, laying down a cover of magical fire that sent him further off course as he twisted and dodged in mid-air while reconstructing his defences.

Nerida had hit him with a damn sledgehammer of power and he needed to conserve his remaining energy. Instead of engaging them, he relied on raw strength to carry him straight up. Cold shivered across his wings as the air grew thinner. He watched as the guards banked en masse and headed after their lady. They'd achieved their aim of running him off. Apparently, they weren't trying to kill him. That was something.

He used Nerida's trick of screening himself in the upper atmosphere to follow them, using just a touch of his power to enhance his vision enough to keep an eye on his mate. Not that he needed to see her to follow her. Their connection was now strong enough that, even when she was unconscious, there was a tug deep inside him that would always take him to her. Bast tried not to think about what that meant for the rapidly escalating severity of her reaction to the souls. First, he needed to get her free. They could keep worrying about the soul taint once she was safe.

He released a breath he didn't realise he'd been holding when he watched Nerida direct the guards to take Hel into the Water Stronghold. At least they weren't flying her straight to Ty or Aliya. This delay might give him the chance to get to her. If he could navigate the heavily guarded, sentient underwater maze to find her. Bast swore and pushed back the wave of despair that threatened to overwhelm him. One wingbeat at a time. He needed to figure out an angle for attack.

Knowing he'd need good intel to pull this off, he reached into his pocket to call Ra on the satellite phone. His fingers closed on nothing and despair almost buried him again as he let loose a much longer string of curses. Somewhere in the various attacks and aerial acrobatics, he'd lost his damn phone. It was probably at the bottom of the ocean somewhere.

He had no back up. No surveillance. Fuck.

Hovering in place, high above the floating stronghold, he reached for the comfort of his connection to the woman below. He could tell she was still unconscious, but at least she was no longer at risk of dying. Yet. It was probably just as well she hadn't woken up or she might have panicked and tried portalling. With the way her sensitivity had worsened, that would probably be a death sentence at this point. She might not have told him anything about why this guy was hunting her, but he knew how she felt about him, regardless. Her desperation to stay free. He needed to reach her before she gave up hope of escape.

With his focus already below the ocean wherever they'd placed Hel, he stretched his awareness out from her body, seeking for he didn't even know what. A weakness. An entry point. Anything. He could no longer tell where his power ended and Hel's began when he worked like this, their magics melding together almost seamlessly.

His search was immediately rewarded by a familiar dark taint near where Hel rested. He blinked in surprise. How had they missed that last time they were there and why hadn't Nerida asked for his help to contain it? He hadn't known the contagion had reached the Water Court. It meant Hel's hunters had portalled there sometime in the past. They were lucky they hadn't still been there to attack while they'd slept in the stronghold.

Bast reached out to the souls who lingered in the strong-hold for an explanation. He could feel their reluctance to talk to him lest they betray their lady to an enemy, but that was why he carried loyal old souls with him. They made sure his access to the wellspring of his power flowed free and, between them, they could compel the answers they needed. That was a worst-case scenario, though. As with the living, it was usually easier to tell half-truths and cajole the information from them. *I can contain the contagion so it won't spread, but I need to know what happened,* he explained, careful to keep his true emotions hidden.

The darkness formed in one of the outer storerooms. The Lady had to amputate part of the Stronghold. It screamed for days and accidentally added to the death toll in its grief, a female soul replied. There was no accusation in her tone despite the fact Bast could feel she was one of those the Stronghold had killed when it was supposed to protect.

Why has she stayed so close to the contagion? he asked.

She's always responsible about what we leave behind. She wouldn't leave something like that for someone else to stumble across, the dead woman said.

She's measuring its growth to see how it progresses in the ocean. Salt water can sometimes act as an accelerant to power and she couldn't risk leaving it unobserved. You can see the darkness from one of the tunnel windows. That's part of why it took so long to calm the stronghold, another soul added.

How deep is it?

Only one level down. Due south of the stronghold, the soul offered.

Bast thanked the dead and lapsed into silence, staring down at the idyllic green artificial islands floating far below. A plan was forming in his mind. It was reckless. Dangerous. Probably too dangerous. But it was the only one he had.

There was a chance Aliya or Ty or the whole fucking

council would get involved in this, and he couldn't face them all together. He needed to act while Hel was alone with only one ruler in reach. He could feel she was somewhere near the contagion. Close enough that she must be on the same level somewhere off that tunnel that looked out on it.

The sky had turned into a pastel palette of pinks and oranges while he thought. It would be dark soon. He was all but invisible in the night sky, especially when he screened himself with his power that few could sense. He knew he could avoid the scouts on the way in. And, hopefully, the chaos of his entry would distract them enough from giving chase after. Even if he successfully mitigated the damage, Nerida might hate him for what he was about to do. That was a risk he'd have to take. She'd taken his fucking mate from him. She might think she was doing the right thing, but she deserved everything he gave her.

Hel was his.

Plan made, calm descended on his mind as he waited for night to fall. When the first stars became visible, he felt Hel stirring along their connection and pushed a wave of reassurance to her, letting her feel his confidence. He smiled a little when he felt her panic lessen. She might not want to trust him, but she did. Her reactions proved it.

Clouds had been gathering throughout the evening and the first drops of rain hit his face as true darkness fell. The water was cold despite the warm climate in the area. He would be a lot colder and wetter soon.

He waited to make his move until just before the change of Nerida's guard shift, when her people would be tired and less alert. Their surveillance targeted normal elemental magic, not his soulweaving. They had no way of sensing his power. Wrapping a cloak of darkness around himself, he dived straight down, arrowing toward where he could feel the absent darkness of the contagion and the alluring warmth of Hel's presence.

His power helped propel him through the water as he dived beneath the ocean's surface. Elementals were not made for swimming and, without magic, his wings would have dragged him down in moments. He shivered a little as the last of his body sank beneath the waves. In the darkness, the vastness of the ocean could hide multitudes, not least the dangerous contagion leaching into the water nearby. He didn't have time to think about that, though. Elementals had good lung capacity, used to flying hard at high altitudes where there was less oxygen. Even so, there was a limit to how long he'd be able to hold his breath to get this done.

Between the soft silver glow emanating from his wings and the lighting of the stronghold, he easily found the window nearest the contagion. It appeared unguarded, which was a stroke of luck. He would still have gone ahead if it was guarded, but this way there was less potential for loss of life. It was a delicate balance with Nerida. She would understand his actions within reason. But if he took it too far, she would retaliate against his city.

He'd been gathering his power with every kick downward, and he immediately lassoed it around the contagion. Unlike the previous times he'd wrapped the darkness in his power, it didn't fight him. It seemed eager to be moved back toward the stronghold, eager to feed on either the sentience itself or the people it contained. He made his containment sphere broader than usual and left a single opening to slice into the stronghold's side. Wincing, he prepared to act counter to his every instinct and let it eat into the window of the Water Court, but the stronghold must've noticed the impending danger. Before the darkness had moved more than a hand's width, the entire underwater pod that formed this outer part of the stronghold detached to avoid the contagion. It was an amputation much the same as when Tir had detached their hand to avoid Hel cuffing them months ago.

He'd never been able to communicate with the sentiences, but he knew it would be in turmoil from the loss, especially if it was already traumatised from the last time. He was counting on that and the need to rescue its own people from the encroaching ocean to keep the Water Court occupied and distracted. With any luck, it wouldn't realise he was here until it was too late. At least it wouldn't have to feel the contagion eating it away. He wouldn't let the contagion spread any further than it had already. Gritting his teeth, he used his power to repel the contagion away from the structure before creating a small opening in glass to enter.

Water rushed into the detached section of the stronghold through the hole he'd opened, and he gritted his teeth as he let his body sweep inside. Judging by the flow of encroaching ocean entering the space, the sentience had sealed the point on the far side where this pod had shorn away from the bulk of the stronghold before it detached so no one would drown.

Hoping he didn't come to regret it, he left the hole he'd created open. There shouldn't be too many people around in this outer section of the stronghold and he needed any guards to be focused on getting clear of the rising saltwater instead of stopping him. He stumbled to his knees as torrents of water crashed against his back. Taking the opportunity to gasp in quick breaths before the ocean devoured the space, he surged to his feet to run towards Hel's presence ahead. Her fear was growing. The water was probably seeping under her door by now. He could see it up ahead. Hel's soul calling to his grew louder with every second as he half raced, half swam closer to her.

The walls of the corridor started rippling around him as he neared her room and he swore quietly. The pod was losing stability without the sentience's magic to hold it together. They needed to be out before it collapsed altogether.

By the time he reached the door, the water was up to his waist and his grip on the handle was the only thing keeping him from being swept past. He didn't bother with finesse, just blasted the lock with pure ice-cold soul magic until it cracked under the pressure and the current slammed the door open.

Hel was crumpled on the floor clutching her head, although she was aware enough to look up when he entered.

"Are you okay?" Bast asked, his feet almost washing out from under him as he slogged through the quickly rising water to scoop her up in his arms.

"The souls are everywhere and the Stronghold is ... not good," Hel said, her face tight with pain.

"That's my fault," Bast said absently, already striding to the far wall of her cell and testing it with his power.

He didn't really have the reserves to be blasting everything in sight like this, but he didn't think they could fight against the water to get back the way they'd come, and every second they spent here was another chance for Nerida to catch them.

"You almost fed it to the contagion," Hel whispered, sounding a little horrified.

"There is *nothing* I wouldn't do for you. And it detached this section before it got hit. Hold your breath," he replied, waiting only long enough to check she'd followed his order before stretching a hole in the wall with his power.

It took another huge surge of power to propel them out into the darkness of the ocean against the incoming seawater. Bast's muscles protested every stroke as he drove them back up to the surface, taking strength from the feel of Hel's body finally back in his arms where she belonged. Knowing he needed to keep Nerida onside, he sent a shot of power he couldn't really spare back toward the contagion and pulled the noose tight until it was completely sheathed and contained. He couldn't anchor it like he had the others. He was leaving behind the equivalent of a naval mine, but at least it couldn't grow any larger. Now, they just had to hope the distraction of dealing with the stronghold screened their escape for long enough to get clear.

The process of getting back into the air was where things started to fall down. There was no way he could get airborne by wing-power alone while swimming with a weakened Hel in his arms and he couldn't afford to use what little of his power remained when he might need it for defence. It took vital minutes for him to swim to one of the satellite platforms just outside the stronghold and drag them up onto it. It was one of the many of the technological additions Nerida had made after the Melding to clear rubbish and pollution from the waters, lacking the softness and comfort of the main stronghold. With firm metal beneath his feet, he could finally shake the water from his sodden wings.

A loud crack followed his movement, and he thought the platform was damaged for a moment until a dull ache in his arm followed the sound. The sight of blood dripping from a hole in his jacket surprised him.

He'd been shot. With a human bullet.

Elementals tended to use blades in aerial combat. There was too much chance of friendly fire in the chaos of open-air battle if projectile weapons were used. Apparently, one of Nerida's guards was armed and willing to risk it. The shot had come from one of the towers on the stronghold proper nearby. Hoping the chaos and the drive to stay close to the traumatised stronghold would keep them from giving chase, Bast clutched Hel close as he adjusted his shields to account for the new threat and launched them up into the air.

CHAPTER 13
HEL

The metallic smell of Bast's blood filled her nose, coating the back of her throat. Hel gripped tight to his arm to keep pressure on the wound. It seemed to be a through-and-through. Her hand could barely stretch wide enough around his muscled biceps to staunch the blood-flow from both sides. Rain beat down around them, drenching her already soaked clothes. It was lucky her body could deal with the cold better than a human, or she'd have been hypothermic in no time.

Between the darkness and the sheets of rain, they couldn't see a damn thing, which meant no one could see them either. The patter of the drops against her skin acted as an anchor, holding her awareness to the world when her soul felt adrift. It was a reminder she desperately needed.

She could feel the boundary between her soul and the place between dissolving as the dead rolled across her consciousness in response to the danger they were in. Images flashed in the surrounding storm she knew weren't really there—a building collapsing above her head, a stream of magical fire arrowing toward her heart, a blade slicing at her neck. Only long practice at hiding any weakness stopped her from twitching at each death. She wasn't feeling them yet, but it was only a matter of time. The promise of pain lingered on an invisible horizon.

Hel bit her lip hard enough that the copper taste of her own blood filled her mouth and forced her attention back to the man straining to fly them free, using her concern for him as another tether to reality. She waited until she was certain they'd passed the outer reaches of where Nerida's people scouted before talking, and even then she kept her voice low.

"You're still bleeding. We need to bandage this. Is there somewhere we can land?"

Bast just grunted and kept up the punishing pace he'd set. Hel rolled her eyes at his self-sacrificing hero complex and wrapped her legs tighter around his waist. Relying on the one good arm Bast had wrapped around her body to keep her stable, she let go of her hold around his neck and reached down to tear enough fabric from her tank top to create a makeshift dressing. She swore as her half-numb fingers tried and failed to shred the cotton. Giving up on that approach, she just ripped down the seams until her entire top was bunched in her hands. The rhythmic pulsing of Bast's wingbeats stuttered as she used her leg muscles to lever herself higher so she could wrap his bleeding arm.

Glancing at his face in question, she could barely make out his expression despite the soft glow coming from his wings in the storm-swept night. His eyes were locked on her now exposed skin where the rain was trailing a path down to her bra.

"You trying to kill me?" he growled, adjusting his hold on

her until his arm wrapping around her nestled beneath her jacket.

"You're doing just fine at that without me. Would you let me stop the bleeding already?" she said, pulling herself up higher.

She told herself the tremor in her voice was from concern and not from his effect on her. The mating bond wouldn't be denied despite their precarious situation. When she finally got decent coverage over his wounds and pulled the fabric into a tight knot to secure it, his wingbeats barely hitched. Apparently, the tough guy was only bothered by a little naked skin in his face, not what had to be an increasingly painful hole in his arm.

"There. All done. Tell me if it slips," she said.

"Thanks. Do up your jacket," Bast growled back.

Hel smirked. "Why? Am I distracting you?"

"You're going to freeze like that. Do up your damn jacket," he repeated.

Even as her thoughts rebelled at him ordering her around, Hel had to work to hide the warmth that filled her at his protective words. It had just been her against the world for so long. It was kind of nice to have someone worried about her. Someone who'd single-handedly attack a fucking stronghold to save her.

"Thank you for coming for me," she whispered, almost too quiet to be heard over the storm.

Bast's arm tightened around her for a moment and she felt his lips brush against her temple. "Always," he said. "Now, zip up the jacket."

Somehow, despite everything, his actions incited a smile she knew the night would hide. She zipped her jacket before nestling into the warmth of his body. She didn't have the heart to tell him the shivers that were wracking her body weren't from the temperature, but from the threatening dead that surrounded him like a second aura.

The rain let up a few hours into their flight somewhere over the expanse of the South Pacific Ocean stretching below them. Once again, they were flying in a direction that would stretch the night and its darkness out as long as possible. The world was fading as Hel's head spun with the pressure of holding off the riptide of the dead pulling at her soul.

"So, what's the plan?" Hel asked, needing Bast's voice to cling to.

"We need somewhere to regroup and figure out how to deal with these structures. If I were the council, I'd be waiting to ambush us at the edge of the City of Souls. Nerida already has scouts there. We need to hunker down somewhere, recover, and get back in touch with Ra so we can figure out what's going on."

"They won't attack the city while you're gone?" Hel asked.

"They'd need to be desperate to risk that kind of loss of life just to take you," Bast said, and Hel couldn't quite hide the irrational flash of hurt at his words. Warm lips pressed to her cool neck as she felt his responding reassurance whispered across her skin. "That's not how I feel, Hel. There's nothing 'just' about you."

"So, where to then?"

"I've got an old friend near Mount Taranaki. She'll put us up for a night or two while we figure out if it's safe to return to the city and get us new comms gear."

Hel couldn't hide the stab of jealousy that statement engendered. Fuck. She was losing the ability to regulate her emotions and responses as she sank further and further beneath the pressure of the souls. Bast's amusement at her poorly guarded secret turned to unease as he decoded some of what she was feeling. He kissed a path up her throat and along the line of her jaw.

"You're my mate. I only want you. You have nothing to worry about. How bad is the soul taint getting?"

Hel shrugged and let her hair fall down to screen her from his view.

Bast touched a finger to her chin to tilt her face back up until she was staring into the deep black of his eyes. In the darkness, she could clearly see the ring of silver between his pupil and iris that was all but invisible by daylight.

"Tell me," he said, his voice a low rumble.

"It's near continuous now, even without a threat. I have to focus constantly to keep myself present."

Bast swore and clutched her tight enough that she knew she'd have bruises where his fingers dug into her skin. She felt the pressure of souls lessen a fraction as he tried to shove them clear.

"Just hold on, okay? I'll try and contain it again once we're somewhere safe."

Hel nodded, but both of them knew it was useless. It was only a matter of time before she succumbed. She might have given up when Nerida had taken her rather than risk being returned to her father if it wasn't for the fact she knew she'd take Bast with her.

"I have an idea for the shards," she said, eager to change the subject to something, anything, else.

Bast's fingers loosened their grip a little and he shifted her in his arms. "What are you thinking? If we can show the courts we've got that covered, we might get some breathing room."

Hel wasn't so sure that was the case, but she pushed on regardless. Whatever happened to her, the world didn't need another Melding. Especially not one she could've prevented by surrendering herself to her father. She needed to sort this out before she could give up fighting. For little Kaia and her mother. For Ra. For all the people they would leave behind when the inevitable finally caught up with them.

"We could use the same approach you tried with the Water Court—push the contagion into the structure and let it destroy it for us."

"I like it," Bast said immediately. "We can head back to Patuna Chasm and give it a shot once we've got things sorted at Taranaki."

Hel nodded agreement and kept the rest of her plan to herself. This was their last chance. They couldn't keep hoping a solution would present itself. They were risking too much. If this didn't work, the Council wouldn't need to hunt her down because she would portal herself straight to her father and give herself up without them. She was going to die anyway. She'd rather remove the danger of the structures before she went, but she needed to accept that might not be possible. She couldn't let her father cause another melding.

As if sensing the tenor of her thoughts, Bast bit down on her earlobe hard enough to jolt her from her thoughts. "Don't give up. Don't leave me," he whispered.

There was nothing she could say to that. She didn't have a choice. It was really just a matter of how she went at this point. Turning her face, she pressed her lips hard to his, kissing him with all the desperate bitterness filling her.

It wasn't fucking fair.

He kissed her back just as hard, just as desperate. And they flew on in silence.

The clouds closed in again as they hit land hours later. At least, Hel assumed that's what it was. The air felt different and the salt-tang scent of the ocean faded. She still couldn't see much of anything in the darkness and Bast was keeping them screened with his power in the hazy, damp mist, out of sight of any threats below them.

They had to cross most of the North Island of Aotearoa to reach the mountain on its western coast. She wasn't sure where exactly they were approaching from, but she could tell their flight path was taking them over multiple inhabited areas, or at least areas that used to be inhabited. It felt like her organs were trying to drop out of her body every time they passed over a mass of lingering souls. The dead called to her with silent voices, clamouring for her attention. If it wasn't for the warm steel of Bast's muscles wrapped tight around her and the downward pull of those souls, she would have been adrift as all other sensation lost its meaning. Nerves and synapses misfired under the pressure. Gravity became a dizzy mirage. The wind pulling at her hair became razor blades of nausea.

"Stay with me, sweetheart," Bast murmured into her hair. She could feel the tension in him as he pushed his body to fly harder, faster. "You'll feel better with some rest. We're almost there."

"No more people," Hel said, the pleading words more of a whimper.

"Only Ivy. Her safehouse is away from the town. Isolated. Just hang in there."

There was nothing to hang onto, though. Nothing except the presence of the man holding her. His power both her saviour and her executioner.

The black of his hair and wings blended with the night,

his physical form obscured. Hel's eyes slipped shut, and she let the darkness seep through her mind until there were no more thoughts.

HEL WOKE to the relief of crisp clean sheets against her skin rather than the bruising pressure of the long flight in Bast's arms. Gentle birdsong drifted through what sounded like an open window nearby. Through her still closed eyelids, she could see that light had returned to the world. Gravity that had seemed so ethereal the night before now pulled at her limbs like a leaden weight, holding her down.

The taint of the souls that had almost overwhelmed her as they flew still threatened on the edge of her awareness, but at least there were few dead to call to her wherever they'd landed. Isolated, Bast had said. She could feel the truth of that in a way she shouldn't be able to. It was in her every breath that wasn't halting. In the absence of deaths flashing in the dark. Even so, she felt like someone had slashed the veins of her soul and she was slowly bleeding out her essence. Fighting to prise her eyes open, she winced against the pain of light on her too sensitive retina before letting them roll closed again.

"Oh good. You're finally awake," a husky female voice said from nearby.

Hel's eyes snapped open and she forced her fatigued muscles to sit up in a crunch as adrenaline filled her. Waking to an unfamiliar voice was never a good thing. The elemental who'd spoken perched in a window seat, her metallic wings a mixture of rose and white-gold draping around her like a feathered cloak. Long hair, a similar colour, tumbled in flawless curls around her face, contrasting against the sleek, black lounging dress she wore that clung to every curve. Her soft lips pulled up in a smile more calculated than welcoming as Hel stared longer than was polite.

Hel could feel this woman's power, but she'd somehow avoided taking the most obvious colours of a court when she was trained. She was as unique as Bast that way. With the metallic colours glinting in her feathers hinting at golds, oranges, and coppers, she could've been from the Air, Fire, or even Earth Courts. It would be a warm counterpart to the cold silver of Bast's power. They'd look exquisite together, wings outstretched and brushing.

He should have mated with someone like her. As perfect as she was, she probably would've figured out how to avoid the soul taint in no time and they would have had perfect little babies. Hel pushed the surge of bitter jealousy down deep and kept her face neutral. She could feel Bast's concern from somewhere nearby and instinctively turned her face in the direction she could sense him.

"He was by your side until ten minutes ago. He's taking a shower. I told him I'd keep an eye on you," the woman said.

"You're Ivy?" Hel asked.

The woman nodded.

She didn't look like an Ivy, other than the way she'd crept into Hel's room to spy on her. Hel suspected it was an alias, and she wondered who she was hiding from. She wouldn't be the first powerful elemental to come to Aotearoa to avoid the Elemental Ruling Council and their courts.

Swinging her legs over the side of the bed, Hel paused to let the room stop spinning. As sensitive as she'd become to the dead, she could confidently point to the nearest grave-yard—almost due north and probably only a ten-minute flight. She could feel the souls creeping closer. Drawn by her or Bast, she couldn't tell. It wouldn't make any difference once they arrived. She used tendrils of Bast's power to draw the tattered remains of her protections back into place.

"You're not what I imagined," Ivy said, and Hel started as she realised she'd become lost in her head again and forgotten all about the other woman.

"How so?"

"I always thought he'd fall for someone full of warmth and life. His opposite. Someone like Ra. You have a darkness to you. And you look ... faded."

Hel raised an eyebrow. Full of warmth and life. Much like Ivy herself, who looked like the gentle rays of dawn turning the sky to peachy colour, compared to the core of Hel's power that was like the searing hot plasma of a blue star's core.

"Better faded than blind. You think him cold like the bodies of the dead? He's literally overflowing with the power of innumerable lives. He shines with it. The dead gift him that power because of his care for people—his warmth—not because he's cold. My faded, dark self *is* his fucking opposite." She managed not to add *bitch* to the end of that sentence. It was a near thing.

"You are neither faded, nor dark. Your soul is literally bleeding out of your body into the place between and you still burn bright," Bast interjected from the doorway. "Can I really not leave you alone with her for five minutes without you trying to test her?" he added, addressing his question to Ivy.

"I needed to make sure she was good enough for you," Ivy said.

"You really fucking didn't. She has enough to deal with."

Hel glared at an unrepentant Ivy, who merely shrugged. She could tell she wouldn't get anywhere arguing with that woman.

"How long was I out for this time?" Hel asked, turning her back on the annoyingly beautiful woman.

"Just the rest of the night and the morning. It's early afternoon," Bast said.

He came to sit next to her on the bed as he spoke, brushing her hair away from her cheek and searching her face for something. Signs of impending death, probably. Hel resisted the urge to lean into his touch.

"Did you get hold of Ra?" she asked.

Bast patted a lump in his pocket she assumed was a new phone and nodded. "There's a perimeter of Nerida's scouts just outside the city's borders watching for us and the usual spies inside. They're not arming themselves for an assault. Yet. They've probably hacked the satellites and vulnerable camera feeds as well."

"Will you take out her scouts?" Ivy asked.

"I'm not discussing details with you, Ivy. What you don't know can't be used against us."

Hel couldn't help the surge of satisfaction she felt at his rejection of the glamourous elemental and immediately regretted it as Bast looked down at her with a smug expression. His hand snuck around her waist to stroke at a patch of bare skin where her shirt had pulled up in her sleep. The teasing contact amplified her awareness of his power and the sensation of souls rocketing towards them returned like a sledgehammer to her nerves.

"We need to leave," she rasped.

Bast frowned in concern and Ivy's protest droned in the

distance, the words barely registering as Hel fought to stabilise her spinning soul.

Bast's voice alone penetrated the chaos of her essence, sounding far distant. "I'm fine, Ivy. The wound is barely a scar. My energy levels are good enough to make the flight."

She noticed when Ivy stepped close enough to put a hand on Bast's shoulder, though. Even as disoriented as Hel was, with a haze slowly descending on her vision, she reacted. Or perhaps it was because of how disoriented she was that she reacted. Either way, the effect was the edge of her blade pressed to Ivy's throat as her other hand gripped tight to her perfect dawn-coloured locks. A buzz of power registered in the distance and it was second nature to grasp for the entwined strands of her and Bast's magic to block whatever the woman was trying as a thin ribbon of red dripped down her throat.

"Helaine. Love. Come back to me," Bast's voice murmured.

Warm lips pressed just below her ear and her eyes fluttered shut. Her hand loosened and her blade dropped. Turning towards him, her eyes searched out Bast's as she calmed her ragged breathing.

"*Mine*," she silently mouthed.

"Yours," he agreed.

A little of the blind need to kill left her. Maybe someone like Ivy would be better for Bast. Someone whose presence didn't put his entire world at risk. Someone whose love grew from friendship rather than hatred. She didn't fucking care. She was done fighting this thing between them. If she only had hours or days left in this world, they would be hours or days where he belonged to her, and her alone. If that meant she belonged to him too, so be it.

"We need to go," he said, echoing her earlier words as his eyes dropped to her lips and his strong fingers traced a line along her jaw. "Go shower and change. You're still covered in my blood."

Hel blinked and came back to herself a little more, fighting to drag her awareness back into the world. Her steps dragged as she headed to the bathroom.

Ivy's quiet voice echoed through her thoughts as she pulled the door closed behind her. "She's becoming rabid."

Hel pressed her ear to the wood to hear Bast's response. "No more than any other newly mated person. You asked for that."

The fading sound of Ivy's flirtatious laugh almost had Hel storming back out into the room, but the sooner she got clean, the sooner they could fucking leave.

"Are you going to ask me?" Bast said as they flew over the tip of the near-perfect triangle of the mountain and powered up towards the scattering of clouds drifting overhead. The effervescence of his amusement was almost enough to distract her from the soul taint's erosion of her mind, which she knew was what he intended.

"No," she snapped back, annoyed at the defensiveness she couldn't keep from her voice.

"Ivy helped me out when I was running from Ty's assassins before the Melding. I'm still not sure why. We've helped each other on and off over the years since then."

"Is that what they're calling it these days?" Hel snarked, immediately regretting the jealous words.

Silence fell for a moment and then Bast threw his head

back and let loose peals of laughter. His chest vibrated against her where he carried her until she couldn't help but smile wryly.

"It was never like that. At least, not for long," he said when he'd got himself under control. "She wasn't interested in my casual approach to sex, and I wasn't interested in anything more."

Hel squirmed a little in his grasp as she resisted the urge to ask what he was interested in now. She could feel the answer in her soul. The words were a reassurance she shouldn't need.

"I think you made her almost as jealous as she made you, Hellcat. She just hides it better."

"So modest," Hel replied, even while she wound her fingers instinctively tighter into his shirt, holding him close.

Bast smiled and leaned his face closer, running his nose up her throat until she shivered in his arms. But when she turned into him, his expression had changed to concern.

"Your skin is freezing," he said, peering closer at her. "And it's taken on a grey tinge."

Hel glanced at the skin of her wrist where it rested on his shoulder and winced. She'd thought it might just be her deteriorating vision slowly turning the world monochrome that made it look grey. It was more translucent as well. She could make out each too-slowly pulsing vein running down her forearm.

"How bad is that?" Hel asked.

"We should go home and—"

"No!" Hel interrupted. "No," she said again, more calmly. "Dealing with the shards is more important. They're too dangerous."

Bast growled in frustration, but she could feel his reluctant agreement. "Ra said Tir might have something to try and help you, but they need to talk to you first. We're heading there by nightfall, no matter what. You're just as important as those shards. If we weren't passing over the chasm anyway, I'd leave it until tomorrow."

The familiar cool tingle of his power thrummed through her as they flew on, pushing back some of the greyness. But as soon as she told him to conserve his energy, the colour started fading from herself and the world again. She didn't have much longer. Nightfall might not be soon enough. The chill sinking into her bones only deepened when they reached the familiar chasm and her mind flashed back to the tortured deaths of their scouts. That memory was all she needed to start to freefall, or perhaps those souls still lingered. She whimpered as phantom limbs were torn from her body.

"Stay with me, sweetheart," Bast whispered, kissing her cold lips and breathing raw power into her lungs to hold the pain at bay.

They landed on the chasm's lip overlooking the dead wyrm and the pinnacle of meteorite that was her father's structure. She could barely process the images as she clung to Bast, sliding down his body until she was crouched on the ground. One hand was pressed hard to the limestone and the other pressed to her temples, as if she could hold back the souls with just that touch.

Bast didn't waste any time. She could feel his power uncoiling to fill the space around them, latching onto the sphere of absence that was the contagion below them to try and use it to damage the shard. She watched through slitted eyes as the ball of darkness throbbed in the river bed, fighting Bast's efforts to move it. The sphere containing it grew in a lurching movement, stretching to consume more of the wyrm skeleton it was nestled inside.

The stream flowing along the chasm had split to travel around either side of the darkness. Now, where the contagion brushed against, it dissolved to nothing. The remaining water reared back from the poisonous absence, directed by Bast's power to find safety and leaving a new line of exposed streambed dry and accusing in the afternoon light.

Bast was crouching next to her now, sweat beading his brow and his breathing ragged as he fought to shift the contagion, even the small amount he had in Nerida's ocean while keeping it tightly contained.

"It's fighting me. There's no living beings to draw it forward," he ground out.

"We need to use my power, too," Hel said.

"No! You're too vulnerable. The souls would swarm you as soon as you reached for it."

Bast's power surged again as he desperately tried to shift the darkness. Hel bit her lip to keep from crying out as the torrent of magic drew the souls surrounding them closer, threatening to drag her soul from her body. She could feel the dead like a whirlpool spinning around their connection. The view of the chasm faded before her and instead there was only death. Everywhere.

Burning contagion speared her abdomen and she twisted in vain with a body of scales trying to free herself.

Wings tore from her back.

The beak of an ancient griffin disembowelled her as she twisted through limestone.

She screamed in silence and endless darkness. The sensation of rock against her fingers told her she wasn't dead yet. She needed to stay strong a little longer. Bast needed to concentrate. This was their last chance. She would have to leave from here to go to her father if he failed. Maybe she could use the shard to reach him. She wasn't sure she could manage her own power in her current state. And she didn't have a clue how to reach his home planet. She wouldn't have to portal far, though. Any distance would draw his hunters and then she could collapse instead of their reality collapsing in another melding.

"Can you do it?" she whispered, knowing the answer would determine whether she had to hold on or whether she could let go.

CHAPTER 14

BAST

Bast almost didn't hear Hel's words over the rush of power flowing through him. The contagion hadn't shifted an inch.

A soft thump next to him tugged at his attention and he pulled his gaze from the river below them to the woman by his side. He blinked in confusion. Her body sprawled on the ground, her skin a sickly colour not unlike the grey-white of the limestone that lined this section of the chasm. As he watched, the definition of her cheekbones became sharper and her closed eyes became sunken. It was as if her body was collapsing in on itself, losing all its moisture and softness. If he didn't stop its progress, she'd be nothing but skin pulled taught across a skeleton.

Fear stabbed through him as he felt her essence drifting into the place between, barely a wisp of her soul clinging to her body. Grasping with his power in panic, he held tight to that tiny piece of her. Even when it threatened to dissipate like smoke into ether.

Bast released the contagion he'd been fighting to move

and scooped his mate up into his arms. Her weight barely registered as the soul taint stole her muscle. Staring down at her face in desperation, he knew his power wouldn't be enough to pull her back this time. Ra's words from that morning echoed through his mind as panic threatened—*Tir knows about her. He won't betray her secrets, but he said he'd found something that might help anchor your protection to her.*

Time seemed to slow as Bast grasped for Hel's power. It was too late to worry about her hunters or the souls swarming. She was all but dead. Holding Tir's image in his mind, Bast focused his mate's fading magic on his desperation to reach the Archivist. They'd just have to hope Tir was still safely inside Soul Tower's wards. If Bast needed to fight off Hel's hunters to save her, he would. The alternative was unacceptable. Unbearable.

The familiar taste of Hel's power sprung up on the breeze, the heat of a sun's core twining through the air before him. His hands clenched tight on Hel's weakening body and his muscles tensed in protest as he waited for the shimmering rift in reality to stabilise before them. Red eyes flashed in the scrub nearby and he strode through the portal the second its edges became defined. When he released Hel's power, it made an audible snap as tiles replaced the earth beneath his feet and the rift closed. A fading hound's yelp drifted in the study they'd emerged into.

Tentacles wrapped tight around his throat before he had a chance to say anything and a terrifying array of hinged jaws lined with razor-sharp teeth filled his vision. He flared his wings wide, heedless of the objects he was knocking to the floor, and the tentacles loosened.

"You're lucky I didn't kill you before I realised who it

was," Tir said, their sibilant voice chasing the last of the chasm's echoes from the room.

"She's dying," Bast said. As the words passed his lips, the desperation that had been keeping him going collapsed and he fell to his knees with a ragged cry.

"She's not dead yet. Put her down and give me some space," Tir snapped.

"What are you going to do?"

"Ra said you anchor your wards in the structure of your wings?" Tir asked.

Bast nodded.

"I'm going to return Helaine to her true form," Tir said.

"You ... what?" Bast said, staring uncomprehendingly at the being who was unique in their world.

"Her mother used her power to shift her shape when she was a baby. A power we shared. I can give Hel back her wings. You'll need to do the rest."

Wings. Hel's wings.

Questions whirled in Bast's mind as he struggled to process. He could ask them later. If there was a later.

"Do it," he said, already preparing the protective ward against the soul taint that Ra and Zee's scans had shown him how to weave.

A tentacle winding around his wrist reminded him he was still holding his mate clenched tight in his arms. Taking a deep breath, he set her down gently on the wool rug in the centre of the room.

"Not on her back," Tir murmured, their face taut with concentration.

Bast rolled Hel onto her front and twined his fingers through hers. He couldn't have stopped touching her if he tried. The feel of her icy, clammy, skin threatening to rip if he gripped too hard was heart breaking.

Like he had that night in their apartment when he'd last tried this, he opened himself fully to their connection and let her power wend through his own as he reconstructed the multi-dimensional protections that kept the soul taint at bay for him. The vaccine to the infection of his power. With Hel unconscious, the process was slow and draining. He was grateful they'd tried this once before so he already knew the places her power could reinforce his efforts, re-shaping the ward into one that would work for her if they could just find a way to anchor it to her body.

Throughout, he kept his eyes trained on the interdimensional being leaning over Hel's prone form. The liquid shadow of Tir's power filled the space and Bast had the sensation of an unanswered call growing progressively stronger. The tentacles drifting from their head, medusa-like, undulated independently as they touched every part of Hel's body, almost like each one had its own sentience. Bast gripped Hel's hand tighter and resisted the urge to shove Tir away.

"She is not there to respond to the call," Tir said, real concern now evident in their voice.

"Can you shift her anyway? She might not return until the protection is in place."

Tir's nebulous eyes met his and Bast could see the doubt there. "You will have to make the response for her, soul-weaver. And we will have to hope that your efforts at holding back the mating bond were unsuccessful, because it will only work if there is a part of you in every cell of her."

Bast swallowed hard. Had he destroyed her by trying to

save her? Beneath his fingers, Hel's pulse fractured and stumbled.

"Call," he growled at Tir, and then he dived deeper into the connection between him and his infuriating, beautiful, vulnerable mate than he ever had before.

Here in the tower where his magic was strongest, he drew deep on the silver of his power to send it surging through her body. It forced the blood to keep pulsing through her veins and formed thick strands that stood in for the muscles that had faded to nothing in the space of less than an hour.

With his awareness absorbed in the shell of Hel's essence, he could feel exactly what Tir meant by the call now. That liquid shadow encasing her body was pulling, cajoling, entreating her cells to take on the form of their birth. Holding tight to that last part of Hel's soul that still resided in her, he sent that call further, letting it reverberate into the place between where his Hellcat drifted in a haze of unknowing. He refused to let up, adding his own essence to the call and begging her to accept the change. Begging her to fight for herself. To fight for them.

Her answer to that call was barely more than a whisper—a fraction of a memory of a thought. All he could feel of it was her need to protect him from their shared death. It would have to be enough. He amplified it, transmuted it, turned it into the instruction her cells needed to survive. His power wove her faltering answer back into her essence until her body stopped fighting them, even if her soul still drifted elsewhere.

Hel's fingers gripped tight in his own twitched, a subconscious response, and the taste of Tir's shadow magic grew stronger. Bast breathed in his mate's fading scent and held fast as he felt her cells tremble and start to shift. He held fast as her magic screamed in pain when her body could not. He held fast as that last piece of her soul threatened to tear away from the anchor of a physical form that was becoming unfamiliar, other. Refusing to let her go, he sheltered the dying ember of her soul deep inside his chest where it settled with a snap like a dislocated limb finally settling back into its place.

"It is done. Work your ward quickly Bastion, or we're going to lose her," Tir said, their voice so distant that Bast wondered if they'd slipped between dimensions.

A piercing pain in the hand not holding Hel brought him back to himself and he looked down to see his blood dripping from Tir's jaws.

"Now!" the Archivist snapped.

Bast rewound his essence that had unravelled into Hel and found the magical construct he'd made for her waiting for him, held whole and present by the souls infused into the tower's defences. Without them, it would have been lost in the same way he'd lost himself in Hel's body.

Thank you, he sent to them.

The last part of the working was almost anti-climactic. The ward integrated into her new body like it had been purpose-made for whatever she was, because it had. He'd woven every piece he knew of her into its design. He could feel the places where Hel's power had fused with his own, paving the way for the magic to wend through her new wings that he hadn't had time to even glance at. With his eyes closed and focused deep inside her, he could feel they weren't like his own. Not anything like elemental anatomy. But they still held the hollow spaces and nested power that would feed and anchor his protections, allowing the ward to self-reinforce and maintain itself.

Bast blinked his eyes open as he severed the last connection between himself and the ward he'd created. His pulse thundered in his ears as he waited to confirm the protection would hold. One breath. Two. Three. It was still there; had already become just another part of a new body that his mate wouldn't recognise and a connection impossibly deeper between them she might reject. The whispers of the souls in his mind confirmed his success.

It worked. We can resist her now. And she can resist us.

Thank fuck, Bast sent back, and grinned as one of the old souls slapped him with a painful zap of power for his language.

The grin only held until Tir's tentacles pulled back from Hel's new form and he realised she was still limp. Still unresponsive.

"Did it work?" Tir asked.

"It did. But she's lost deep in the place of the dead. I might not be able to pull her back."

"You will," Tir said, their conviction ringing in the room.

Bast bent forward to scoop Hel into his arms and almost toppled forward over her body. Even with the wellspring of power stored in the fabric of his tower, he had overstretched. Where before, he might have pushed through to carry her through sheer force of will, that would no longer be possible. Wings almost as broad as his own flared out from between her shoulders. They were a bright silver, the exact shade of his power. At a distance, he guessed they might fool people into thinking they were feathered, especially given they were overlaid with the black feathered tattoo of his mating mark, but this close they looked almost bio-engineered, made of angled shards of overlapping metallic ... something—bone, cartilage, stardust, who knew.

Reaching out, he stroked the surface, surprised at how warm and soft it felt despite its appearance. Where his fingers touched, the blue lightning of her power danced. He let his hand drift higher and pushed strands of her now pure silver hair from her face. The ever-widening lock of silver hair that she'd blamed on their mating had taken over and there was no black left, except for the deep black of the twin curved horns now nestled in her hair, twisting into sharpened points.

"It's like she was made for me," Bast whispered as the full effect of their silver/black symmetry became apparent.

"That will be the effect of how much of your power was involved in the shift," Tir said. "She's probably going to be pissed off about it."

Bast winced. Yeah. Hel wasn't exactly forgiving when she thought he'd messed with her body without her consent. And rightly so. The thought refocused him. First, he needed to get her conscious again. Then she could rip him a new one for the colour scheme.

A portal of shadow opened nearby and Tir bent down to pick up Hel, their tentacles wrapping around her wings to keep her stable. Bast gritted his teeth hard as he fought not to snap at the being for their presumption. It wasn't like he could carry Hel in his current state, he reminded himself. He drew the line at letting Tir precede him through the portal they'd opened, though. Who knew where it might lead? Staggering to his feet, he stumbled through the rift alongside them, and into his bedroom several floors above the study.

Tir placed Hel on the bed and turned to face him. "Bring

her home. She deserves to have one," they said, and then they stepped back through the portal and left.

Bast looked down at the woman on his bed and studied her body that was so familiar and yet so different. He'd never experienced a magic that could shift someone's body like that, but, as he looked closer, he could see the clues of Hel's true form had been there all along, had probably even been part of her appeal to him when they'd first met.

Whether from Tir's shapeshifting magic or his own power, she had regained the familiar muscle tone he'd always admired in her. Muscle tone that he'd never quite realised was more similar to an elemental than the human he'd assumed her to be. She'd always had that extra sleek density to the muscles in her torso. As if even with her wings missing, her body still accounted for their absent drag. It had been there in the way she moved as well, her weight poised further forward than a human might to counterbalance those beautiful structures now gracefully folded at her back. And it had been there in her joy in flight and her surprising stamina for staying with him in the air, even if it she could only do so in his arms.

Sitting down beside her, he stroked the beautiful silver of her wings, revelling in their softness. They were both creatures of the air and, even when neither of them had known it, that fundamental aspect of their natures had called to each other.

Bast added that realisation to the myriad other ways in which they fit and merged the whole into the now too familiar process of pulling back his mate from the depths of the place between life and death. She really needed to stop fucking almost dying. It occurred to him he couldn't really talk because he actually *had* died on her, but that had just been the once.

Guilt at what his power had done to her threatened to dilute his focus. He forced himself to concentrate only on Hel and that ember of her existence still flickering inside him as if the slightest breeze would extinguish it. Feeding that tiny ember every drop of passion he felt for his bewitching mate, he immersed himself in memory—each stolen kiss, each clash of wills, each unexpected moment of protection.

Tir had said she deserved a home. She did. The day they'd mated, they'd unwittingly become that home for each other. Regardless of whether it was what either of them would have chosen, he was damned if he'd ever leave her out in the cold. Bast stoked that ember inside him with power and memory until it flared bright in the darkness of the place between, forming a beacon she could follow. A bastion of light and warmth to draw her back.

His head spun. His energy reserves were failing. Gritting his teeth, he held fast even as he slumped onto the bed beside her, so near that his eyelashes brushed her cheek when they fluttered closed. Her soft breaths were icy cold against his skin and it was only when they finally warmed and he couldn't hold on a moment more that he let everything go. She still hadn't woken, but if he kept going, he would follow her into the depths.

His last thought before he succumbed to exhaustion was a silent plea to the unreachable dead beyond the veil that it had been enough.

THE SOFT BRUSH of wings against his own was what finally pulled Bast from the darkness of his unconscious. He blinked in the shadows, the peach blush of the light reflecting on the ceiling suggesting it was either dawn or dusk, but who knew what day. The woman beside him slept on, despite her movements waking him. He brushed a lock of metallic silver hair behind her ear, unable to resist the urge to let his fingers carry on to gently trace the unfamiliar horns that now graced her scalp. His fingertips stayed pressed to her as he tried and failed to make himself disconnect from the tactile reinforcement that his mate was alive. Time lost meaning as his awareness of the world narrowed down to that single pulsing point of connection against his skin.

He was finally jerked from the state of meditation by Hel's voice, barely more than a whisper, and gravelly with fatigue.

"Tickles," she complained.

But instead of shifting away, she turned her body into his.

Bast reached out his other hand to stroke down the still unfamiliar wing draped over her side and regretted it immediately as Hel's body stiffened in shock and she tried to bolt upright. *Tried* being the operative word, because the hand she attempted to use to push herself upright was resting on her other wing, effectively pinning herself to the bed. He couldn't quite hide his chuckle as he watched the endearing confusion on her face.

"What the fuck did you do now?" Hel hissed, not impressed with his reaction.

Her eyes widened as she tried to make sense of the no doubt confusing sensations coming from her new wings.

"You were dying. Tir shifted you back to your true form

so we could anchor my shielding in your wings," Bast said, schooling his face back to neutral even though her anger had shifted her from adorable confusion to sexy as hell and all he really wanted to do was kiss her until she stopped freaking out. Well, that and eat his body weight in meat and wash the mud and sweat from his skin. It had been a long few indeterminate number of days.

"And did anyone think to ask me if I fucking wanted that?" Hel fumed.

"Did we ask your completely unconscious and dying body if you wanted to live? No. I try not to make a habit of talking to myself and I just figured I'd go with you not dying. If you can't bring yourself to be glad I'm still alive, maybe you can cope with the fact that the next time the contagion pops up here I'll still be able to stop it from killing everyone and destroying the world."

He regretted the defensive words as soon as he spoke them. The reminder of what the world was facing seemed to crush all the fight out of her and he watched as the beautiful glint of her raging emotions flickered out of her eyes and her expression slackened.

"I need to go," she whispered, pushing away from him and struggling into a sitting position.

"What are you talking about? You just almost died. You need to rest and eat. A shower wouldn't hurt either." Even that comment didn't get him more than a dull glance as she limped toward the bathroom letting her new wings drag along the floor behind her.

Frustrated at her silence, he followed her into the en-suite, both of them ignoring the intimacy of the moment as they worked around each other. At least, he thought that was what they were doing. Hel seemed more like she was working so much on auto-pilot that she wasn't even conscious he was there. When she started struggling to get the shreds of her shirt off around her wings, he stepped in to help. As the last scraps of fabric drifted to the tiles, he gently propelled her into the shower and wordlessly took over washing the days of travel and fighting from her, starting with her hair. If he'd thought that might have brought her back to life, he was wrong. Even his hands brushing over the curving black horns she probably hadn't yet noticed existed had no effect on her malaise.

"Talk to me. Please," he whispered in her ear, pulling her body back against him as he rinsed the shampoo from her hair.

Her head fell back against his shoulder and he felt her take a shuddering breath. "The hunters. The shards. It's all my father. We can't let him start another melding. I need to go to him."

Bast's hands stilled where they had been stroking down her arms. "Your father," he repeated, his mind swirling with the implications of this new information.

"Yes."

"And how will he use you to stop the contagion exactly?"

"By sacrificing me. My guardian ... my mother ... always told me he would kill me if he caught me. She just never told me why. I guess it makes sense now. The contagion needs to be fixed. I'm not even sure I can hate him for it anymore."

"He wants to kill you," Bast said, incredulous and fuming.

"To save everyone else," Hel replied, no intonation in her words.

"That doesn't fucking work for me," Bast growled.

"Have you got another option? One that will work before

he causes a melding?" Hel asked, spinning to face him and glaring into his eyes.

He opened his mouth to reply when for the second time in his existence his reality was plunged into darkness and absolute silence stretched taut with pressure across the world, as if the darkness was an inverse strike of lightning and every living being awaited the thunder to follow.

"It's too late," he whispered.

The second Melding had begun.

His words were silent, eaten by the absence that surrounded them, but his mate was part of him and he could feel her hear the words, accept them. The burning flame he so cherished in her flared back to life as if it was pushing back the surrounding darkness.

The moments of primordial chaos as the realities combined and all frame of reference disappeared could have been endless or a single breath. They hung together on the precipice of a new world, poised against an attack it was too late to avoid. When everything else around them was in a state of flux, he'd never been more grateful for the constant of Hel's presence as the sun around which he orbited.

Light snuck back into the world in shards and whispers. They both sensed the tsunami of dying souls from the crashing of another world into their own already damaged and fragile melded realities. So many lives extinguished. So many people lost. Again.

His mate's response, when it came, sunk into his bones. It was devastating guilt and raging vengeance; endless grief and staunch endurance. He could taste her power gathering, all fiery plasma and heat. They'd been too late to prevent the Melding. With its advent came the freedom of having nothing more to lose by resisting.

"I'll never submit to him. I will drive his power out of our world and never let it back," she growled.

Bast clung to her as the first swells of the vast numbers of the newly dead threatened to tear his mind adrift.

"We will. Together."

CHAPTER 15
HEL

Somehow, the shower was still functioning despite reality itself collapsing around them. Hel was distantly aware of warm water falling on her skin, running in rivulets down the wings on her back that felt as awkward as they did right.

When their world's essence had broken and re-formed, she'd instinctively reached for Bast with her power. They'd reached for each other. And even through the terror of absolute darkness and the moment, the age, where there was an absence of everything, he'd been there. Their connection was so much deeper than it had been and her head was frighteningly clear after months of the looming dead constantly in the background dragging her under.

Bast's arms were still wrapped around her and she buried her face in his chest where her mark was indelibly etched into the skin over his heart. Through Bast's power running through her, she could feel the massive roiling energy of so many deaths around the world, and through her own power that was born of the connections between worlds, she could feel the surging energy points that had come from the melding of another reality into theirs. The new reality tasted of blood and violence tempered with swathes of too-silent shadow. Only time would tell what that meant for the Melded Earths where three realities now needed to co-exist.

She winced as pain distracted her from her thoughts. Her magic felt too full—burning paths of fire through her she could only survive because of the chilling waves of Bast's soulweaving power holding her steady. It would take time for the realities to stabilise and a new balance to form. Until then, they would compete with each other. The mental strength of the Melded Earths' occupants, new and old alike, would determine which came out on top. Reality was once again in the eye of the beholder—fluid. And her power would surge where the points of conflict arose.

In the first Melding, the elementals had come out on top by virtue of an instinctive understanding of the premise of this magic, but they'd had to compete with the influence of the sheer number of humans that populated the Earths. If another magical intelligent species came with this new Melding, elemental supremacy might be challenged.

The thought didn't scare her with so much magic flooding through her. She could feel the City of Souls around them held stable by the network of souls Bast had established at the last Melding.

"We'll never have access to as much power as we do right now," Hel murmured, her lips brushing against Bast's pec as she spoke into his chest. "At least, I hope we won't."

"We'd better make use of it then," Bast replied. His words reaching her ears as if from a vast distance even while they felt like they were sinking into her skin. "Last time, I used the power released to stabilise the city, but this time our defences have held. We're fine, even if the rest of the world wasn't so lucky. I hope there were no people here in the other reality because they would've been annihilated."

Hel was only half listening to him, the other part of her immersed in the new sensations so much power brought with it. She felt like if she just reached a little further, she could speak to the world itself, just like Bast did to the dead. Pulling on that part of Bast's power, she wove it through her own as he fed it to her, the sensation of their magic wending together every bit as intimate as the way his hands caressed her.

The response that came back from the world when it came was nothing like speech. It was flashes of understanding, stark images, and deep emotion. It was a juxtaposition of patience in the face of apocalyptic change, and the wrench of an identity subsumed and forced to become something else. The world was broken, fragile, damaged, and enduring. What was time to something so vast? The universe exploded into being yesterday. Continents formed tomorrow. Life sprung into being sometime before it dragged itself to land.

Fangs flashed with blood in the darkness. The beat of a thousand elemental wings filled the sky. A high-rise crumbled into dust and the dead swirled inward faster and faster.

"Hel!" Bast's voice called her back from the timeless, referenceless sensation.

As she pulled away a little from the connection with the melded earths, she could feel more of the whole. The new third reality was harshly distinct where it pushed tight against the two that were more integrated. The world felt balanced on a knife-edge of sanity, the forced transformation threatening to catapult it into being murderously inhospitable with wildly changeable personalities. Reaching out with the vast power available to her, she comforted and calmed. She knew what it felt like to wake in a different form she hadn't chosen, and she knew what it was like to want to burn everything down to the ground. She couldn't let that happen.

If you own this, you take his control away. Your evolution can give you strength. Don't let him win, she told the vulnerable Earths.

Her words were not enough to heal the world. They weren't even enough to stabilise it. But they focused the Earths' attention on her instead of the chaos inside them and she, in turn, focused on finding an outlet for their shared torrent of power and grief.

Through her connection to the world, she could sense each dark spot of contagion around the globe and the spheres of Bast's power holding them contained. She could sense the shards of stasis her father had built, now spent and devoid of magic but still tasting of his power. And she could feel the link between those points and *him,* far in the distance. With power burning through her, begging to be used, it took mere seconds to follow that trail in her mind until her father's location set in her brain like a galactic GPS.

"I found him," she told Bast.

"I know. You're using both our powers, both our senses. I can see everything you see. There's a huge concentration of contagion not far from him. A huge concentration of death," he replied, although she couldn't have said if either of them had actually spoken aloud.

Hel twisted in frustration as she floated in awareness. The solution was on the tip of her brain, but she didn't have the experience using magic that Bast did to know how to pull it off.

"What do you want to do?" Bast asked, sensing her annoyance, or perhaps hearing her thoughts as closely as they were linked in that moment.

"Send all the contagion and his shards back to his world," Hel said.

The vengeance in the statement was carried on a tide of determination from the world she was still communicating with. It couldn't ever go back to what it was, but it wanted the darkness gone. It knew the contagion would mean its death.

She felt Bast nod as he twined even more strands of their power together. "Then that's what we'll do," he replied, and the way forward spread through her awareness like a channel directing the floods of magic submerging them into its path.

With the help of her connection to the world, they could see everywhere the contagion existed. And with Bast's power magnified by the multitudes of dead, they could contain each dark taint. The Melded Earths themselves formed the anchor they needed to hold firm against the overwhelming volume of magic at play as Hel shaped a dozen portals across every continent and Bast lifted each spot of contagion, shepherding them toward the gates. It couldn't fight their power this time, and with her senses stretched wide, she could feel an eagerness in the darkness to shift back to a world where it might break free of Bast's constraints.

Every time her mind splintered as she worked, the three strands of realities that now made up her world pulled her back together, saving her even as she saved them. And every time Bast faltered, she did the same for him, wrapping him in her essence so he couldn't fall apart.

The silver and plasma blue of their powers wove so

tightly into each other as they worked, it was almost as if they'd melded together in the same way the earths had. It wouldn't have worked if they weren't mated. Or if the world itself hadn't responded to Hel's compassion. It was like every moment of her life, of their lives, had led to this one point where their relationship, their power, and their history created the conditions necessary to win through. That and the unwilling sacrifice of so many lives.

When the absence that was the contagion clung tight onto the boundary of the portals, it was the Melded Earths that gave the final push. They expelled the diseased reality from their essence and across light-years of space before helping knit the rent tears in existence back together and collapse every portal so nothing else could sneak through.

As her mind slowly returned to the room her body still stood in, Hel shivered in the now cold water of the shower and stared up at Bast's face leaning down close to hers. The silence of the second Melding and the space in which they'd woven their power faded. She became aware of the noise of the water, the soft sigh of Bast's breath against her cheek, the distant bang of a door in another room.

"We did it," she said, still buzzing from the remains of the excess power that had flooded through them, although she knew they would likely both soon crash from the overload.

Bast smiled down at her and reached past her to turn the water off before grabbing two giant towels and wrapping one around her. Before she could do more than return his smile, the door to the bathroom crashed open and she was being shoved behind Bast's large frame.

Ra's frantic voice echoed against the tiles. "We're under attack!"

Bast strode toward the bedroom ahead of her, wings held tight to his back with taught control as he yanked on his clothes. Hel was just as fast, but paused in the doorway realising she had nothing that would fit around her new appendages until Ra chucked something soft in her direction.

"Tir got some clothes for you," he said, a hint of kindness sneaking through his focused expression.

"Thanks," Hel replied, securing the elemental fabric in a soft drape around her neck and stroking its edges until she found the seam that would make the magic secure the garment around her wings.

She grinned a little as Bast flared his wings out to screen her from Ra's view. The hint of jealousy and protectiveness in him even as their shared overwhelming need to protect the city dominated their connection warmed some of the chill she was feeling.

"Report," he snapped, as Hel heard more footsteps enter the room.

It was Morrigan's voice that replied as Hel dragged on a pair of jeans and her boots.

"Three squadrons from the Air Court converging on the Tower. The south, east, and west scout outposts have engaged them, but they're outnumbered. I don't know how, but they timed it with the Melding. They must have been waiting nearby."

Bast's power flared and Hel could feel him activating the magical protections on the Tower that would extend from the building's crown down through the twisting metals of its sides to sheathe it in sparkling silver soulwoven power. Gently pushing his still flared wing aside, she squeezed his arm in support as she felt the beginnings of burn-out in her mate, in both of them. They were running on fumes.

It was only the sheer volume of still surging power flooding the world that was keeping them upright, and it was that same power that would burn them to a crisp if they let it. Hel's connection to the new world had helped anchor them both to consciousness, but it was fading. Such fragile temporary beings as they were couldn't hold the attention of an entire world for long.

A low whistle sounded and Hel glanced over at Ra leaning against the doorframe.

"Holy shit. I didn't get a good look at you before Bast went all gentleman. You look badass," he said.

"Focus, Ra," Bast chided tiredly, but Hel could feel the slightest release of tension in him as Ra's words brought back a fragment of normality. "Can we hold them off?" he added, addressing Morrigan.

"Our people are shaken but largely unaffected by the Melding thanks to your protections. We've got emergency plans to deal with this and we can pick them off in a fight through the city, but there will be a lot of collateral damage. The city is built to withstand heavy wind, but it's not the same as an elemental air attack. There's already glass everywhere from the shattered windows. I lost a scout impaled by a flying power pylon. It's going to be messy as hell," she said.

"I need to draw them away from the city," Bast said, striding toward the door.

"We won't do well in open-air combat with them unless you can shield us. You know we don't have the mages for that," Morrigan snapped.

"He doesn't have the reserves to shield you as well as himself. He'd lose consciousness," Hel said, frowning.

Bast glared at her for outing his current state, but she ignored him. She wasn't going to let him do some self-sacrificing bullshit when there were clearly contingency plans in place for this kind of thing. If only there was a way to corral their attackers somewhere there were no non-combatants to get hurt. Her mind flashed to her first hunt for Tir, and an evil grin stretched across her face.

"Oh. I like that look. What's that look?" Ra said.

"We draw them to the Spiderhive. Trap them in the shields there," Hel said.

The advantage of the City of Souls being shunned by the rest of the elemental courts was that very few of them understood its history or its dangers. It was highly unlikely that Aliya's squadrons would know Bast had shielded the building to keep the winged arachdryn that nested in its depths from going on a murder spree through the city. Even with its insides now a cavernous hole, it still looked like a landmark building. With any luck, they would assume it had some strategic importance and follow them right in. And get stuck inside with the murderous spider-creatures.

Bast's eyes widened in surprise at the suggestion as Morrigan burst into bloodthirsty laughter. "Genius," she said. "Also, remind me never to get on your bad side."

"That might work, but there's no 'we'. There's no way you can learn to fly, or even run, with that unfamiliar weight in a combat situation," Bast said.

"And how are you planning to get out safely without me making a portal?" Hel asked.

Bast snorted. "They're my shields. I can get through them. And even if I couldn't, I'd just borrow your power."

Oh yeah. How had she forgotten about that?

"You can use each other's powers?" Morrigan asked,

intense curiosity in her eyes as her gaze flicked between the two of them.

A crashing explosion from outside interrupted whatever response they might have come up with and sent them all rushing towards the rooftop. Hel watched Bast for signs of fatigue as he pushed a comms device into his ear and hurriedly slung a short sword on his back. Ra passed her another comms device for her to listen in as he paused beside her on the terrace. Someone without their connection probably wouldn't notice, but she could see the effort it took Bast to lift the sword he usually wielded like it weighed no more than a soul.

"Protect him," she growled at Morrigan, both of them probably surprised at the possessive edge of violence in her voice.

"Of course," the scout-captain responded, and then the two of them were launching through the curtain of soul-woven magic and out into open air.

Overwhelming fear filled her for the half of her soul that was flying away.

"He'll be okay," Ra said.

Hel just gave a terse nod. She could feel the lethargy in Bast's flight, the fragility to the personal shield he'd extended around himself. As the first sharp arrow of pure magic shattered against it, she flinched, too conscious of the entire construct flickering like static.

"He's too drained," she whispered as they both focused on the words coming through their comms devices.

"Tornado incoming on your right..."

"Eastern squadron converging on your position."

"They're using invisible nets of air. The scouts at Midland Park are down."

Hel staggered as Bast drew deep on their shared energy to extend his protection to his people. The city had few mages thanks to the way elementals trained those with power. They were only trained in the courts and every aspect of magical learning was focused on securing their ongoing loyalty, most obviously through the changes wrought to their wing feathers to take on the colours of their liege. Even if mages wanted to move to their city, they wouldn't have been allowed to.

That was a problem now because there was at least one mage with each of Aliya's squadrons, the tell-tale white and gold of their wingspans reflecting the morning light. The only mage of any power Bast had at his disposal other than himself was Zee, and they couldn't risk drawing attention to their presence in the city.

Speaking of Zee, despite the oxidised copper colouring of their wings being nowhere in sight, Hel could see the elemental buildings they'd engineered throughout the city joining the fight. The structures might not be sentient like the courts' strongholds, but they were imbued with Zee's power and were a vital part of the city's defences. As the scouts dodged air missiles they could sense but not see, they lured the attackers lower until the causeways that crossed the golden mile of streets could fire iron-like shrapnel into the air and send vines of thick cable undulating out to snare those who flew too close. Twin five-storey buildings constructed of power, native greenery and local bedrock leaned toward each other over a narrow laneway as if seeking to kiss, crushing two Air Court soldiers flying between them.

It wasn't enough.

"Bast. The other two Air Court squadrons are heading for the bunker where the non-combatants are evacuating."

Morrigan's voice was strong and calm, but Hel could hear the fear that lay underneath.

A string of swear words came through as Bast cursed in response. "Fucking cowards. They must know it's only children and elderly there. And mostly humans."

A wave of elemental citizens took to the air as they realised where the attackers were heading. Not trained scouts now, but just the everyday people of the City of Souls. They were a city of the non-conforming. A city of people who didn't fit into the elemental world of blind loyalty to tradition. A city of survivors. And there was no way they would let Aliya's squadrons get near their vulnerable.

"Call them back! They're sitting ducks for a magical attack flying so close together," Morrigan cried.

"I didn't call them out!" Bast shouted back, even as Ra set the tsunami siren blaring in the hopes it would deter their crazy brave people from throwing their bodies in front of the attack.

A flash of familiar rose and white-gold in the distance preceded an explosion that sent a squadron scattering. Ivy must've followed them back to the city and joined the fight. Her magic wove protections above the humans and children. She could save those around her, but there were still too many Air Court soldiers. Too much space to defend.

It wouldn't be enough.

A cold clarity settled on Hel as she watched the scene play out. She couldn't let this happen. For the first time since she'd woken hours before, she stretched her new wings wide. The sensation was such a physical relief she would have revelled in the feeling of sunshine and the soft breeze against the unfamiliar surface if she wasn't watching a tragedy about to unfold before her. Despite the new nerves and feelings, they didn't feel unwieldy. In fact, it felt like they'd always been there, invisible, waiting. All she had to do was not fall.

How hard could it be? she thought, staring down the twenty-nine storey drop. *Not as hard as the ground,* her traitor brain responded.

Before she could rethink, she stepped off the edge of the building. Pulling the dregs of her power together to half-form a rift in the air above her that clashed with Bast's shielding, she sent a shower of blue-hot sparks edged in silver into the air. Hopefully, it would be enough to get all the squadrons' attention.

"Incoming," Hel choked out as she cleared the haze shielding Soul Tower and gained an unobstructed view of just how high she was.

Gravity was an anchor dragging her down. Her wings screamed in protest as she fought to keep them stretched out, catching the air. Was she supposed to flap or glide?

Fuck.

"Hel! What the fuck are you doing?" Bast yelled, making her wince in pain from the volume and spin sideways as she lost her focus.

It was just as well the majestic centre was so much higher than all the buildings around them or she would already be a bug splattered on a window.

"Three squadrons heading your way, Helaine," Morrigan's voice came hard on the heels of Bast's cry, calm and collected.

She was still losing altitude and not making any forward momentum. With a deep breath, Hel focused inward, remembering the feeling of being in Bast's arms in flight and his surging motion that had become so familiar. Stretching her awareness into each trickle of power running through the bones and membranes that stood between her and death, she let instinct and the residual memory of Bast's power running through her veins take over. A gust of wind caught beneath her wings and she pushed into it, stabilising her lurching flight.

Ahead of her, she could see the black of Bast's form speeding toward her carried on a tide of his fear. Morrigan's scouts' dive-bombing had scattered the squadron that had been pursuing him to either side, temporarily distracted. It wouldn't put them off for long. They were already regrouping, five to each side and more trailing behind. She knew if she could've glanced behind her without spinning out of control, there would be more coming in fast from behind. A surge of elemental power from that direction sent her barrelling to the left as a concentrated shard of air passed through the spot her wing had been moments before.

Just as she spun wildly out of control, two powerful hands gripped her arms, holding her steady.

Bast's breath tickled the hairs on her neck as he spoke. "You crazy, reckless woman."

"Love you, too," she snapped back. Wait. What? She shook her head as if that might shake the unintended words from existence. There wasn't time to deal with it. "We need to go."

"Fold your wings back so I can carry you," Bast said, resignation clear in his tone.

"Just until we're closer. I'm sure I can manage a controlled fall that won't kill me," Hel replied as she did as he asked.

If she didn't already know that she trusted him, this would've proven it. Mid-air, surrounded by attackers, she pulled her wings in tight and tucked herself into his body.

He took her weight and dragged them through the air toward the stacked circles of the Spiderhive in the distance that seemed so close and so impossibly far at the same time.

Bast was slowing. Too tired. Not nearly fast enough to evade even the slowest of Aliya's scouts. She could feel his muscles trembling against her body as he let them drop closer to the relative safety of the city's buildings.

"OK. The whole flying thing might've been a stretch, but if there's one thing I can do, it's run. Put me down on Lambton," Hel said.

"You'll be a sitting duck."

"No. I'll be a moving target. And I know the streets here."

CHAPTER 16

BAST

B ast cursed quietly at his stubborn mate and launched into a steep dive, the ground rushing closer as they plummeted. Waves of searing heat pushed down against him as the air itself burst into flame where they'd just been. The sound of semi-automatic weapon fire rang out from a nearby balcony. Thankfully, it was the city's human defenders joining the fray to lay down covering fire while the two of them slammed into the tar seal of the road with an impact that jarred every joint in Bast's exhausted body.

Dashing for the nearest awning to take cover from the aerial attack, Bast tried to shelter Hel's body with his wing, but she shoved it away.

"I can take care of myself. We need to move," she said, pulling her modified baton from its sheath at her thigh and twisting it to form the two long blades she was so deadly with. Not that they'd be much use if Aliya's squadrons kept to the air. There was something to be said for projectile weapons.

"Morrigan, report," Bast snapped into his comm as the two of them took off at a run.

They'd ended up near to where Bast had doubled-back to save her. He fought to rein in his fury as he noticed the crumpled forms of his scouts on the pavement next to the small area of grass at Midland Park where their attackers had taken them down.

"You've got five landing ahead of you, and ten behind. The rest have formed a defensive circle above your position that we can't get through without either Zee or Ivy getting out here or breaking out an RPG. We can keep them focused on us, at least."

"No grenades, and tell the defenders to stop firing. We'll hurt our own people. Just make sure they can't ambush us and herd them in the direction we want them to go," Bast replied, shifting a little further from Hel's side and drawing his short sword as he twisted to avoid a motorbike one of the air mages had thrown with their power.

They were probably only a two-minute run from their destination if there had been nothing in their way. Unfortunately, they were fast approaching an obstruction of half a dozen white-winged elementals stretched across the wide, empty road.

When they'd first re-shaped the city for protection decades ago, Zee had gently coaxed the trees planted down this stretch of road into forming a living shelter. Thick trunks wended down the middle of the road, their branches stretching across the entire space between buildings, screening their path from the predators above while their roots protected them from the predators below. The woven canopy lent an ethereal glow of green-shadowed sunlight to the surrounding air, but the efforts of the wind mages facing them had already stripped trees nearest them bare of leaves. Detritus spun so fast through the air he wouldn't be surprised if it sliced them open if their shields dropped—death by a thousand cuts.

From the corner of his eye, he saw Hel glance behind them.

"Too many," she gasped, pausing to catch her breath.

Neither of them were in any state to fight. Her new wings were dragging on the ground as they slowed. He felt a rush of concern from the souls in this part of the city reacting to his fear for her. There was only so much power a physical form could channel before it consumed you, and they were both on the tipping point. He couldn't use the power the souls offered.

Without words, they placed their backs against each other and faced the encircling threat of Aliya's soldiers, their blades up in a guard position. Sparks of their magic shot between their wings like a current jumping between exposed wires where they brushed against each other.

They both tensed as the air pressure around them dropped sharply and the sensation of gathering elemental magic surged. Bast was poised on his toes, ready to charge forward and at least go down swinging, when the tree branches opened up above them and a flutter of electric blue dropped to their left.

"Kaia, no!" Bast yelled, feeling Hel's panic responding to his own as they realised who'd joined them.

They'd both forgotten there was another mage in the city. Untrained. A danger to herself as much as anyone else. He would've done anything to keep her away from there. Why hadn't he made sure she was safely away from the city?

The twelve year old ignored his words, totally focused on

weaving her magic through the surrounding branches until the trees themselves had cocooned them in a sphere of safety.

She then promptly fainted.

"We can't keep her safe here," Bast said.

"I think I've got enough juice to portal us a bit further on. With any luck, my father's too busy with the contagion we sent to his world to send any hunters after me."

"Get us as far as we can go and still be in sight," Bast replied, before pushing a finger to his comms device. "Morrigan, Kaia's here. We're portalling out to draw them away. I want this position secured as soon as we're clear."

Ra's swearing filled the comms channel briefly before Morrigan's clipped voice came through. "Copy that. Ivy's en route."

The barrier sphere Kaia had created around them was big enough for them to stand comfortably, but wound so tight that not a drop of sunshine could sneak through. Bast gently shifted the girl at their feet clear of them by touch alone, placing a finger against her pulse as he did so to feel the reassuring but too-slow pulse of the girl's heartbeat.

The familiar sensation of Hel's power filled the air as she drew on the dregs of her power. He didn't know how she was still standing when he could feel what the effort cost her. The rift opened just inside their wooden enclosure, preserving its protection for the girl they were leaving behind. The portal was a jagged rent that smelled like burned ozone and flickered an alarming black colour at the edges. It did the job, though. Hel shoved Bast through ahead of her, already turning to close it before he'd even processed the fiery discomfort of the place between worlds they passed through.

Bast watched in horror as a dagger thumped into her shoulder as the portal disappeared and left them exposed to the attackers behind them.

"Freak out later," Hel hissed at him as they staggered back into motion.

He could almost feel the pain himself through their connection as she gripped the hilt of the blade and tugged it out of her body. The sound of steel on bone had him grinding his teeth.

"It's fine," she said, even though they both knew the blood would draw the arachdryn to her too quickly once they reached the building they were careening toward.

"Almost there. Are they following?" Bast replied, pulling her back into a run with her good arm.

She shook him off, holding tight to her shoulder through her leather jacket to try and staunch the wound as she loped forward. Bast kept his eyes on her and the road ahead as Hel checked behind them.

"Yeah," she replied.

"Good."

"That sentiment may be premature."

Bast could only nod in response.

As they emerged into the plaza where the old human cenotaph loomed high overhead, the shadows of their aerial hunters flitted across the pavement, growing larger by the second.

Movement flashed in Bast's peripheral vision and he slashed up with his blade, his aim confirmed by the cry of pain echoing against the stone column and the sound of a dismembered limb thunking to the ground. A quick glance showed Hel was still keeping pace, her own blades also dripping red, though he hadn't noticed her wielding them. They both pumped their wings for added speed as they scaled the three flights of tiled stairs that stood between them and the shielding on the building that squatted before them. Now they just had to hope their pursuers would be stupid enough to follow them in.

Even with the brown and grey flashes of Morrigan's scouts dropping onto their attackers, it was still only instinct and luck that meant they were still moving. The magical attacks on their shared shielding had become constant, and each one threatened to shatter the now gossamer-thin protection they'd woven around them.

Hel dodged another wild swing of a blade from above and Bast caught her as she stumbled sideways. Below them, the bricks paving the plaza trembled as wisps of air magic ripped them from their moorings and spun them in a whirlwind. Things were about to get messy.

"Fuck. Run," he whispered, as if they both weren't already moving as quickly as they could.

Somehow he managed a burst of speed, gripping Hel tight to pull her along behind him.

"I'm having a flash-back to the night we met. Fitting I guess," Hel murmured.

Bast growled as he felt the acceptance of potential death in his mate through their connection. That was not happening. Ever. He gripped her arm in a bruising hold and hauled them both skyward enough to reach the nearest ledge of the Spiderhive. They teetered there on the edge of the building for a moment before staggering into the looming shadows of the triple-height open space.

The sudden abatement of the onslaught against their joint shielding just *before* they crossed the Spiderhive's boundary should've been a warning, but he was too exhausted to do more than slump his shoulders as the relentless draining pressure ended.

A draft of air rifled his feathers. He barely had time to register it and twist himself around Hel protectively before a heavily muscled elemental body slammed into him with the force of a bird of prey dive-bombing. Breath rushed from his lungs and his knees screamed in agony as he fell forward. That pain was nothing compared to the searing burn of the short-sword now impaling his wing, pinning it to his thigh.

Somehow, Hel disentangled herself from him, falling into a roll on the concrete floor. Bast winced as he watched the tangle of her wings wrenching away from her back. Clumsily regaining her feet, she launched one of her lethal blades at his attacker who was still recovering from their shared fall. Bast ducked just in time, the sharp metal whistling past his head so close he could swear it cut a few strands of his hair and sent them drifting to the floor. A gush of warm liquid against the back of his neck said Hel's blade had found the carotid artery.

"Thanks," he muttered as he shoved the dying body off him.

It was the wrong move. He almost lost consciousness as the guy held tight to the sword still piercing his wing even in his death throes, dragging the blade back out through the already ragged injury.

"Idiot," Hel whispered in his ear, her voice tight with concern as she slipped in close to put pressure on his wounds and support his wing that now hung useless from his back, making the pain even worse.

A pattering series of thumps sounded to either side of them like the first ominous cracks of hail on a rooftop—the sound of too many attackers landing. Bast forced himself to look away from his mate and staggered them away from the ambush and further into the building, closer to the internal wall curving into the distance. Each step took them further from the outside world they needed to return to on the other side of his one-way shielding if they wanted any hope of survival.

What looked like a dozen elementals had landed on either side of them, the well-trained soldiers fanning out to block their escape. He wasn't sure how large a force Aliya had sent against them. More would've fallen in the fight raging outside. Ivy and Zee were both powerful. Hopefully, it was enough. It had to be.

Mass casualties were rare in elemental warfare. A race of immortals understood the changing tides of enemies over time. Today's foe would be tomorrow's ally. When the courts fought each other, they usually did so to show strength, to disable. And then they healed to fight another day. When they fought outsiders like him and his city who threatened their power structure, though, they fought to kill. The only way to keep his people safe had always been to be so ruthless it wasn't worth the damage of attacking him. It looked like Aliya had forgotten that lesson. He sighed as he watched the ageless, beautiful, sneering faces that encircled them. They didn't have a clue what was coming.

"Really? You're feeling guilty about killing them?" Hel asked, her tone snarky but the emotion hidden beneath saying her heart ached for his pain.

She was stalling for time. The nocturnal arachdryn would've been sleeping in the depths of the building and had yet to emerge from the darkness of their nest. There was no chance they, or their attackers, would hear the near-silent predators over the noise of the squadrons. Bast kept his gaze subtly trained on the ceiling, all too conscious of the open wounds they sported that would make them prime targets for the winged spiders.

The elemental who stood between them and the shielding they'd passed through let out a cool laugh, the malicious sound echoing off the concrete walls of the abandoned building. He had the markings of a captain on his tailored jacket. Bast's vision was darkening from exhaustion, or maybe blood-loss, but he could still make out the flash of reflected sunlight on the gold-tipped white of his primaries. The man's voice was flat, almost bored, when he spoke and Bast wondered if he'd even had a chance to be something better, kinder, having grown up in the court of the most vicious of the elemental rulers.

"I hate to break it to you, but your man hasn't killed us and we could have killed you a hundred times over if we didn't have orders to take you alive. Now be a good girl and step away from him, or I can't guarantee he'll stay that way."

Bast stretched his good wing out protectively, partially screening Hel from view. Was that smear of darkness behind the elementals the arachdryn arriving or was his vision getting worse?

"I'm curious how you're planning to get her away from here," Bast said, straining to keep his voice nonchalant and hide his laser focus on the space behind their attackers. They just needed to keep them talking long enough that they couldn't mount a proper defence against the threat they weren't yet aware of.

The squadron captain frowned and cocked his head. "What do you mean?"

"These shields are one of my more-accomplished constructs."

The man scoffed. "It didn't take even a drop of magic to get through them."

That was the thing with the arrogance of the courts, especially the Air Court. They really couldn't imagine someone being competent outside their training structure. It meant they made all kinds of wrong assumptions.

"It wasn't designed to keep you out," Bast said, letting his lips tip up in a tiny smile.

The Captain frowned again and flared his wings out behind him, or at least he tried to. He was still close enough to the shielding that it blocked the motion, sending sparks of silver magic scattering where he connected with it. He still looked smug as he shrugged, though.

"I guess we're killing you, after all," he said.

"Okay. But that won't have any effect on the shield," Bast explained, starting to enjoy himself despite everything.

He loved cutting these arrogant pricks off at the knees. Now, if only he could figure out how to get him and Hel out before the bloodbath started. There were too many attackers blocking their way.

"Magical constructs don't survive past their creator's deaths," the Captain shot back, but behind his smug statement was a growing seed of doubt.

Bast smiled wider. "I'm a necromancer, remember? Death is nothing to me. I anchored the shield in hundreds of souls. One more will only make it stronger."

"And there will be way more than one," Hel added cheerfully, which was the point at which a strangled scream washed over them as the first arachdryn dropped onto the furthest attacker.

"What're the chances we're going to get out of this

alive?" his mate whispered in his ear as their attackers pivoted to face the oncoming predators.

"Got enough power left to portal us somewhere?" Bast asked, but he already knew the answer.

They had nothing left.

"What the fuck is taking you two so long? Get out of there." Ra's voice echoed through their comms as Bast watched an arachdryn creep along the ceiling toward their position, ignoring the struggling fighters for the more tempting injured prey.

"Our exit's blocked and I'm not really mobile right now," Bast grunted into his mic, before bracing himself on Hel to sweep his sword out and up.

He was rewarded for his efforts with a segment of spider leg falling onto his exposed face, searing him with its stinging spines. He swore and kicked the thing into the wing of the nearest elemental, distracting the fighter long enough for one of the other arachdryn to sever their arm before shooting webbing around their body to trap them.

The momentary pain of the lost leg had made the predator above them pause, but it wouldn't keep it back for long. Everywhere Bast looked, horror images flashed in the shadows and a symphony of tortured sounds filled the air—spider fangs piercing flesh, throbbing skin reddened with spider venom as their victims screamed, the eerie shrieks of dying arachdryn pierced by so many invisible spears of air. That last one only seemed to spur on their brethren, who were now not just after a tasty snack but swarming to defend their nest.

The air mages finally seemed to clue in to the fact that a good offence is *not* always the best defence, joining together to encase their fighters in a sphere of solid air. The arachdryn surging against it were burned to a crisp, their skin bubbling as if a cruel child had focused the sun's rays through a magnifying glass on a hot day. Seemed like the kind of thing the Air Court would be into. Unfortunately for the elementals, the monsters were cunning but incapable of calculating odds. This nest was vast and the creatures would continue to sacrifice themselves against their barrier until they broke through.

Bast slumped to the ground, no longer able to support himself on his injured leg. He'd long since tuned out the voices coming through his comms, so it took him a moment to realise Hel wasn't talking to him when she spoke, her voice low and urgent.

"We're still stuck. His leg's got a hole the size of my fist in it. I couldn't portal a foot away right now and our attackers are not going to be happy when they finish with the tourniquets and cauterising. Even if we could walk, their shielding is blocking us from leaving."

Sure enough, as if he'd heard her words, the Captain overseeing the remains of their force turned and stalked towards them. He drew power to himself until it coalesced around both clenched fists, making them glow golden in the dim light. "This is your fault."

Hel's warm arms wrapped around Bast where he now lay half-prone on the ground, blood pooling beneath him. Leaning his head back against her chest, he couldn't make himself care he'd left his throat exposed. He could swear he saw a tentacle undulating in the darkness just behind the Captain, but he suspected it was just another sign he was sinking into unconsciousness.

Or maybe not, because a moment later Tir's sibilant voice sounded from nearby.

"If you two could stop being so dramatic with the certain-death situations, that would be great," Tir whispered.

The screams started up again partway through their sentence and the Captain twisted to redirect his gathered power at the three arachdryn bearing down on them.

"Can you get us out?" Hel asked Tir.

"You will owe me a life-debt. Do you accept?" the incomprehensible being replied, and the heavy truth of their words seeped into Bast's bones.

"Yes," Bast gasped, desperate not to save himself but to preserve the woman holding him.

He barely heard Hel's echoing assent before the floor disappeared from beneath them and they were falling.

CHAPTER 17
HEL

Hel groaned and clutched at the throbbing wound in her shoulder as they crashed down onto the rooftop she'd recklessly launched herself off not long before. Ra's voice echoed in surround sound as she heard him both in her earpiece and from his position overlooking the city nearby. Tir had already disappeared to wherever it was they went when they weren't in the city.

"The lovebirds are back. I need medical assistance on the roof terrace. Status on Kaia?" Ra said.

"You did *not* just call us that," Hel muttered as she struggled up into a sitting position to check on Bast beside her.

She didn't like the way his blood was oozing from his leg in a steady stream and the flickering weakness she could feel along their connection. A hiss escaped her as she tried to reach out to put pressure on it, forgetting her own injured shoulder.

"I've had worse. A bandage and some sleep and I'll be fine," he told her, squeezing her leg reassuringly.

266

Dammit.

That touch should not have sent her body tingling the way it did. This mating bond was ridiculous. They were injured, exhausted, about to suffer the king of all magical overdose hangovers and still mopping up the last of the attack. Now was not the time. Bast's mouth twitched in a way that said he knew exactly what she was thinking.

"Shut up," Hel growled.

"I didn't say a word," he shot back with false innocence.

Morrigan's voice through the comms responding to Ra's query interrupted them—"Ivy couldn't get through Kaia's shield. We've just cleared the city of the last of Aliya's people, so Zee's heading up there now to help. Even if their power isn't enough to break her construct, they should be able to get the trees to listen and release her."

"How powerful is she, exactly?" Hel asked in surprise, but the question went unanswered as two of Morrigan's field medics finally dropped onto the roof and started working on her and Bast.

Relief flooded through her a minute later as the pain in her shoulder was finally washed away by the magic-infused dressings they carefully wrapped around her abused joint.

"Nice wings," the young woman leaning over her murmured as she worked, but her tone sounded wary.

Hel kept her face neutral, well aware her unique transformation would make her a sideshow attraction to elementals and humans alike. She'd never felt like she belonged to this world, but now that was painfully evident to anyone who looked at her. Strong arms wrapped around her from behind as Bast felt her spiralling thoughts and she felt a surge of possessive affection.

"I don't know exactly where your thoughts just went, but you belong with me. Always," he growled in her ear.

Hel let her head fall back against his chest. The discomfort of the cold solid tiles beneath them and their tangled wings felt far distant as she let everything go to sink into the new comfort of their connection now it didn't promise certain death.

"Come on, lovebirds. We've got this. Let's get you to bed," Ra said, offering a hand to pull Bast to his feet and slipping under his arm to support him.

Bast pulled Hel up in turn, and somehow Ra navigated the three of them to the penthouse suite without anyone tumbling headfirst down the stairs.

The world around Hel was fading into a blur of fatigue and she was barely aware of drinking the high-energy liquid nutrition elementals kept on them during long-haul flights that Ra pressed into her hand. The sugar kick was just enough to allow her and Bast to struggle out of their clothes and take a perfunctory shower. If she'd had a bit more energy, Hel would have had to process the strange sensation of warm water on new wings and the fact she was naked with a man she definitely no longer hated.

As it was, she only managed a brief sense of gratitude that Bast's shower had enough space and showerheads to comfortably fit two people with significant wingspans, followed by gratitude his bed was just as large and accommodating. She fell asleep pressed tight to his side, head cradled on the mark her power had left on his chest when they mated as she felt the reassuring pulse of his heartbeat against her cheek.

The last sensation she had was of soft lips pressing a kiss to her forehead and Bast's whispered, "Sleep well, love."

Hel woke to the tantalising, peppery smell of stimulant tea and feathers tickling her nose.

"Auntie Kitty Cat! You're awake! You've been asleep *forever*," a too loud, too high-pitched voice said next to her ear.

Hel groaned and tried to roll away from the torturous noise.

"Kaia Selene Archer. Give the poor woman a chance to wake up," Ana scolded.

Hel finally dragged her eyes open and blinked as soft cream feathers filled her vision until Kaia shifted back to give her some space.

"Where's Bast?" she asked, too tired to beat herself up over that being the first thing out of her mouth. As soon as she asked the question, she knew the answer. His presence was a soft pressure on her awareness coming from somewhere below her.

"He woke a couple of days before you. He's down in the council chamber sorting out repairs and dealing with this new Melding," Ana answered, confirming what Hel had already sensed about his whereabouts. It took her a moment to process the rest of the information in her statement.

"A couple of *days*?! How long was I out?" Hel asked.

"A week. You had a drip in, but Bast said you'd wake today so they took it out this morning. Hungry?"

Hel groaned again and rubbed gritty eyes. "Shower first. Then food."

Ana looked like she was going to protest when Hel insisted on showering without help, but she reluctantly left when Hel successfully staggered to the bathroom unaided. Someone had dressed her in a soft singlet and pyjama pants at some point, and it took far longer than it should have for her to find the right threads to stroke to get the magical fabric to unravel and pool on the floor.

It was worth it when she was finally standing under the streams of hot water, face tilted up as if the spray could wash away her fatigue and weakness. She didn't hear the door open, but her innate awareness of Bast meant she didn't jump in surprise when his arms wrapped around her from behind. His hands brushed her hair to the side as he pressed a kiss to her neck and she tilted her head to give him better access, sighing as she realised the annoying truth that she'd been missing a piece of herself until he was touching her again.

He didn't say anything, just grabbed the shampoo and massaged it into her scalp in firm strokes that made her moan before carefully washing every inch of her body. She looked down at him as his hands brushed over her calves. Her fingers stroked through his hair, making him glance up at her in a way that left her breathless. This man was now so tightly woven into her soul that she didn't know where she ended and he began. He was achingly beautiful as he knelt at her feet, drips of water glistening on his black wings half-spread behind him as he focused every inch of his attention on her.

"Hey," she said, dizzy with the emotions ricocheting between them.

Bast's lips pulled up in a sweet smile she'd never seen from him before, and she knew this expression would only ever be for her.

"Hi," he replied, heat sparking in his eyes as the sensation of his fingers on her skin suddenly turned from innocent to carnal.

She gasped as he traced a soft circle on the back of her knee that should not have been as arousing as it was.

"You need food and we need to talk," he said, removing his hands and chuckling as Hel groaned in frustration.

Bast was as thorough and frustratingly gentle in drying her as he had been washing her and before she knew it, she was curled up in a soft, fluffy towel in bed with a tray of waffles piled high with bacon, cream, and berries. She ignored Bast and his satisfied smile as he watched her devour the food. When she finally finished, there was no more ignoring him because he set the tray aside and all but pounced on her, straddling her where she lay propped up against the headboard.

He was careful to keep most of his weight off her, but the warmth of his mostly naked body resting on her pelvis was an excruciating tease that only got worse as he leaned forward to brush a strand of hair from her face. His familiar scent she couldn't get enough of washed over her and her eyes fluttered shut as his thumb trailed down her cheek to run across her lips.

She resisted the urge to pull him down for a kiss, but her appearance of control was shot when she instinctively opened her lips to suck his thumb into her mouth and bite down. Who was she kidding? He could sense her arousal just as well as she could sense his. There was no hiding it. What she didn't know was what was causing the hesitance she could feel from him.

Hel sighed. "What is it?"

Bast didn't immediately answer and when she glanced

up, she saw his eyes were laser-focused on her lips where she was still gently biting his thumb. Whoops. Pulling free, she tried to sit up straighter so she could focus, but he didn't shift an inch.

"I don't want there to be any ... misunderstandings between us. About what this is," he finally said.

Hel's heart rate picked up as her anxiety surged. She preferred not to think about what was between them. It was less scary that way. Her eyes dropped to her lap where her fingers were twisting at the hem of the towel still wrapped around her.

"We're mates. You explained it already. At length," she said.

"What do you want with me? What do you want us to be?" Bast asked.

Hel scowled up at him, an ache starting in her chest. Habit made her react as she always had, defensively. He'd spent weeks trying to sever their bond. Was he regretting failing? Was he happy to let her go now she wasn't in danger of dying and killing him along with her?

"It doesn't matter what I want. We're stuck as we are."

"It matters to me."

"It never seemed to matter when—" Hel cut herself off mid-sentence. She couldn't keep blaming him for everything. She knew that. They'd both caused this bond to form and she was firm in her resolve to stop fighting it. That didn't mean she had to lay herself bare, though. She could feel Bast's frustration growing, but he gave no sign of it as he let his hands trail down her arms leaving goose bumps in their wake. Finally, he swore softly and looked away.

"Fine, I'll start," he said. Silence fell between them as he closed his eyes and took a deep breath. "I want us to be partners. By choice and not just circumstance. I want to wake up with you in my arms every morning knowing that it's because you *want* to be there. I need you because of this connection we share, but I love you because of who you are. Your strength. That compassion you try so hard to hide. You make me feel as protected as I hope you feel with me. You make me feel like there is beauty in life as well as duty. At some point, you became my everything, and it had nothing to do with when we mated. So, don't tell me it doesn't fucking matter. You matter. *We* matter."

A teardrop ran down her cheek as Hel stared up at Bast —his eyes still closed like he couldn't stand to watch her reaction, face turned away as he braced for rejection. Her hand trembled as she reached up and traced the line of his collarbone before letting her fingers drift down his muscled torso. She felt him tremble in response, but he still didn't open his eyes.

"Those squadrons were coming for me. People died defending me. The courts know who my father is now. No one will trust me in this body. They'll call me a traitor and a freak. You'd do better if I left. You'd be safer. The city would be safer," she said.

"This city has always welcomed the outcasts of our Earths. Our people chose to defend you. And I don't care what anyone else thinks, I only care about you. You belong here. With me. With Kaia and our family." Bast was watching her now, his eyes holding her captive as he refused to let her hide from what he was telling her.

Hel banged her head against the headboard in frustration, her voice rising to a yell as it all became too much. "I can't be the reason you're hurt!"

"Why?"

"Because I love you, too, you bastard," she shouted.

Bast gave that sweet smile again and it was like a river of calm flowing through her, soothing all the anger and hurt she was relying on to stay staunch against the temptation of his words. "No one is going to rush to attack us after that massacre. You're the only one with the power to hurt me, sweetheart. Let me love you."

Hel blinked, face blank as she stared up at him. Her whole life she'd hidden and run. She wanted a chance to belong. Even if it was only another day or week until her father's hounds caught up with her. She needed this. Needed him.

"Okay," she whispered.

"Okay, what?"

"Okay, I want to be here. With you."

"Forever?"

Hel swallowed hard. "For as long as it doesn't put you or your family in danger."

"*Our* family. And don't think for a second I'm ever going to let you go," Bast muttered, and then he was yanking her body down the bed to lie beneath him, his lips pressing hard to hers, frantic hands pulling at her towel.

Hel arched her body up into him, every bit as desperate as her mate. It had been too damn long. She moaned as he trailed nibbling kisses down her neck and helped him push the infuriating material out of the way until they could finally press their bodies together without barriers. Skin on melting-hot skin.

"Yes," she groaned as Bast curled over her, connecting them from chest to feet as his wings spread and enclosed them in a cocoon of feathered shadow.

The lightning storm of his kisses travelled further down

her body, worshipping each curve and dip. He was resting his weight on one arm pressed into the pillow by her cheek and she turned her head to kiss his taut biceps as his other hand trailed down her sensitive inner wing surface, sending shockwaves of desire through her. A gasp fell from her lips as the warmth of his mouth closed around her nipple followed by the curl of his teasing tongue.

Her fingers wrapped tight in his hair, pulling him closer as if she could meld them together if she only tried hard enough. Bast's responding smug smile against her skin was enough to bring her back to herself and she took advantage of his distraction to hook a leg through his and flip their positions.

The vibration of Bast's silent laughter made her smile despite herself as they ended up almost surgically attached by the tangle of her wing trapped underneath him. She'd wondered if it would be uncomfortable having someone lying on it, but it was flexible enough that the only discomfort came when she tried to pull away too quickly.

"Shut up. It's not like I've had them long enough to practise," she mumbled against his lips as she started kissing him again, teasing his mouth open.

"Mmmm. I think you need a lot of practice. I volunteer as tribute," Bast said, his free hand brushing against the side of her breast as he stroked down her body to trace tantalising circles by her hip.

Hel groaned in frustration as she tried to grind against the steel of his erection so close to where she needed it, only to find her movement too restricted.

"You're going to have to get off my wing if you want me kissing anything that's not your mouth," she said.

"I don't know. I kind of like you like this. Helpless.

Pressed so tight against me I can feel your heartbeat like it's my own."

Hel pinched his nipple. Hard.

"I'm never helpless," she snapped.

Bast's laughter rang out through the room. "Alright, Hell-cat," he said, his abdominal muscles flexing delightfully against her torso as he supported both their weights while curling up into a crunch so she could extract her mutinous wing from underneath him.

"How do elementals deal with these damn appendages anyway," Hel grumbled as she resettled herself into a sitting position on top of him.

"I mean, missionary isn't super popular? And beds are definitely optional." He'd finally calmed his laughter, but she could still see the amusement dancing in his eyes.

Hel tilted her head to the side, studying him. He'd let his wings stretch out on either side of him to lie flat on the covers. The contrast of all that smooth skin and muscle against the dramatic backdrop of his unnaturally black feathers absorbing the light around them was enough to steal her breath.

"Did you have a suggestion?" Hel asked, rolling her body against him that was now positioned just right.

Bast's hands snapped to her hips, gripping tight as he dragged her over his hard length again and groaned in appreciation. There would definitely be bruises where his fingers dug into her. At least she hoped there would be. It seemed she'd thoroughly lost any pretence they were anything but extremely possessive of each other. She leaned down to kiss his neck right above where any shirt collar would rest and sucked hard, marking him.

"Fuck yes," he groaned, completely distracted from her original question and no doubt sensing the possessiveness that had driven that move.

"Is that a position?" she teased, sitting back up.

Bast followed after, chasing her lips with his own as he wrapped his arms around her waist. Somehow, he kept her in his lap as he got his legs beneath him so he was kneeling with his wings now safely tucked away at his back.

"This avoids any pesky knees pressing into wing bones and gives me some leverage," he said, demonstrating exactly that as he started grinding them together again in a way that had Hel's eyes fluttering shut. "But if you really want the full winged experience you need to get on your hands and knees," he finished, voice dropping to a low growl.

"We've done that one before," Hel said.

"Not like this. Trust me."

Hel was struggling to focus on his words, the feel of his body moving against her too distracting. Her eyes snapped open when Bast's strong hands lifted her away from him, holding her just out of reach.

"Fine," she said, shifting back and smirking at how fast Bast moved out of her way to make space for her in the centre of the bed.

Her body trembled as she settled onto her hands and knees, remembering that night when they'd first come together. The night they'd both accidentally become the missing pieces of each other. Dropping even lower onto her elbows, she arched her back to present herself to her mate and stared over her shoulder at the man who was showing every sign of being about to totally lose control.

"Well?" she asked.

"Let your wings relax down by your sides," Bast said, his voice strained as his eyes darted across her body, watching her everywhere.

Hel did as he asked and was immediately rewarded with his warmth pressing against her from behind. She knew instantly what Bast had meant. In this position, their wings curved against each other, fitting seamlessly together until she could feel his feathers brushing against every single tantalisingly sensitive inch of her wingspan. It was beyond exquisite, not least because his mating mark now stretched across her wing surface instead of her back, making the sensations almost overwhelming.

One of his hands trailed down her spine, carrying down until his fingers were brushing through the wetness pooling between her thighs, teasing her just right. Bast's teeth bit her uninjured shoulder gently as he leaned further forward and stroked down her arm, pausing at the slight raised bump of her contraceptive implant.

"This is coming out one day," he growled in her ear.

Hel snorted. "Nope. But you can pretend if you like," she said, pushing back against him.

Bast braced himself over her and she felt him grip his shaft to trace his head over her entrance. She'd waited long enough, though. She was done with the teasing and she was pretty sure she might literally die if he continued demonstrating viable sex positions without actually following through.

Reaching behind herself to grab him, she shoved her hips backwards, impaling herself on his cock. They both froze for a second as the mating bond between them surged, amplifying and echoing the sensations between them until they were nothing but aching pleasure and need.

There was no talking or thought after that. There was just a perfect harmony of movement, connection so intense they lost any sense of self, and a peak when it came that seemed to echo into eternity.

Into forever.

EPILOGUE: BAST

Bast pressed his lips to Hel's silver hair and traced a single finger along one of the gracefully curved horns that now twisted out from within its strands. The soft dawn light gave her skin the appearance of rose gold wherever it reached. Shifting slightly, he revelled in the now-familiar feeling of their wings brushing together. She'd fallen asleep cradled in his arms, her wings tucked in tight so he could wrap them both in the warmth of his feathers like a living blanket. It was how they'd fallen asleep every night for the last month as they healed the damage done to themselves and their city. Both of them had worked themselves to the bone to protect their people and to counteract the guilt of feeling like if only they'd tried harder they could've prevented the second Melding.

The vibration of his phone nearby had woken him early, but he was ignoring it. Hel needed to rest. While the power that had reshaped her body meant she had the muscle-tone to fly, it couldn't overcome a lifetime of inexperience to make her instantly competent. It was only in the last week that she was starting to reliably get where she wanted to go without damaging anything. And that amazing achievement was all attributable to Morrigan's relentless drills and the infuriating, endearing stubbornness of his Hellcat.

His cock swelled and he traced a path down her skin as he thought about the way she'd applied that same focus to navigating her wings in the bedroom.

The vibration of his phone starting up again had him cursing softly at the interruption as he stretched to snatch it up.

"What?" he said quietly into the phone as he smoothed out the frown that had formed on Hel's forehead with his other hand.

"Good morning, Bastion," Mica's too-polite voice said.

Bast waited silently, unwilling to wake up his mate for the sake of manners. Their relationships with all the elemental council were strained after they'd voted for Nerida to take Hel from him on that island and hand her over to her father. He couldn't assume anyone was neutral anymore. Although the courts were more respectful than they'd ever been, thanks to their show of power in ejecting the contagion from their world and keeping their city stable through the second melding.

The City of Souls had come through largely unscathed because of the network of Souls he'd established to stabilise their reality after the first Melding. They'd had their own challenges repairing the damage from Aliya's attack, as well as reinforcing their defences and sending support to their allies in other parts of Aotearoa.

"You received our invitation?" the Earth Lord continued when he realised Bast wasn't going to say anything more.

"It was more of a demand."

"And yet you are not here," Mica said, a hint of impatience sneaking in.

Unlike the City of Souls, the rest of the world was unstable and reeling as it tried to absorb the third reality to collapse into their Melded Earths. The courts had been kept busy dealing with collapsed buildings, lost food production, and ambushes by the new and varied creatures they now coexisted with. His spies among the couriers reported that the violent new predators across the other continents seemed to universally subsist off a diet of blood, but either the isolation or the concentration of aerial predators in Aotearoa had helped keep them safe. Whatever new animals came with this new reality were avoiding the City of Souls.

There had been whispered reports of a new intelligent people and even the suggestion they were behind some of the attacks. But if they were out there, they were staying quiet for now. Probably wise given Ty and Aliya's tendencies to kill first and ask questions later.

The courts had finally found enough breathing space to hold a council session to deal with their shared problems, and they'd notified Bast of the meeting a week ago. He was intending to show up to the Council at some point, if for no other reason than to learn as much as he could about this new reality that had melded into theirs, but he didn't trust the courts and Hel had needed more practice before she could make the flight. They still couldn't risk portalling if it would draw her father's attention, despite the absence of his hounds since they'd sent the contagion back to his world. Hopefully, that would keep him busy for a long time.

"I wasn't sure what kind of welcome we'd receive given the damage we left behind at the Water Court and how many of Aliya's people we sent home in body bags. Even you didn't seem all that keen to invite us along last time. Something about us being compromised? Was that before or after you voted in favour of abducting my mate and delivering her to her death?"

To his credit, Mica sounded a little sheepish as he responded. "Yes. Well. Your mate is clearly a liability, but we all felt your power pushing out the contagion and we are grateful for it, even if it is quite possible her actions caused the Melding."

Bast growled loud enough that Hel stirred in his arms and blinked up at him. "Would you blame the victim for the crime, then? If you touch her, you die. Did you not feel her power saving your asses as well, or was that fact too inconvenient for you to notice?"

"She's wanted by someone who has catastrophically attacked our world twice now, and all indications are he would have left us alone if someone had just given her back to him. I'm sorry, but in a choice between millions of lives and your mate, I will choose the former every time."

"Did you ask Aliya how her attacking force could invade at the exact time of the Melding if she didn't know it was going to happen in advance? I'm guessing she didn't bother giving you a heads up. Maybe direct your attention at the viper in your nest who's actively working with this so-called emperor instead of helping sacrifice his victim. He would've left our world to succumb to the contagion. Instead, we saved you. You're welcome."

Mica sighed. "It is too late to revisit past decisions, regardless. The Council is willing to overlook your reckless choice of mate given your actions on behalf of the greater good."

Bast's hand gripped his phone so tightly his knuckles

turned white and he clenched his jaw hard to avoid saying something he'd regret. He only calmed enough to continue speaking when Hel started pressing soft kisses to his chest to distract him. "I don't give a fuck what the Council thinks about my mate. Let me guess, you're overlooking Aliya's actions as well? She launched a full-scale assault against us."

"And she paid for her impulsiveness with their lives," Mica said, voice calm.

"They mean nothing to her. If she gave a shit about them, she wouldn't have sent them." So many lives lost. Another cloak of guilt for him to bear. And for what?

"Bastion, you know how this goes. You cannot afford not to be part of this discussion. There is a whole new reality to deal with. If nothing else, I would think you would care that young Kaia is a danger to herself. She needs to be assessed and allocated to a court urgently."

Bast flinched. Was Mica backing off from his commitment to take her in? It certainly sounded like it. Bast had been trying to teach Kaia enough control to stay safe, but she was so powerful and her magic was nothing like his own. Zee was helping too, but without a stronghold to help anchor the girl as she learned, there was only so much they could do.

Most elemental magic came from the ley lines that crisscrossed their world and the strongholds of the four courts existed at the largest nexuses of that power. It wasn't just politics that meant elementals always sent their young powerful mages to the courts to train. The strongholds were so steeped in magic they'd developed their own sentience, which helped guide and contain those learning within their bounds until they could channel their power without burning out. Mica was right. They were out of time. As impressive as Kaia's display had been, she'd almost died, and next time she probably would. She needed training now.

"Fine. But if we're travelling with Kaia, we can only go so fast. We'll be there in two days," Bast snapped.

"Your mate is welcome, too," Mica said, the words sounding like they were dragged out of him. "Do you intend to bring her?"

"Yes, Mica. I intend to bring my fucking mate. She rules by my side. Her power is every bit as great as mine. Frankly, you should be honoured to have her and you're lucky she's even willing to attend."

"As you wish. Be sure to tell your demonic viper of a right-hand man the invitation was extended. We will see you then."

Bast threw his phone somewhere on the floor nearby and buried his face in Hel's hair. He should call Ra and ask what the fuck he'd done to make Mica invite Hel to the council session, but he couldn't get up the energy. Knowing his friend, he'd probably tracked down something to blackmail the Earth Lord.

"Do I?" Hel asked when he finally pulled away.

"Do you what?"

"Rule by your side."

Bast blinked in surprise. "Why do you think Zee was asking you about pedestrian urban design priorities yesterday? And Morrigan was getting you to review her defence strategies for portal-based warfare?"

"Because I'm a captive audience?"

Bast smirked and shook his head. "No. Because I wasn't kidding when I called you Lady Soul. And now you're going to come stand by my side at this stupid council meeting, so you'd better get ready because we need to leave this morning if we're going to make it in time."

THE RAIN SHEETING against the invisible barrier of his power around them from the moment they'd flown out over Wellington harbour seemed like a bad omen for their trip. They hadn't extracted themselves from the Tower until midday, mostly because Ana kept repacking Kaia's small travel pack that was being carried by one of the two scouts he'd agreed could accompany them.

He would've preferred to travel with fewer people so he could conserve his power but with both Kaia and Hel potentially needing to be carried part of the way, he hadn't had much choice. As it was, even though he'd mostly recovered from their efforts after the Melding, he could still feel the drain of the magic he was using to accelerate their speed and keep the weather away from them.

The scouts each had a sling infused with Zee's power that ensured the weight of their packs, and Kaia when she needed it, and didn't drag them down. He had a sling for Hel too, but she'd managed on her own and no way was he carrying her anywhere but in his arms if she needed help. This far into the trip, she was showing signs of strain despite the numerous stops they'd used for brief rest breaks as they hopscotched across the Australian continent and various landmasses en route to Mica's court in Southeast Asia. Not that the rest breaks had been particularly restful. None of them had been able to relax on foreign soil that was so unpredictable as the three realities vied for precedence.

As they reached the large continental landmass, they

passed the border of Nerida's territory and entered Mica's. He wasn't sure if that made them more or less safe. At least he hadn't actively attacked Mica's stronghold. Yet. Shit. How had he got into conflict with three out of four of the courts in the last few months? But they'd started it, dammit.

They dropped lower to the ground as they approached the final leg of their journey, preserving some of the energy he would've otherwise used keeping them warm at high altitude. They'd been flying around ten minutes at that height when movement below them distracted Bast from his thoughts. Something was drawing his attention when the distant movements of the predators and other elementals they'd given a wide berth hadn't registered as more than an instinctual risk assessment.

"Hold," Bast called to the rest of their party, reinforcing his command with a raised fist as he pulled up into a hover to watch the subtle shifting of the tall grasses in the abandoned farmland below. Someone was there, running, but he couldn't catch more than a flash of shadow.

"They're shifting the reality," Hel said from his left, and he realised that sensation through her magical senses was what had caught his attention.

They'd done their best to steer clear of civilisation on their flight, so they'd yet to see many obvious signs of the second Melding. One stretch of ocean was much like another regardless of the world and it was hard to tell whether a wilderness had changed when you had no reference for what it used to look like. But below them, the land was subtly shifting as they watched.

The sight of reality switching like that had become rare in the decades after the first Melding. The world had fallen into a natural equilibrium once the beings that resided in it developed a shared memory of their surroundings that held them stable. But now there were new people again, new memories. Whoever was passing beneath them was reshaping the world around them in a thin swathe as they travelled.

Given he still hadn't caught a good glimpse of them, he probably wouldn't have even noticed their passing if not for the shifting landscape. The change was slight, merely the difference between a landscape of long-abandoned agrarian fields that had returned to their original state and a landscape that had never been tamed from that state in the first place. He guessed the untamed landscape only stretched as far as whoever it was could see. Focusing on Hel's power where its tendrils spread through his essence, Bast could feel the nexus of the joined and shifting realities below them.

The tell-tale churn of disturbed earth arrowing in the trail's direction told him why the still-hidden traveller was running so fast. They must have stumbled over a wyrm's territory. Probably a nest of young ones by the looks of the incoming disturbance. A quick glance in the direction of whoever was running showed there was no safety ahead, no outcrop of rock that would block the tunnelling path of the mostly subterranean earth dragons.

It was dangerous to get involved. He hadn't even laid eyes on whoever or whatever was fleeing the wyrms and he had no way of knowing if they were friend or foe. He'd never been one to stand by when someone needed protecting, though. And he really couldn't stand the thought of one more death in this shitty month.

"Need a lift?" he called loudly, wrapping his words in power to ensure they were understood. It was the same trick of translation that even the youngest and least powerful of his kind were capable of that had allowed them to communicate with the humans when they'd first come into contact.

The shifting reality paused its progress. A glance up reassured him his two scouts still hovered high above keeping Kaia clear of any danger and watching his back, ready to intervene if needed. Hel had dropped down near him, the backdraft from her heavy wingbeats a welcome breeze in the humid heat.

"Who are you?" a voice called from the ground, and Bast finally caught sight of the figure they'd been following.

They looked vaguely human, but he could tell this was someone from the new reality. They felt different to his power, like their magics were distantly related.

The figure had textured straight dark hair that swept down the side of their face to brush their collarbone on one side. Their skin was pale but swollen with a hint of red Bast was pretty sure was sunburn rather than their natural colouring. They were flat-chested and their clothes, head-to-toe black, looked like they were fashioned from leather they'd probably hunted. He could just make out a collection of piercings on their face that glinted white in the sunshine like they were made from bone.

A thin scrap of gauze wrapped around their head, covering their eyes. Bast doubted they could see well through it. Possibly nocturnal then, and struggling with the light and UV. Even without his power, he would only have briefly mistaken them for human. Their ears twitched independently like they were monitoring both his approach and the wyrms' as Bast dropped to the ground near them, and their movement was unnaturally fluid.

"I'm Bastion. My mate, Hel, is the one circling at your

back looking violent. It's best not to get on her bad side," he said with a smile to soften the threat.

The person before him barked out a laugh that revealed wickedly sharp transparent teeth. "Women are like that. You feel like a predator. You both do."

"Takes one to know one. The wyrms will be on us in less than a minute. If you want a ride, make your mind up quick."

The person lifted the gauze wrapped around their face and squinted into the light to get a better look at him. As their gaze held his, Bast was surprised to see their eyes looked a lot like his own uniquely black irises, although where his pupil was ringed in the silver of his power, this person's were ringed in blood-red.

They inclined their head in agreement and Bast strode forward the three steps needed to grab them. Thankfully, he still had the sling for Hel tucked into his belt or this would have been a lot more awkward. Laying the fabric out on the ground, he hooked the carabiner hooks to the harness he was wearing around his waist for just this reason.

"Get in. We need to get altitude fast. The wyrms can lunge high."

"Bast, stop messing around. You've got ten seconds max," Hel called to him, and he heard the soft snick of the hidden blades she carried in the staff at her leg being released as she positioned herself between them and the incoming threat.

The person leaped quickly into the fabric and Bast powered up from the ground using more of his magic than he usually would to shoot them airborne. He'd made three surging wingbeats when the snap of teeth sounded below him, hopefully clear of the sling.

The wailing scream of an injured wyrm filled his ears.

"Your mate is magnificent," his passenger murmured and

Bast glanced down to see Hel dragging herself clear of a brilliant azure wyrm who was now short an eye, one of her blades dripping with viscous liquid.

She'd dropped too low when she attacked, though, still learning the constraints of her new body. Bast ground his teeth. There was nothing he could do to help without putting the person hanging below him in too much danger.

He breathed a sigh of relief as a blur of black and brown shot past him and Tijmen, one of the scouts, ran interference with the rest of the angry earth serpents until Hel got herself out of trouble. As they flew clear, he looked back down to see seven wyrms surging out of the earth below them like so many homicidal garden eels swaying in the dry grass.

"What did they say?" Hel asked, having caught up to them.

"I think they have a crush on you," Bast replied with a smirk.

He felt Hel exploring the translation spell he was using before borrowing a touch of power to apply it to herself so they could all be understood. "As long as they don't make a move on *you*. I'd hate to have to hurt them," Hel replied, smirking at the person hanging below him before banking to the right to go check on Kaia. Her words didn't seem to bother his passenger at all.

"I owe you a life-debt. My name is Kairon and, if I've understood the nuances of your language through whatever magic you're weaving, you can refer to me as he," the man below him said, his words reminding Bast he'd seen no sign of Tir since that slightly ominous promise he'd extracted before saving them.

"Nice to meet you, Kairon. I'm afraid we're running late to a meeting and don't have time to drop you anywhere."

"I can hear the deception in your voice. What aren't you telling me?" Kairon asked.

Bast glanced down at him in surprise. Although with ears like his and the indications he preferred to live in darkness, perhaps acute hearing shouldn't be so surprising. He decided he had nothing to lose by being honest with the man. It's not like he could run away.

"I'm heading to a council meeting of the rulers of my kind. I think they'll want to hear from you. And bringing you with me will help distract them from some ... disagreements ... we've been having."

Kairon laughed. "I guess it's only fair that I play distraction for you. Will I come out of this meeting alive?"

"Almost certainly," Bast said. And he meant it. As long as he and Hel came out alive as well.

"And will I come out of it still a free vampyr?"

"If I have any say in it, yes," Bast said, noting the word Kairon had used for his people.

The echo of the human tales of vampires didn't surprise him. That was the nature of multiple realities. They all had echoes of each other—stasis points of stories and myth as well as location.

"How much say do you usually have?" Kairon asked.

It was Bast's turn to laugh. "It varies. But they will fear me more now than last time we met."

"Then I'm willing to take my chances with you. I need to meet these rulers of yours, anyway. And there is an advantage to allying with the scariest guy in the room."

"They don't rule me. No one does."

"We have that in common, Bastion."

BAST HADN'T CALLED AHEAD, but Mica was waiting for them at the entrance to the cave system that made up his stronghold when they arrived. Kairon, apparently not wanting to rely on Bast's landing skills, launched himself from the sling as soon as they were within ten feet of the ground, landing with lithe silence. He'd ditched the scrap of gauze over his face when Blaine, the other scout travelling with them, had offered him some mirrored aviator sunglasses a half hour back. The substitution took him from looking like a ragged refugee to appearing much more like the apex predator he no doubt was.

"The stronghold's registering him as a threat," Hel murmured, quiet enough that Mica wouldn't hear.

With the deeper connection they now shared, Bast could feel a little of that sentience himself through his mate's senses. Hel was right. It felt poised to lash out at the perceived threat; protective of the man who held its loyalty. Bast landed next to Kairon and placed a firm hand on his shoulder, silently hoping the man wouldn't take offense.

"Rein in your home, Mica. He's just one man, and he's under my protection. A rockfall here wouldn't take him out, but it would make us late."

"Greetings, Bastion. Welcome to the Earth Court. Still full of surprises I see," Mica said, his tone slightly chiding at Bast's lack of manners as the Earth Lord demonstrated once again he was a stickler for the courts' classist welcome etiquette that said he only needed to acknowledge the leader of their group.

Bast frowned. "Greetings Mica," he replied, purposefully omitting his title again just like the Earth Lord always left off his own. "I thought for sure you'd at least include my mate and co-ruler in your welcome even if you can't lower yourself to being polite to the rest of my party. It's not like you to make a faux pas like that," he drawled.

Mica stiffened in affront, but to his credit seemed to realise his guests wouldn't be coming any closer if he didn't bend a little. He inclined his head to Hel.

"My apologies. Welcome, Helaine. We are honoured to host your people," he said, eyes flicking back to Kairon in a clear indication he did not consider the unknown being to be one of their people.

Kairon pulled away from Bast's grasp to step forward and Bast let him go, hoping he wasn't about to regret offering his protection.

"Thank you for your welcome. I am Kairon, one of the twelve voices of my people—the vampyr," he said, adding the slightest of bows to his words as he held eye contact with Mica.

Bast kept a poker face as he hid his surprise at the words. He wished he'd had that nugget of information a little earlier so he could plan better.

Mica paused before inclining his head in what could pass for a polite greeting before gesturing for them to follow him into the depths of his stronghold.

Kairon kept pace alongside the Earth Lord as they made their way through the soaring limestone tunnels and caverns towards the council-chamber. Bast hid his smile as the vampyr seemed to charm Mica despite himself with his compliments and questions on their surroundings. With violence at least temporarily diverted, Bast checked behind him to see Hel had put an arm around Kaia and was whispering something in the girl's ear that made her giggle. He wished he had time to reassure her. He knew she must be nervous about entering what could be her home for the next five years if Mica pulled his head out of his ass. Their scouts flanked the two of them on either side three steps back, protecting them from anyone coming up behind them.

Mica paused at a vast chamber that was lit only by thousands of glowing rainbow-coloured tendrils hanging from its roof. A dozen holes at various heights around its walls shone with magical light where pathways curved out into the rest of the subterranean stronghold. A constant stream of the Earth Lord's people flitted above them, flying between the points of light as they traversed the room.

"With your permission, I'll have someone escort young Kaia and the rest of your party to somewhere they can rest," Mica said, raising an eyebrow in question as he turned towards him.

Bast nodded. "Thank you. We gratefully accept. Hel and Kairon stay with me, though."

"The council only voted to invite you, Bastion."

Bast just met Mica's gaze and held it silently until the Earth Lord sighed. "Very well."

"I don't want to leave you, Uncle Basti," Kaia said, her voice trembling as her wide eyes took in the strangeness of the world they'd entered and the number of unfamiliar people around her.

Bast leaned down to give the girl a hug. "You'll have Tijmen and Blaine with you. And Mica is too old and staid not to honour guest-right. You'll be safe here."

Bast hid a smirk as Mica's jaw tightened in annoyance at the words Bast hadn't bothered to keep quiet.

"You've got this, sweetness," Hel added, holding her hand out to fist bump with Kaia.

"Okay, Auntie."

Bast reached out to entwine Hel's fingers with his own as they watched Kaia until she was out of sight.

"There will be no room for that hesitance when she is training," Mica warned.

His mate glared at the Earth Lord. "That hesitance is her survival instinct. She doesn't need to lose it. Whoever's training her needs to earn her trust," Hel shot back.

Mica shrugged. "To be trained by a court is an honour. Especially if the payment is favours rather than loyalty. It's her who will need to earn people's trust if we let her stay."

"Come. We have kept the others waiting long enough," Mica added when Hel showed no sign of conceding the point.

"Remind me again why we have to put up with this," Hel growled softly in Bast's ear.

"Because her life depends on it, Hellcat," Bast sighed, noting Kairon's curious look in their direction. They'd have to be careful what they said within the man's sensitive hearing.

BAST HAD NEVER BEEN in the council chamber of the Earth Court. It was everything he expected of the showy rulers. Three times larger than the nexus of passageways where they'd left Kaia, this chamber stretched high enough that its peak was open to the sky above them. Stalactites had merged with their counterpart stalagmites to form thick columns that surrounded the council table in an unnaturally perfect circle.

If the stronghold's magic hadn't clearly been a factor in their creation, their sheer size in circumference and height would have placed them as impossibly ancient phenomena.

The table itself and all its chairs appeared to have grown from solid mineral rock. Not the limestone that abounded in the cave, but glittering layers of the crystalline mica the Earth Lord was named for. Dangling bioluminescent strands of light draping from the ceiling's surface were the brightest he'd ever seen, refracting off the latticework of the mineral's structure to make it appear lit from within even as it sent rainbows scattering across the space. The table, the light, and the columns were the only use of the vast space. Everything else was cloaked in dramatic darkness that made one acutely aware how deep within the Earths the chamber was.

It was a hugely inefficient use of an area solely for the purpose of impressing the three other rulers on the council.

Someone had added an extra chair near the only empty crystalline seat at the head of the table. It was in between where Mica would sit and where the Water Lady Nerida had casually draped herself with her legs crossed beneath her. Just one spare seat. Bast swept past the three rulers eyeing them up and pulled the chair out for Hel.

"Your seat, my lady," he said, letting the chill of his anger at their effort to snub her ring clear in the words.

"Thank you," Hel murmured, as she sank gracefully into the seat.

Bast was tempted to take Mica's still empty chair, but instead he positioned himself to Hel's left and Kairon mirrored his move to stand at her right. Knowing the rulers would do their best to keep the unknown vampyr out of their conversation, Bast let his power drift out to fill the surrounding air, ensuring everyone's words would be translated for Kairon.

"Really, Mica. You can't just let any old riff-raff in here. Those two aren't even elemental," Aliya snapped from her place to the right of the Earth Lord.

"Bastion is entitled to be accompanied by his mate. And Kairon is one I am sure we are all keen to question. Unless you have finally captured one of his kind like you promised weeks ago?"

A low growl issued from Kairon that somehow literally chilled Bast's blood, slowing its passage through his veins. The uncomfortable shifting of the rulers around the table suggested he wasn't the only one.

Hel jumped in before Kairon could follow the noise with a threat. "Don't judge her failure too harshly. I hear she's down a few squadrons. Probably just as well if the rest of Kairon's people are like him. He doesn't seem the sort to roll over for a homicidal, narcissistic traitor," Hel said, her voice sugar-sweet.

Bast winced inwardly at the harsh words. Not that he disagreed with her approach. The time for making nice was over. The council needed to treat them as equals. He just would've liked the chance to assess who might be sympathetic to them before eviscerating the Lady of Air with their words. At least Kairon was smirking at his mate in appreciation now instead of looking like he was about to launch himself across the table at the threat to his people.

"I refuse to sit here and be insulted by a ... whatever she is," Aliya said, sneering as she shoved to her feet.

"Is she wrong, though? Did you not betray us?" Nerida asked, surprising Bast who'd been sure she'd hold a grudge over the damage they'd done to her stronghold escaping it.

"It was you who sent us chasing down Helaine for the emperor and then your territory was coincidentally the least affected by this Melding. Exactly what relationship do you have with this man who has killed tens of thousands of our people and millions of humans on two separate occasions?" Nerida continued.

"Aliya's squadrons attacked us within minutes of the Melding. They would have had to travel the better part of a day to be in position. She must have had advanced knowledge. I do hope she warned you all," Bast added, helpfully.

Even Tyson was glaring at Aliya now. Interesting. Would this be the wedge that finally drove apart their alliance?

"We had an arrangement. I helped him find his errant child and, in return, he stayed his hand from the destruction he could have otherwise wrought here," Aliya said.

"Except Lady Nerida is correct that your territory is the only area where he stayed his hand. And even then, your human population was decimated," Mica said.

Aliya's lip curled up as if she couldn't understand why anyone would even mention the human population. "Any reduction in damage to the Earths as a whole makes it easier to recover," she said.

"Sure, because you're such a humanitarian helping out your neighbours," Hel said.

"I'm not the reason millions died. You put everyone around you at risk when you refused him. Just like you've put that poor child at risk," Aliya said.

Was she talking about Kaia? Bast frowned and stepped closer to Aliya. "What are you talking about? It was your attack that did that," he growled.

"You really should keep a closer eye on your people,

Bast," Aliya purred, just as Bast's satellite phone started buzzing with the emergency ring. Tijmen's name flashed on the screen.

"Report," he said as soon as he answered. The scout wouldn't have interrupted them unless it was urgent.

A gargled wheeze sounded through the speaker, followed by a strained rasp, barely audible. "They've taken Kaia."

"Who?"

"Half a dozen Air Court scouts. They knocked us out. They're maybe five minutes fast flight east."

Bast shared a horrified glance with his mate as they processed what had happened. Kaia was so young. So vulnerable.

"You're faster than anyone. Go. We can't lose her. I'll keep an eye on this lot," Hel said, voice low and urgent.

Bast hesitated another second, instinct holding him back, but they couldn't afford to wait. Wrapping his power into every aspect of his flight, he launched himself up toward the distant gap in the cave above until he was breaking out into the sunlight. He heard Mica's angry voice echoing behind him as he left. The Earth Lord would not tolerate such a breach of guest-right, but whatever he did in retribution wouldn't bring Kaia back.

Frantically, Bast called to the souls surrounding him who responded with a sharp pull on his psyche in the direction Kaia had been taken.

He'd cleared the edges of the Stronghold and was closing the distance with the group of would-be kidnappers flying just ahead when he felt a vast resonance against his sense of Hel's power weaving through his own.

Someone had opened a portal to another world inside

the Earth Stronghold behind him. Not someone—Hel's father. He'd recognise the taste of that power anywhere.

Bast's flight faltered and he twisted mid-air, tumbling toward the ground as the sensation cut off. His heart skipped a beat. He'd lost access to Hel's power. Lost it because she was suddenly too far away. Her constant reassuring presence in the back of his soul now stretched like a vast chasm, impossibly distant from him.

Her hunters had found her.

She'd finally been taken.

THANK YOU FOR READING!

If you'd like to hear about my new releases and read the prequel short story of how Bast came to the City of Souls during the Melding and met Ra, sign up to my newsletter through my website and I'll send you the free ebook From the Ashes.

About the Author

Mel Harding-Shaw is a paranormal romance and urban fantasy writer from Wellington, Aotearoa New Zealand. Her debut novel *City of Souls* won Agent's Choice in the RWNZ Great Beginnings Contest.

She's also a widely published award-winning writer of short speculative fiction as Melanie Harding-Shaw and has published five books under that name: a trilogy of near-future novelettes, a story collection *Alt-ernate*, and a witchy urban fantasy novella *Against the Grain*.

Mel won the award for Services to Science Fiction, Fantasy and Horror in the 2020 Sir Julius Vogel Awards. You can find her at www.melaniehardingshaw.com and on social media.

Printed in Great Britain
by Amazon

37262265R00179